Darling

Darling
Brad C. Hodson

ANAHEIM - CALIFORNIA

FIRST EDITION

Darling
© 2012 by Brad C. Hodson

Cover Art © 2012 by Phillip Simpson

Book Design
by César Puch

Copy Editing
by Steve Souza & Jamie La Chance

Bad Moon Books Logo Created by Matthew JLD Rice

ISBN-10: 0988447819
ISBN-13: 978-0-9884478-1-3

 BAD MOON BOOKS
1854 W. Chateau Ave.
Anaheim, CA 92804
USA

www.badmoonbooks.com

For Shannon
Our 7 is an upside down 2

Acknowledgements

Writing has been called that "dirty thing you do by yourself behind locked doors," implying a certain amount of mental masturbation. I won't debate the truth of that (at least not here), but in order to move past that stage and make your work not only readable but publishable requires some intervention. Books are not produced in a vacuum and no matter your opinion of *Darling*'s literary merits (or lack thereof, for those whose cup of tea tends toward a lighter shade and less bitter taste), it would have been far worse without the support, advice, and even intervention of some mighty fine folk.

First and foremost, I'd like to thank the late and amazing Michael Louis Calvillo, a brilliant artist who not only believed in this book but also recommended its new and unknown author to his publisher. I also have to thank Lisa Morton for becoming a kind of unofficial mentor to me. Her talent and keen head for the business side of this bizarre pursuit have learned me gobs of invaluable information. I'd also like to thank all of the members of the *Dark Delicacies* writing group for their ceaseless support and consistent criticism: Del Howison, John Palisano, Joey O'Bryan, Jodi

Lester, Maria Alexander, Benjamin Kane Ethridge, Martel Sardina, and all other members, past, present, and otherwise.

I'd be remiss not to thank Thomas F. Monteleone, Elizabeth Monteleone, F. Paul Wilson, Douglas E. Winter, John Douglas, and all of the grunts at the Borderlands Bootcamp. "Bootcamp" is the best name for their program because it's truly like doing pushups for your writing. Thousands of them. While someone screams at you and someone else beats you with a rattan cane. And you love them for it.

A quick list of other folks I'd like to thank for this particular book: Roy Robbins and Liz Scott, Dan Simmons, Adam Fox, Bryan Shane Best, Currie Adams, Kate O'Toole, James O'Neil, Ross Graham, Irene Lawson, Tim Lawson, Gordon and Linda Neil, and, of course, Shannon. If I missed anyone, you'll have to excuse me. It's been a long road and the backseat only fits so many…

Darling

The man in apartment 333 stopped scrubbing. He rinsed the chemicals from his hands and scanned the bathroom. It wasn't clean enough (it could never be clean enough), but it would do. The cracks separating the tiles were the worst, but the bleach had worked well.

In the kitchen, he rooted around on his hands and knees with an old toothbrush. Confident that the hidden dirt had been exposed, he swept and mopped again. He scrubbed every dish to a shine. He rubbed the silverware down with an expensive metal cleaner. He packed his wife's remains into a large garbage bag. He cleaned the windows.

He stopped long enough to stare at his hands. White spots scattered across patches of reddened skin, a road map of the cleaning fluids he had used. His fingers were raw and bled around the nails. His palms burned from the bleach and the knot of muscle at the base of his thumbs screamed at him. He supposed he was finished with the apartment.

He sat on the couch and pulled the checkbook from his suit. He wrote a check for the next month's rent and drew a smiley face next to his signature. The check went into an envelope along with his keys.

He left his apartment, garbage bag in tow, and climbed into the elevator at the end of the hall. He mashed a button with his thumb and the doors rattled shut. The box threatened to break apart as it descended.

The shaking stopped and the doors creaked open. He stepped out, slid the envelope into the superintendent's mail slot, and left by the back door.

Under the yellow light of the patio he felt disoriented. His head swam. Shadows writhed at the corners of his vision.

It passed and he stared into the night. Ahead of him, past the tacky lawn furniture and broken propane grill, the grass grew wild.

The wind danced through the field and praised him with dry, rustling words. He brushed his hand through the waist-high growth. It was damp and cool.

He removed his jacket, folded it, and placed it on a lawn chair. His shirt followed, then his shoes. Socks. Pants. His boxer shorts were last. He rolled them into a ball that he slid inside one of the shoes. He placed the bag next to his clothes, his wife collapsing to one side.

The breeze came to him, took his hand, and led him in its dance. He smiled and walked naked through the field.

The supermarket rising from the grass was a black void absorbing the moonlight. It wasn't until he was close that he could make out the cracked and vine-covered facade, could read the faded nonsense spray-painted onto its side.

Broken pavement bit into his foot. One of the parking lot's busted lights flickered to life over him. He stood there for a long while, staring into the blackness behind dusty glass doors.

He took a step forward. The doors slid apart along broken mechanical tracks. His view of the shadows was unhindered.

Without looking back, he stepped inside. The doors screeched shut behind him.

The light in the parking lot flickered once and went black.

Across the field, Raynham Place was quiet. His apartment sat, clean and empty, and waited for its next occupant.

PART ONE
JUNE

Do what we can, summer will have its flies.
—*Ralph Waldo Emerson*

Chapter One

The sword fell, again and again. Ripper72 hacked Mike into pieces and there was nothing he could do about it.

"FUCK." He threw his half empty Mountain Dew can across the room. It clanged against the wall, spraying an arc of soda across his movie posters. The syrupy odor filled the room.

He logged off, pushed his chair back, and grabbed a T-shirt from the hamper to wipe his wall clean. He had spent all morning playing the online role-playing game, hours spent adventuring and building up his character, and then some asshole comes along, steals his money, and leaves him rotting in a ditch somewhere.

Kind of like real life.

His blood scorched his arteries. He played these games to escape the real world, yet here he was feeling just as helpless and shit upon as usual. He considered logging back on and exacting vengeance, but the clock told him he needed to leave for work. He grabbed his red vest and name tag and ran down the stairs.

His mother lay on the couch, an issue of *People* open in her lap while Fox News played on the television. "Off to work?"

"Yeah."

"What time will you be home?"

"I get off at six."

"Pork chops for dinner."

Pork chops? Maybe he would try to work late and get a burger. "Dad in his office?"

"Mmm-hmm."

Mike knocked on his father's door and waited for an answer. After a long silence, he knocked again.

"What?"

He cracked the door and peeked inside.

His father's fingers drummed against the keyboard. "I'm busy, Michael."

"Uh…sorry. I just, uh…"

"What is it?"

"I have to be at work in half an hour."

His father sighed. "I can't get out of here for at least an hour. You'll have to take the bus again. Okay?" He turned back to his computer.

"If I take the bus I'm gonna be late."

"You should have left earlier."

"But you said—"

"Goddammit, Michael. Can't you do anything for yourself?"

He had to fight to keep from slamming the door. He left without saying goodbye to anyone.

The air was thick and hot and he was glad he spent his days inside an air-conditioned theater. He had only walked a block and his collar was damp.

His jaw ached, and he realized it had been clenched tight since leaving the house. Why did his father tell him he was going to take him to work if he had so much to do? He'd never understood the man. Sometimes he thought these situations were manufactured, some twisted method his father used to remind everyone who ran the home.

The neighborhood was quiet. Only a scattering of people were out, namely housewives and retirees. The Vick boys played basketball in their driveway. A large German Shepherd tugged all three hundred pounds of Carolyn Peters down the street. Mrs. Montgomery lay on a blanket in her yard, listening to the radio while the sun worked hard to keep her skin brown and leathery.

"Mike?"

He stopped and turned. A woman stood by a silver Celica. The trunk was open and she pushed a box inside. He stared at her for a moment, trying to place her long brown hair and round cheeks.

"Michael Pritchett?"

"Renee?"

She smiled and closed the trunk. "I thought that was you. How have you been? I haven't seen you since graduation."

"Yeah." His hands went to their usual place in his pockets as he shifted his weight from foot to foot. "I'm good. How about you?"

"Not bad. Just picking up some things I'd left with my parents. I'm living in Nashville now."

"What are you doing there?"

She laughed. "Just interning. It's the advertising industry, so it's a start, I guess. But nothing special. Off to work?" She pointed to the Regal Cinemas name badge on his red vest.

Was she making fun of him? "Yeah. Work."

"Well…I guess I shouldn't keep you."

"Yeah."

"Good to see you."

"You too." Mike turned and hurried off, glad she couldn't see the red building in his cheeks. He hated running into old classmates, hated that he seemed to be the only one still working his shit high school job and living with his parents. Every time he ran into someone like Renee he could feel them looking down their noses at him, judging him, *pitying* him.

Fucking bitch.

He hurried on to the bus stop, hoping Renee wouldn't see him waiting on the little green bench as she drove by.

He wished he had a car. He'd talked to his father about it on occasion, but was assured he wasn't ready. "A car is a big responsibility for a man. Car payments, insurance, registration. Maybe you should wait awhile." He had wanted to ask how long he would have to wait (he *was* twenty, after all) but kept quiet. It didn't pay to argue with his father. It never worked in Mike's favor.

There was only one other person at the bus stop, an elderly black woman in a long brown coat. He wondered how she could wear a coat on such a hot day. She stared at her feet and mumbled something to herself. Mike thought it better to stand.

The bus roared up the street. It stopped in front of the bench and black clouds of exhaust spilled out. The doors creaked open and the woman shuffled on board. Mike waited until she was in the aisle before climbing on and flashing his bus pass.

"That's expired," the bus driver said.

"What?" He read the laminated card. The driver was right. It had been expired for three days. "I'll get a new one tomorrow."

"Three dollars."

"C'mon. I used it yesterday and no one said anything."

"That was yesterday. Today? Three dollars."

He sighed and dug into his wallet. He only had four ones. He forked over three of them and stomped to a vacant seat while wondering what Renee would say if she could see him. Thinking of her made him think of high school and he laughed.

I just had my lunch money stolen. Twenty years old and my goddamned lunch money was stolen.

Something had to change.

★ ★ ★

The rolling hills and green pastures reminded Dennis of Thomas Cole paintings. The trees grew large and healthy and a wild array of flowers painted the fields in vibrant Technicolor. The houses out this far were rare and each was magnificent.

Why had he never driven out this way? Between the view and the warm breeze, he was more relaxed than he had been in months. He thought of Eileen and how she hated to drive and was reminded of why he *hadn't* been out this way. This was at least a twenty-minute drive from campus and that time would only get worse with weekday traffic.

Stirring his own hatred for traffic, Dennis almost turned around and headed back to Knoxville. He was slowing to look for a driveway when he saw the road. *Emory Highway* shot off to his left and wound its way up a hill. He turned onto it and had to slow to twenty to stay in his lane.

Not much of a highway, he thought. Must turn into four lanes farther south.

The road twisted even more as he climbed the hill. His knuckles went white gripping the wheel. Finally the hills leveled, the road straightened, and he was able to once again enjoy the view.

Then he saw it, rising from the hills like a beast from a forgotten age. It was giant. Sprawling. It jutted ever more into view and Dennis thought of icebergs floating in arctic seas, waiting for passing ships to collide into them and sink to the depths.

The urge to turn around and leave rushed back. Dennis forced himself up the long drive. The area itself was a sharp contrast to the structure, as idyllic as anything he had seen so far. Magnolias stood like sentries around the drive, their blossoms still white. The branches of apple trees hung low from the weight of heavy fruit. A giant Weeping Willow rose high to one side of the building, its green draped to the ground.

He parked his car with several others in a small, make-shift lot and laughed at the awkward white lines painted onto the cul-de-sac. The convertible's top went up with the press of a button. He shut the engine off but didn't get out. Instead he sat in his space, his eyes taking in the building.

It was off-yellow. He wasn't sure what the original color was but assumed it had faded in the sun. It brought to mind jaundiced children. There was a long staircase leading up a hill and into a deep, narrow courtyard lined with statues. He couldn't make out what they were from his car, but could see potted trees between them.

The courtyard ended in a five-story tower. To each side of the tower a three-story building spread out like an opened book. Dennis did a quick count and, assuming one apartment for each window with one across the hall, guessed that the building must have at least sixty apartments. The sheer size of the place was overwhelming.

"Dennis Logan?"

He looked to the curb to see a fat, balding man in a black T-shirt and gym shorts waddling over to him. He shut the engine off and stood, extending his hand.

"Yeah, that's me. You must be Rudy."

Rudy grunted something that sounded like "yeah" and shook Dennis' hand. "I guess I'll show you around," he mumbled and waddled back toward the building.

Dennis wiped his palm on the front of his jeans. Rudy's hand had been covered in sweat and, now that he was behind the man, he could see giant beads of it glistening on the back of his scalp. Soured musk wafted from him and into Dennis' face.

"This," Rudy said, "is the...uh, courtyard, I guess."

"Definitely interesting." He wasn't quite sure what to think of the statues. Now that he was between them he could make out their Greco-Roman design. He couldn't exactly place them, but thought some might be satyrs. They had the characteristic hindquarters of some hoofed beast, while their torsos were a steroid dealer's wet dream. Each was locked in the midst of a sensual dance, their bodies twisting and writhing. Some of them played the flute, some ate pieces of fruit, and others admired their own creation by rubbing their chests and stomachs. Each smiled and small horns curled from their heads like a ram.

He thought the others were nymphs, with their bare breasts and erotic poses, but wasn't sure. He tried not to stare at them too long. Something about the way their faces were carved suggested a sly malevolence, as though they knew he had stolen a peek of their exposed breasts and plotted retribution.

"A previous owner had those built. I think they're tacky, but the tenants love them. Whatever."

Dennis just nodded. They were fucking strange is what they were.

"This is the main building." Rudy swung the door to the tower open. Dennis stepped around him and into the lobby. It smelled musty, like a closet that had been closed for years. The sunlight bounced from wall to wall and the first impression he had was of a hospital—cold, sterile, and impersonal.

"The tenants call it Eiffel." The door closed and the lobby changed. With the sunlight gone, the only light came from a single bulb overhead. The effect was oppressive. Long shadows ran from the chairs and directory along dirty brown floors and up walls the color of scorched milk.

What was he doing? There was no way in hell he was living in this creepshow. And Mike, or Eileen? Jesus.

"Pool's this way."

Pool? Well, maybe he was being a little hasty…

They walked down a long corridor lined with apartments. "In case you're wondering, we're in the West Wing now." Rudy scratched his hip with a meaty hand. "You're okay with the two bedroom, right?"

"Yeah. Two bedroom's fine. Perfect, actually."

"You and your girlfriend?"

"God, no. We're not even close to that point yet. Just me and my friend Mike."

Rudy snorted. "College students, huh?"

"Yeah. It's Mike's first year, and my first back after a long layoff."

"We don't like loud college parties around here."

Dennis laughed. "Oh, I wouldn't worry about that. Mike's a real quiet guy."

"And you?"

"I've grown out of that phase."

"Good." Rudy nodded. "People like their quiet around here."

"Us too."

"And their privacy. People here don't like folks sticking their noses where they don't belong."

Ahead of them a man stood on a chair and fiddled with something over his doorway. He reminded Dennis of a scarecrow, his scrawny frame only hinting at humanity. His jeans slid down from his waist, revealing a thin, white ribbon of underwear. A gray T-shirt draped over his shoulders like a sheet. As they moved closer Dennis could see he placed roach traps on his door frame. The man stared at them as they passed.

"Is there a problem with bugs?"

Rudy shook his head. "I wouldn't worry about Lloyd. Never seen a roach here. Don't think anyone has. Probably had this whole place fumigated three times in the past year because of him. Here's the pool."

He opened a door to reveal a pool that, while not

Olympic-sized, still looked at least eight feet at the deep end. Pool furniture was scattered around on the concrete next to a large grill. Most of the area was in the shade of overgrown trees and bushes. A small pathway angled off from an opening in the fence and Dennis could see the corner of a bench and the edge of a small fountain.

He smiled at the sight of the Jacuzzi. "Nice."

"I guess. Pool hours are ten to ten, no exceptions. And no college pool parties. People here like their quiet."

"Yeah."

Rudy shut the door. He started back toward Eiffel and Dennis trotted behind him. They stopped at the elevator. Rudy's thick thumb pressed the "Up" button. "Two bedroom's on three."

The whirring of the elevator vibrated the doors. The intermission in the tour was awkward. Dennis shuffled back and forth trying to think up a question to ask about the building.

Finally, the elevator *dinged* and the whirring stopped. The doors parted to reveal a tall woman in a green sundress. Red hair cascaded over her shoulders. The sweet smell of strawberries and exotic flowers pushed Rudy's odor to the side. She smiled and Dennis lost his breath.

"Hi, Karen."

"Hey, Rudy."

"This is Dennis. He's thinking of renting Sam's old place on three."

"Hi. Nice to meet you." She stuck out her hand.

"Hi. Hi. Hello." He took her hand. "Very nice to meet you." Her eyes were the same green as her dress and he wondered if that was intentional.

She turned and slender, tan legs bounced her down the hall. "Hope to see you around, Dennis," she said over a shoulder with a perfect flip of her hair.

"Yeah. You too." *Hate to see you go, but I love to watch you leave.*

She paused at the door and smiled back. He waved. Then she was gone and he was left feeling like an idiot.

"C'mon, loverboy." Rudy stepped into the elevator and pressed another button. Dennis stepped in behind him. The doors creaked shut and the elevator whirred to life.

He was disoriented as the elevator started its climb. He wasn't sure if it was the subtle hint of perfume still lingering in the tiny box, or the way it shook and rattled as it fought its way up the shaft. He was forced to grip the bar running along the wall.

Rudy laughed. "Don't worry about the elevator. Hasn't been an accident on this thing in forty years. Jack, our maintenance guy, looks at it every Friday."

"Is he the only maintenance for this place?"

"Yep."

"But it's so big."

"Believe it or not, we don't get a lot of problems here. The wiring's pretty solid and the plumbing's good. Everything had to be in tip-top shape when they built this place."

"People used to really care about apartment buildings, huh?" Dennis steadied himself as the elevator's rattling slowed.

"This place wasn't built for apartments. My father converted it in the seventies." The doors opened and Rudy stepped into the hall. He pulled a large set of keys from the pocket of his gym shorts.

"What was it?" Dennis stepped out after him. The third floor was only slightly better than the first. At least there was a little more sunlight coming in through the windows.

"It was originally built in the twenties as a tuberculosis hospital." He stopped at apartment 333 and fumbled with his keys.

"A tuberculosis hospital?" Seriously? Could the place get any weirder?

"Yep. Must have been a thousand people die here before they found a cure. Here we go." He shoved the door open and stepped inside.

Dennis stumbled in behind him. All thoughts of the macabre history of tuberculosis vanished. The apartment was huge. The living room alone could fit the entirety of his current place. Hardwood floors, giant bay windows, a fireplace—it was much more than he had hoped for.

Rudy told him the rent and his mind was made up.

"We'll take it."

The fat man laughed. "You don't want the grand tour?"

Dennis smiled. "This place is perfect."

"Good. You're lucky to have it, you know. People here tend to be long-term renters. Nice and quiet out here. People here like their quiet. The last occupants lived here for six years, then just up and left in the middle of the night. No forwarding address or anything. Not gonna have that problem out of you, am I?"

Dennis stared out one of the large windows at the field below. He wondered about the abandoned and overgrown buildings that rested on the other side. "I can't see why we'd ever want to leave," he said, squinting to read the graffiti staining the old supermarket's walls.

Chapter Two

Dennis had written a check for the first and last month's rent, and while his wallet hurt, he felt great. He usually wasn't so impulsive, but goddamn was that a great place. Once he split the rent with Mike, it would be far cheaper than the shit hole he rented downtown.

Mike. How would he react? They had been talking about moving in together. When he finally convinced Mike to sign up for classes, they spoke for hours about how things would be once school had started and Mike was out from under his parents' roof. But all of that had been hypothetical.

He should have consulted Mike before making the decision, but he knew how Mike operated. Give him a choice, a decision to make, and he would always find a way to avoid making it. He had to be backed into a corner, especially with something that would be good for him.

Dennis checked his watch as he drove down Cumberland Avenue. He was tense about the possibility of missing his counseling appointment. He had underestimated how long it would take to get back from Emory Highway. Maybe he had been a little hasty...

He shook his head. The drive time would be a small adjustment. It was a nice drive, especially in the summer. The only thing he regretted was that he didn't have a chance to stop by his apartment and change. He felt a little old to be showing up for an appointment in jeans and a T-shirt.

He pulled to a stop at a red light. A skinny teenager in a wife-beater and baggy shorts walked by, a backpack slung over one shoulder. *Well, I guess jeans and a T-shirt should be fine, after all.*

He pulled into the Campus Center parking garage at five till two. He had exactly five minutes to make it across the parking lot, cross the street, and head up three flights of stairs. He refused to be late. He felt too good today for that.

He shut the car off, grabbed his keys, and shot out the door. He sprinted across the garage faster than he remembered he could run. By the time he made it to the counselor's floor he had worked up a nice sweat. He looked at his watch again. It was exactly two o'clock.

He ducked into the bathroom, rinsed his face with cold water, and dried off with paper towels. He entered the office at two minutes after and was sitting in front of Mrs. Riddell by five after.

Not bad, he thought.

"So, Mr. Logan, I've been going over your grades and your placement exams." She brushed a piece of graying hair from her eyes. "You seem to be a very bright and studious young man."

"Thank you."

"Now, there have been some changes in the curriculum during your, um, *absence*."

"I was afraid of that."

"Well, it shouldn't be a problem for someone like you. You'll have to retake English 103, as some of the required readings have changed. You may be able to test out of the class rather than retake it, but you'll have to speak to one of the English teachers about that."

"I love to read. Shouldn't be a big deal."

She nodded and crossed her legs. He thought she must have been a knockout when she was younger. Even now his eyes were drawn to the shape of her calves.

"Well," she continued, "the foreign language requirements have become more stringent, so you'll need another year of—" A glance at her papers. "Italian, to meet requirements. And then you'll need another Fine Art."

"Mmm-hmm."

"And a physical science."

"I had taken biology."

"And passed. Unfortunately, there was a controversy about the curriculum during the years that you were originally here. The state has mandated that students who haven't already graduated discard their biology credits. So you'll have to retake the class or take another science."

He sighed. "Well, if that's what I have to do."

She handed him a sheet of paper. "Here is a list of all of the current requirements for a Classical Studies major. And here is a print-out of all of your viable credits."

"Thank you."

She paused and stared at him. It was just long enough to make him uncomfortable and he fidgeted in his chair.

"Have you seen a psychiatrist?"

He blinked. "I'm sorry?"

"Here." She gave him another paper. It was pink and

said "EMOTIONAL PROBLEMS?" at the top. "That's the information for the Campus Health Center. If you ever find yourself having another, um…*episode*, please don't hesitate to make an appointment."

He could only nod.

"And if you have any more questions or concerns, please call me."

He muttered a quick "thank you" and headed out the door.

His steps were much slower leaving her office. What information was in her files? He wished he had asked.

No. Better not to know. He felt bad enough as it was. All of the elation was sucked out of his day in two quick seconds like the air from a popped balloon.

Have you seen a psychiatrist?

No, ma'am. I found a different therapy. Time, and alcohol, and poverty, and public debasement. Those did the trick better than any shrink could.

Not that any of those things had worked completely. They had worked in tandem, like the diet, exercise, and supplement programs he gave his clients at the gym. All of those things together had made him hate himself enough to turn his life around. Everything he was doing now was pure determination, an unvoiced desire to prove he was a good, strong person. That he was no longer that self-obsessed boy he had been. That he wasn't his father.

His father. That face was just one of the markers he used to map his life's tragedies. The old man was the first and the last. In between his horrible influences other faces swirled. His mother. Allison.

Allison most of all.

Damn. He had been having a good day.

He pushed all of their faces aside and climbed into his car. He had good news to share, good for him and Mike. And it wasn't just good news, was it? It was a new beginning.

He called Mike at the movie theater. He knew they frowned on personal calls, so made it brief. "What time you get off tomorrow?"

"Ummm…three."

"I'll pick you up at home after. Got something to talk to you about."

Mike laughed. "Like what?"

"I'll tell you when I pick you up. But it's good news, man. Real good."

When he hung up, some of his earlier mood had returned. He lowered the top on the car, cranked his radio up, and headed toward his apartment. Some lunch and a good workout would help erase the tension. Then maybe he'd call Eileen and see if she wanted to meet him and Mike at the new place tomorrow.

It was going to be a good day.

But something tugged at the back of his mind, some sensation that things weren't going in the right direction. He tried to ignore it, but it stayed with him, at times conjuring the faces of his ghosts. He wondered if those faces would ever leave him.

★ ★ ★

"I'm just going out with some friends." Mike jerked his red windbreaker from the closet, bending the wire hanger it hung from. He shrugged it on and stormed down the stairs.

His father stomped behind him. "We need to know where you're going and who with." His voice rumbled through the house like a rockslide.

"What's it matter?"

"It matters because I damn well say it matters."

His mother stood in front of the door. She wrung a dishtowel in her hands. Her knuckles were white and the muscles around her eyes quivered. "Are you going out with *him* again?"

Mike sighed and grabbed his shoes. He sat down on the stairs and loosened the laces.

"Your mother asked you a question."

"I don't know." He pulled his shoes on.

"You know we don't like you hanging around that son of a bitch."

"You've been different since you started spending so much time with him." His mother sniffed.

God, don't cry. Not again. "Different how?"

His father ran a hand through his thinning hair. "You've started disobeying us, for one."

Mike tightened his laces and jumped to his feet. "I'm twenty years old, Dad. I should make some of my own decisions now, don't you think?"

His father jerked forward, his nose less than an inch from his son's face. Mike flinched. "You may think you're an adult, Michael, but your behavior says otherwise."

Mike rolled his eyes. "Fucking Christ."

His father's hand shot out so fast he didn't even see it. It left a red mark on his cheek and a ringing in his ears. "Don't you dare talk to me like that."

Mike tried to pour all of his hatred into his eyes.

The old man's gaze was intense, the result of long years as a Marine. Mike looked away.

"Apologize to your mother for your language."

"Sorry, Mom."

She nodded.

"Now go to your room."

"Dad!"

"Mike…"

"I can't. I've got plans."

"They can wait."

"No, they can't. We're meeting with our class counselor." It was a lie, but he couldn't think of anything else that would get him out of the house.

His father studied him. Mike knew the old man could tell he was lying. Finally, he snorted and asked, "When's your appointment?"

"Five."

"A little late for an appointment, isn't it?"

Mike shrugged.

"How long is it scheduled for?"

"I don't know. It's done when it's done."

"Hmph. Well, go meet with your counselor. But you have to come home after."

A horn honked outside and his mother jumped. "Do you have to ride with him?"

"If you would let me get a car…"

She shook her head. "You don't have a license."

"And whose fault is that?"

"Mike." His father crossed his arms, the signal that Mike should drop it.

"Sorry." He grabbed his house key. "I should go."

His mother sidestepped and he opened the door. Dennis was parked across the street, the top down and his sunglasses on. Mike stepped out onto the porch. His father followed him, but his mother ran up the stairs.

He raced toward the car.

"You better call us after your appointment," his father yelled from the porch.

Mike ignored him. He saw Dennis wave and then his friend looked away. He turned and glanced to the porch, where the old man's eyes were filled with fire as he went back into the house.

The front door slammed shut.

"Just drive."

The car eased down the road. When they were a safe distance away, Mike sighed. "I don't know what their problem is," he said.

"Yeah, you do. We both do."

They drove through the neighborhood in silence. It wasn't until they were on the highway that Mike's anger got the better of him.

"Fuck! I should have started college two years ago. I should have gotten out when everything happened."

Dennis shook his head. "They're just scared of you growing up and not needing them anymore. Especially with Allison gone. You're all they have."

"Yeah, I guess. I just don't know what to do."

Dennis smiled. "I do." He pulled a set of keys from his pocket and dangled them in front of Mike's nose.

"What are those?" He pushed himself back in the seat as though his friend had revealed a dead mouse.

"Keys to our new place." Dennis jangled them.

"What?"

"Yeah. I put a deposit down yesterday."

Mike's eyes went wide. He snatched the keys away and studied them. "You're shitting me. Where?"

"Raynham Place."

"Huh?"

"This big-ass place out on Emory Highway."

"Way out there? That's in the middle of nowhere."

Dennis laughed. "That's why it's so cheap."

"I don't know..."

"C'mon, Mikey. This is the answer to all your problems. You get out from under your parents' noses, get to concentrate on school, and finally get a damn life."

"How will I get anywhere? The buses don't run out into the boonies."

"That's the other part of the surprise. We've got two months until school starts. I'm going to teach you how to drive."

"Really?"

"Yeah. It's ridiculous you don't have a license. Besides, you've got...what? Twenty-two hundred saved up from the movie theater?"

"Twenty-three," he said. "Dad won't let me spend it."

"Well, Eileen's selling her Saturn for twelve."

Mike cackled. "Dad would shit."

"Yes, he probably would."

"Speaking of Eileen...why aren't you guys moving in together?"

"Move in together? We've only been dating for a few weeks. We haven't even had...um, talked about it yet. We haven't talked about our future, I mean. If we're exclusive."

"Do you think she wants to be?"

"I don't know. We're just playing it cool right now. So… what will it be?"

Mike watched the storefronts zoom by. "Fuck it. Why not? It'll piss my parents off enough."

"That's what I like to hear. We move in Friday."

"Friday?"

"Yeah." He laughed.

"You idiot. What if I said 'no'?"

"You didn't."

"But what if I did?"

"I knew you wouldn't."

"How?"

"Because you need this as much as I do."

Mike couldn't disagree. "Well, can I see the place, at least?"

★ ★ ★

"No, no, no." Mike shook his head as they drove through Raynham's shadow.

"Just wait," Dennis said, easing the car up the hill.

"Does it get any less creepy?"

"Don't puss out on me now, Mikey."

He snorted. "Looks like an insane asylum."

"Used to be a tuberculosis hospital."

"What? You didn't tell me that."

"What's it matter?"

"I don't know. It's just…

"Creepy."

He nodded.

Dennis laughed. "You're such a pussy."

"I'm not a pussy."

"Yeah you are." He shoved Mike's shoulder.

Mike shoved him back. "Fuck you."

"Aw, I'm sorry, Mike. I didn't know your vagina was hurting."

"You're an asshole."

Dennis parked the car. "Beats being a pussy."

"Hey, is that Eileen?"

Dennis followed Mike from the car and raised a hand to shield against the setting sun. A young woman pulled a broom and dustpan from the trunk of a green Saturn. Her blond hair was pulled into a ponytail and the gray sweatshirt and paint-splotched jeans hid her shape, but Dennis recognized her car.

"Yeah, that's her. She's gonna help us clean up a bit."

Eileen smiled and waved the dustpan in the air. She ran up and threw her arms around Dennis' neck.

She kissed him. "The drive here sucks."

Mike snapped his head forward and walked toward the building.

Dennis pulled his lips away. "Not in front of Mike," he whispered.

Her brow wrinkled and her eyes narrowed, but she nodded. "Yeah. Sorry."

Dennis smiled and grabbed the broom. He took her hand and headed up the stairs to the courtyard. They passed Mike, who shuffled along staring up at the tower.

"Hey, Mike," Eileen said.

"Hey, Eileen," he muttered, eyes still scanning the building.

"Good to see you." She flashed him a smile.

"Yeah. You, too."

When they were a good distance in front of him, Eileen leaned in close to Dennis. "As charming as ever…"

He pinched her hip. She squealed and slapped his shoulder. They laughed.

"Cut the kid a break. He's—"

"Yeah, yeah. I know." She surveyed the statues as they passed through the courtyard. "Boy, you weren't kidding about this place."

"Told you so."

"Bet it's haunted."

Dennis laughed and opened the door for her. "You think every place is haunted."

"They probably are." She walked inside. "We just can't see by what."

★ ★ ★

Mike paused in the courtyard, eyes drawn to the statues. There was a quality to them that suggested flesh, some sculptor's technique that crafted the illusion of blood pumping through veins beneath the marble. Maybe it was the way their bodies twisted, or the coy smiles and lusty glares. He had never been with a woman, but the statues somehow captured most of his fantasies.

"You coming, kiddo?"

"I'm coming." He rushed into the doorway. He hoped the heat he felt in his cheeks wasn't visible.

Dennis glanced back at the statues and smiled. "You dirty young man, you."

Mike ducked his head low and hurried down the hall.

★ ★ ★

"And here we are." Dennis threw the door wide and sauntered into the middle of the room.

"Wow," Eileen said. "This blows my apartment away."

Mike paced through the room, running his hands along the walls.

"Well?" Dennis placed a hand on his shoulder. "What do you think?"

"It's…it's perfect."

"Of course it is."

"And you know what the best thing is?"

"What's that?"

"My parents aren't here."

All three of them laughed. They took a tour, each impressed that such a building could house these large and beautiful apartments, before sweeping, dusting, and trying to puzzle out where they would place their furniture. Sometime after sunset, Eileen brought a cooler with a six-pack of beer up from her car. After coercing Mike to drink ("I'm underage," he had argued), the three of them sprawled out on the floor and sipped from their cans.

"We should get cable," Mike said.

"Hey, what my roommate wants, my roommate gets."

Eileen wiped foam from the top of her can with her shirt. "I'm surprised there wasn't more cleaning to do. My apartment was filthy when we moved in."

Mike ran his forearm across his lips. "I thought they had to clean apartments before renting them?"

"They're supposed to," she said. "But what are you going to do? Take them to court?"

"You could put some of those burgeoning lawyer skills to use." Dennis nudged her in the ribs.

"*Pre*-lawyer skills, you mean. I don't even know where to stand in a courtroom." She took a long swig of beer. "Have you decided what you're going to major in yet, Mike?"

"I'm thinking Anthropology, with a focus on religion. After Allison...well, I don't know that I really believe in God anymore. But I'm fascinated with why people believe what they do, ya know?"

At the mention of Mike's sister, Dennis stood and went to the window.

Mike leaned against the wall and took another sip of beer. He scrunched his face up. "Still say this stuff tastes like piss."

"Hey." Dennis tapped on the glass. "You guys see these weird buildings over here?"

They squeezed in on either side of him and Mike pressed his face against the glass. "Looks like a strip mall and a grocery store."

"Yeah," Eileen said. "It was supposed to be."

Dennis put his arm around her. "How do you know?"

"You know my uncle Gary?"

"The drifter, right?"

"Yeah. He was working construction, probably around the time they converted this place to apartments. They were going to build an entire shopping center up here, but never completed it."

Mike finished his beer with a grimace. "So it never opened?"

"No. Gary said there was an accident or something. Some piece of equipment malfunctioned and a bunch of workers were killed. Everything stopped for a while. I think the guy that was in charge of it died not long after and they never finished. I don't really remember. Just one of those stories Gary told us when we were kids and would drive past here on Sundays."

They turned back into the room. Dennis gathered up the beer cans and placed them in a small grocery bag. "So where's Ol' Gary at today?"

"Who knows? Probably the same place my father is, wherever the hell that might be."

"Aw, shit." Mike smacked his hand against the wall.

"What?"

"What time is it?"

Eileen glanced at her watch. "Eight thirty."

"Dammit. Can I use your phone?"

"Sure." She handed him her cell. He rushed into an empty bedroom and shut the door.

She whistled. "What was that about?"

"I think he has to check in with his parents." Dennis slid an arm around her waist and pulled her close.

"At his age?"

"Don't rag him about it, okay? That house hasn't been the same since everything happened."

She leaned in and kissed him. Her lips were warm and soft and he tightened his arms around her. After a moment she pulled back. "Are you okay?"

"Yeah. Of course. Why wouldn't I be?"

The door to Mike's room clicked open and Dennis took a step back from her.

"I'm sorry guys." Mike handed Eileen her phone. "I gotta go."

"That's cool." Dennis patted him on the back. "I need to pack, anyway. Dinner here Friday?"

"Of course." Eileen smiled.

Dennis turned to Mike, but he was quiet. "Mike…?"

"Yeah. I…I guess."

Dennis sighed. Eileen leaned in and kissed him on the cheek. "I'll call you later. See ya, Mike."

"Later."

She grabbed her broom and dustpan and went to the door. She paused to smile again before leaving.

When she was gone, Dennis turned to his friend. "You *are* still moving in here with me, right?"

"I…I should…I mean, uh…"

"C'mon, man. You can't live with your parents forever. I was already on my own at your age. Eileen, too."

"I know, I know. It's just such short notice and I—"

Dennis grabbed him by the shoulders. "You have to do this. You know it's the best thing for you."

Mike nodded. "I'm just not looking forward to telling them, that's all."

Dennis slid an arm around his shoulder and walked him to the door. "How do you think they'll take it?"

They both knew exactly how they would take it. Mike's relationship with Dennis was a poison to the Pritchett family.

Mike was quiet as they sped along the East Tennessee highway, consumed by thoughts of how his sister's death had derailed so many people. He should have been a sophomore in college by now. Dennis should have already graduated. As it was, they were behind in life, desperately scrambling to catch up.

He glanced over at his friend. Dennis' lips moved in time to the AC/DC blaring from the speakers, the volume hiding his voice. His dusty hair blew around the sides of his face and his shoulders barely seemed to fit inside his T-shirt. His hand tapped out the rhythm on the steering wheel and Mike could see the large muscles in his fore-arms move with every beat. He looked at his own arms, pale and stick thin, and wondered why Dennis was friends with him.

Dennis only hangs out with you because he feels sorry for you, a voice inside of him said. He heard that voice a little too often. He wished he didn't, but it always lurked around, sneaking out to cajole him whenever his guard was down. *Don't you hate living in his shadow? Don't you hate how he always dates the pretty girls and has the great accomplishments, just to rub them in your face? That even the low points of his life garner sympathy, while everyone looks down on you for yours?*

"What are you thinking about?" Dennis turned down the stereo.

"Huh? Nothing. Just trying to work out what I'm going to say." Mike pushed the little voice back into the shadows. It made him feel guilty. Dirty. Dennis had done so much for him and he should be thankful.

"Wish I could help you, man."

"Me too."

As they took the exit to Mike's house, a ball of acid formed in his stomach. He couldn't do this. There was no way he could tell his parents he was moving out.

He looked to Dennis and his friend smiled.

"I'll have my phone on me. Let me know if you need anything," he said.

Mike nodded. Dennis was right. He had to stand up to his parents. He just wasn't sure how.

Chapter Three

The following was found scribbled on the open page of a notepad inside apartment 114 when the police arrived that Friday:

I dowsed the floor in some chemical that punk rock bitch at the drug store gave me she said it would kill them all but its not working or doesnt seem to be cause their still running round here like they own the goddamned place I cant take the filthy fuking things anymore I went back to the store and spent fifty dollars on more roach motels and put them up everywhere all over my bed the fridge the bathtub the closets even outside on the door frame I havnt had food here for weeks to keep them out but their everywhere there was one crawling across my face when I woke up from my nap a big fat red fuker with these spiny little legs just tapdancing his way across my face I think he even touched my lips I washed my face so many times today that my lips bled but now IM worried it laid eggs in my mouth or up my nose or in my ears or eyes even and I now I cant sleepe again everytime I close my eyes I can here them so IM just going to stay awake allnight and try to catch them I know how their getting in but NO one listens to me or seems care but you no what fuck them cause those littel bastards will be in there apartments soon and lets see how they like that fuking lazy Rudy mite finly do something about them if that happens they nest in that goddamn grocery store and run through the field at night just to fuking torment me I dont know how much of this I can take did I sleepe last night I don't think I did seems like they where running all over me then to I dont know when I sleeped last I mean you cant sleepe cause thats when they crawl between your teeth and shit on your tonque or nest inside your ears I cant take much more of this I swear to fuking christ I cant

Chapter Four

Mike slammed the door. It caught a pocket of air two inches short of closing, slowing it down and stealing any indication of anger. He collapsed onto his bed and sighed. The door had stolen all of his resolve.

The evening hadn't gone the way he had wanted it to. He knew it was going to be a war, but had hoped he could at least mention moving out. Instead his father had erupted the second Mike walked through the door.

"Don't tell me your appointment ran late. And don't try to spin some other lie. When in the hell did you become such a selfish little shit? Is this the kind of influence Dennis has on you?"

They had argued for an hour. Mike had pressed the issue of being treated like an adult, his father argued that he was still a child, his mother sat in the kitchen and sipped brandy, and the shadow of Allison fell on them all. When his father had tired of the old arguments, he banished Mike to his room like he was a teenager.

It did the trick. Mike felt thirteen again, kicking his heels against the foot of the bed and contemplating the repercussions of running away. He chided himself for it.

A grown man shouldn't be "running away." He should be moving out.

And what would he tell Dennis? He'd promised to move in with him tomorrow. Yet here he was staring at the movie posters on his wall while his parents were downstairs, oblivious to his plans.

The building tension forced him to his feet. He paced around the room, his stomach twisting from the dueling responsibilities. Why did everyone want so much from him? Why couldn't he just do what he wanted?

What *did* he want? He shook his head. He wasn't sure. His mind was murky.

A tremor started in his bowels. It shook its way up his torso and into his limbs. When it was too much to bear he lashed out, throwing one of his action figures across the room. It crashed into the wall and exploded, showering his bed with small plastic shards.

"Shit!" Why did he do that? That was his favorite. Now he felt even worse.

"Mike?" His mother knocked on the door.

He ran to his bed and threw his covers back, hiding the evidence of his tantrum. "Come in."

The door creaked open and she peeked inside. "Are you alright?"

"Yeah."

She stepped in and shut the door. "Are you sure?"

He nodded.

"Your father's just trying to take care of you."

He snorted. "I should be taking care of myself."

She hugged him. "You need us. You know that. We need you, too."

He squeezed her back and tried to think of what he would say to Dennis.

Friday morning, after his father left for the office, Mike crept into his parent's room and stole his check card. He once again felt foolish and childish, stealing his *own* check card, but his father kept it hidden to ensure Mike's money wasn't spent. He always gave his son a line about helping to save for the future, but Mike suspected it was a way to maintain control.

He walked a mile to the closest shopping center and withdrew a few hundred dollars. Then he went to the street corner where he had told his friend to meet him and waited.

At a quarter past the hour, a small U-Haul truck pulled up. Mike opened the door and hopped in.

"Morning." Dennis handed him a cup of coffee and took a sip from his own. He had a giant smile plastered across his face.

"Hey."

"So, why did you want me to pick you up here? Your Dad going to work late?"

"No. He left already."

"Well, let's go pack your stuff."

Mike stared at the lid of his coffee.

"Fuck, Mike. You didn't tell them, did you?"

"I was going to. I swear. It's just that Dad tore into me as soon as I got home and—"

"Okay, okay. So when are you going to tell them?"

"I don't know."

"How about tonight?"

"I guess."

Dennis sighed. "This is what you want to do, right? I'm not pressuring you into anything, am I?"

Of course he is. The voice returned. *He always pressures you. Everyone does. Tell him that's what he's doing.*

"No, you're not pressuring me. I want to."

Pussy.

"Good. So tonight, then?"

"Yeah." Mike pulled the wad of twenties out and handed it to Dennis. "That's the most the ATM would let me get, but I can give you the rest tomorrow."

"Cool. Then you and Eileen can talk about her car."

Instead of the usual talk about Mike's parents, they discussed what movies were coming out that week and which were worth seeing. Dennis came in and out of the conversation as he struggled with the rental truck. He shushed Mike while maneuvering up the curved roads to the apartment building. They crested the hill intact and Dennis parked in front of the stairs.

"Well," he said as they undid the gate on the back of the truck, "I guess I get first pick on where my stuff goes." The gate rumbled upward and he jumped into the back of the truck. "Let's start with the couch." They wrestled it down.

Sirens sounded in the distance. As they carried the couch onto the sidewalk, the wail grew louder.

"I think it's coming up here."

The ambulance roared into view. A police cruiser was behind it. Both screeched to a halt in front of the truck and two EMTs sprinted up the steps toward the apartment. The cruiser doors opened and two officers followed.

Dennis sat his end of the couch down and sprinted after them.

"Shit. Dennis!" Mike fought his end to the ground and followed.

A tide of bodies pressed into him as he entered the lobby, a sea of anxious faces staring down the hall. Mike caught up to Dennis as he pushed his way through.

"What's going on?" Dennis asked.

"It's Lloyd," someone said. "He's—"

"Put it down, Mr. Trent." One of the cops circled through Mike's view. He craned his neck to get a better look.

The EMTs crouched on the ground and pulled gauze from their bags. The cops stood in a defensive position, their hands hovering over their guns. Ahead of them a thin man, more bone than flesh, paced back and forth in the hallway. He was shirtless, his skin striped with red. His bare feet tracked blood in circles on the tiled floor.

He waved a butcher knife in front of him.

"Lloyd, please," someone pleaded.

"They're everywhere." He motioned with the knife. "Don't you see? They're crawling all over me. They're so goddamned filthy." He pressed the knife against his forearm and sliced off a thin ribbon of flesh. It hit the ground with a wet slap and blood drowned his arm.

Someone screamed.

"Fuck!" Dennis turned away.

Mike didn't want to look, but his eyes were drawn to the scene like magnets.

The cops made a move toward Lloyd. He waved the knife again and they hesitated.

"There are no bugs, Lloyd," one of them yelled. "I swear it."

The sight of blood, the tightness of bodies pressing in around him, the screaming—it was too much for Mike. His stomach lurched one way, then the other. Acid bit at the back of his tongue and the bitterness of his coffee bubbled up into his mouth. He pushed away from the crowd and emptied his stomach onto the floor.

"They're not just bugs." Lloyd pushed hair from his eyes, streaking his face with red. "They're fucking filthy cockroaches. AND THEY WON'T GO AWAY." He dug the knife into his arm again. The loud scrape of metal on bone echoed down the hall. Blood poured onto the floor like a water hose running and his arm dangled limp to his side.

The cops rushed in, tackled him to the ground and ripped the knife from him. He screamed, thrashed, painted the floor with his blood. The EMTs produced a needle. He bit at one of them. A cop wrenched his head back.

The injection only took seconds to work. When he was out they went to work bandaging his wounds.

After they had stopped most of the bleeding they wheeled him to the ambulance and sped off. The police took statements and searched his open apartment. The gruesome show was over and the crowd disappeared behind closed doors.

Dennis walked a tall redheaded woman to the elevator. Mike stared at the blood on the floor. His face had gone bone-white and cold. The image of red-on-white blurred into and out of focus.

Is this what we're filled with?

The blood stole him, pulled him into its pattern. The walls melted away and he was left in darkness.

A pool of light washed in, gleaming across the porcelain of a bathtub. Steam rose like fingers from the water. The red-on-white branched out over the tub, into the cracks of the tile on the walls and floor. In the water a crimson flower bloomed and grew until it pressed against the tub's walls. It kept growing, forcing bucketfuls of bloody water over the sides and across the floor, under the doorway, down the hall, staining the tan carpet as it made its way to the stairs, blossoming wider as it covered the walls of the house, so much blood, he would have never guessed that she had had so much blood inside of that tiny body, that she—

Dennis squeezed the back of his neck. "You alright?"

"Huh? Yeah. Yeah. I mean, I didn't even know the guy, right?"

"I'm sorry you had to see that."

Mike was silent.

"Hey. Let's get out of here and let them clean the hall up. We can go get a bite to eat or something and then unpack later."

"I don't think I could eat anything right now."

"Still…"

"Oh. Yeah. Okay."

Mike headed out the door. Dennis took one last look at the hallway before following him.

No one noticed the fat red cockroach scurry through the blood and under Lloyd's door.

★ ★ ★

The mop bucket squeaked like a dying rodent as it wound its way down the hall. The front wheel was warped and Reynaldo had to fight to keep it from slamming into the walls. He ground his teeth together as it squeaked along. He hated that sound more than anything, more than he hated his wife's nagging or his children fighting. No matter how many times he tried to repair it, or how many times he begged Rudy for a new bucket, he was always left listening to the bent wheel.

It could be worse, he reminded himself. He could be back in Juarez, shoveling shit from clogged toilets at pennies a day for gringo tourists. At least the plumbing worked here and his pay was decent. Not great, still below minimum wage, but under the table. Rent was free, so that was something. Not bad for an illegal groundskeeper.

Groundskeeper? Fucking janitor is more like it. Most of his time was spent cleaning up messes. The closest he came to "groundskeeping" was cleaning the pool and supervising the landscaping crew that maintained the yard. Lately, it had mostly been the messes. They were often mundane—a burst pipe, a leaky roof—but sometimes they were strange, like today. Too many of those involved blood.

He plunged his mop into the suds and splashed a figure eight on the tile. At least it was only blood this time. He knew how lucky he had been last time. He had buried the garbage bag in the field with Mr. Henry's clothes. He never opened it to see what was inside; he had long ago stopped being curious.

When the hall was clean he pushed the bucket back to the elevator and down into the basement. There he dumped the contents into a large sink. He turned off the light, undid the locks on a forgotten door, sat in a cold steel chair, and lit a cigar. It had been a long week and he needed this.

He reclined in the dark, letting the cigar's earthy taste roll around in his mouth, and waited. He grew impatient and almost left, but when the cigar was down to a stub his nose was tickled with a light breeze of cologne.

"Darling," he whispered as cold lips descended on him.

Chapter Five

Dennis fell into the couch and let the cushions swallow him. Most of his things were inside but didn't even fill half of the apartment.

Mike inched his way to the floor and leaned against the couch. He was drenched in sweat and fought to catch his breath. "Please tell me we're done."

"We're done."

They sat for a few minutes and relaxed. A knock at the door made them both sigh.

"Well?" Dennis tapped the back of Mike's head with the toe of his shoe. "You gonna answer your door?"

Mike shuffled over and opened it. A plate of brownies was shoved into his arms.

"Welcome to the building." A stocky woman in a jogging suit stepped into the apartment. Her brown hair was pulled into a ponytail and a smile almost split her face in two. She looked to Mike to be around his mother's age, but in much better shape. "I'm Margot, in 328. Kind of the unofficial welcoming committee."

"Uh, hi. I'm Mike. This is Dennis." She turned to Dennis and waved and Mike's eyes were drawn to the sway of her breasts.

Dennis stood. "Hi, Margot. Nice to meet you. Thanks for the brownies."

"My pleasure." She turned back to Mike and caught him staring at her chest.

He snapped his eyes up and prepared to apologize. The corner of her mouth turned and Mike was confused. He thought she looked a little like one of the nymphs in the courtyard.

"I love to bake," she went on, her eyes boring into his. "Anytime you wanna come by, I'll whip something up for you."

Mike swallowed. "Uh…great. Yeah. We'll, uh, we'll do that."

"Good. Now, I really gotta be going. I just wanted to introduce myself and welcome y'all here. It was nice meeting you boys." She ran her hand along Mike's shoulder on her way out.

He shut the door behind her and grinned. "She was nice."

"Yep." Dennis snatched the plate of brownies from him and crammed one into his mouth. "You flirt. Mmmmm. Good."

"I wasn't flirting."

"Don't be ashamed. I like that move."

"Move?"

"Yeah. Letting her catch you drool over her tits. That's good."

"I didn't—"

"Very subtle."

"So, I don't need to be home for a few hours." Mike's

voice cracked as he changed the subject. "What do you want to do?"

Dennis returned to the couch. "Man, I just want to lay here for a while. I gotta go get the rest of my shit later."

"Why didn't you pack it all in the truck?"

"Huh. I don't know. Maybe because someone else's furniture was supposed to be crammed in there."

"Why don't you show me around? I haven't seen the pool, or the laundry room, or—"

"C'mon, man. Let me rest."

"Yeah, but I haven't—"

"Just go look around. You don't need me holding your hand."

Mike nodded. "Fine."

★ ★ ★

The stairwell swayed under him. The steps rose and fell like heavy breathing and the walls twisted and swelled. Mike grabbed the railing and steadied himself. Blinked twice. Attempted to focus.

He had avoided the elevator because of its shaking and jostling, but the stairs were worse. Whoever had originally laid out the tile and painted the walls must have been a fan of MC Escher. The stairs were an odd jumble of black and gray tiles assembled with no known geometric pattern, while the walls were the same faded and stained yellow as the rest of the building. The difference here was that there were spirals painted on the wall in a slightly different shade of yellow; no doubt someone's misguided idea of art deco. Add to all of this a single, filthy yellow bulb per floor and the effect was startling.

He fumed at Dennis' remark and the nauseating stair-well just worsened his mood. *Fuck him. What if I don't move into this shit hole? Yeah, the apartment is great, but the building… And do I want to live with someone like Dennis that expects—*

Expects what?

Expects him to act his age and start taking care of him-self. He knew that no matter how harsh Dennis was at times, he always had Mike's best interests at heart. Mike just didn't know how to take responsibility for himself. The idea of it turned his stomach.

At the second floor he had had enough and decided to take his chances with the elevator. The heavy metal door screeched into the hall, its black trail carving deeper into the floor. He stepped out and had to push hard to shut it behind him. He stopped to catch his breath and cursed himself for the shape he was in.

He passed an open apartment and couldn't help but peek inside. A TV tray sat covered in dishes, a large, shirt-less man behind it shoveling food into his mouth. His head was shaved and he wore a salt and pepper goatee. Tattoos ran up and down his arms, over his chest and back. Mike thought he saw a swastika, but sprinted off when the man turned toward him and so couldn't be sure.

He pressed the elevator's button and listened to the sounds of the building as he waited. The box hummed its way down the shaft. Laughter echoed behind one of the doors. The faint sounds of a talk show murmured from the skinhead's open apartment. Music played somewhere, gentle notes of piano accented with violin. The deep bass rhythm of feet pounded up the stairwell.

The elevator doors opened. He stepped inside and almost pushed the button for the ground floor, but hesitated when he saw "5." Wasn't the building only three floors?

Of course. The tower. It was higher than the rest of the building. Curious what kind of view it offered, he pressed its button.

He regretted it as the box struggled to climb through the shaft. It finally ground to a halt and the doors split apart to reveal a small room. He stepped inside, shuffling through bits of drywall and kicking up clouds of white dust. Long beams of sunlight danced through the shadows. Mike took three steps into the room and paused. What he had thought was a wall to his right was nothing more than a giant piece of filthy white canvas nailed to the ceiling.

He pulled the edge away from the wall. Through tiny gaps between crisscrossed two-by-fours, he saw the back of a red sofa splotched with mildew. Bits of stuffing escaped here and there. It sat facing another sheet of canvas. This one breathed, its contracting and expanding hinting at an open window somewhere beyond it.

Where would that window be? He tried to get his bearings. Imagined the front of the building. Was there a window there? No, it was just brick. The elevator was in an alcove positioned to the left of the front doors. He had taken a left from the elevator, so would the window open onto the back of the building? Why would a window open onto that field? And whose couch was that?

Not one for puzzles, he climbed back into the box.

Once on the ground floor, he stepped outside and made his way through the courtyard, hands in his pockets and head down to avoid the statues. He felt ridiculous doing so, but the values his parents had driven into him ran deep. To think lustful thoughts was to invite guilt and he didn't want to be caught doing so in the open.

Instead of taking the stairs, he walked around the gently sloping hill to the side of the building. Flower beds encased the place like a moat and were filled with a wide array of blossoms whose names he didn't know. Allison could have rattled them off. She'd had a great love for nature and her mind seemed to trap every scrap of information it ever came across.

The heat pressed down on him like a wet coat. He spotted the Weeping Willow not far from the building and made his way over. The vines hung to the ground, mostly wearing their summer green, but a few white blooms were still visible here and there. They caught the light like silver buttons.

His grandmother had a tree like this in her yard. He and his sister had spent a dozen summers cradled in its low, wide branches reading. Allison had taught him to read using faded copies of "Dick and Jane" from their grandmother's basement.

The vines parted like curtains and he crept into the shade.

Stepping into the shadow of the Willow was like stepping into a memory. He was five years old again, following his sister around everywhere she went. He was a Prince, she had told him, and she was his protector.

"No one knows I'm really a girl," she said while skipping over the humpbacks of giant roots erupting from the earth like sea monsters breaking waves. "I cut my hair off like Jonah Arc and beat all the other knights in a duel to be your bodyguard." She swung a stick around in her hand like a sword and he had no trouble envisioning her in her role, covered with silver armor and defeating his foes.

Only now she was gone and he had to fight his battles on his own.

He grabbed one of the thick branches and, planting his foot against the side of the tree, hoisted himself up. It took three tries to mount the limb, but he finally straddled it and leaned back against the rough bark. He closed his eyes and took in the smell of dirt and wood. A squirrel scrambled somewhere above him.

They used to nap like this after defeating dragons and trolls, the hard day of fighting exhausting their tiny bodies. Allison would nudge him awake, produce a peanut butter and banana sandwich from her "My Little Pony" backpack, and give him his reading lesson. He realized that most of his favorite memories occurred in the embrace of his grandmother's tree.

The high-pitched laughter of children playing rushed by. The squirrel chattered above. He opened his eyes and glanced up, looking for the rodent. Bright blue slashes carved up the shade toward the top of the tree. He blinked at the brightness, his eyes finding a glowing orb sailing skyward. A giant silver balloon splotched with red and blue came into focus. It climbed higher and higher, sunlight glistening from its surface, a breeze jerking it back and forth, until it vanished from view.

He closed his eyes again, the image of the balloon projected onto his lids. He should get down soon, he thought. Explore the rest of the grounds before heading home. But for now he was relaxed. Calm. Tranquil.

I could do this every day if I lived here.
He smiled.

★ ★ ★

After making plans to meet Eileen at his old place that afternoon, Dennis gathered together a small basket of clothes that had failed the sniff test and took the elevator to the basement. It was a labyrinthine structure of mesh-fenced storage units winding past giant pipes and the occasional locked door. Harsh yellow bulbs were hung every few feet and the floor was dotted with shallow puddles. Dust-filled beams of sunlight washed through from tiny windows scattered around the room.

The laundry room was a slate gray concrete box with six washer/dryer combo units and a folding table covered in floral print wallpaper. It was colder than the rest of the basement by a few degrees and damp. He didn't care for it, but conceded it was still a big improvement over the laundromat.

A pile of clothing rested atop one of the machines. He opened the one next to it and shoveled in his own clothes. He poured a cap full of detergent, slid three quarters in, and hit the button. The machine shook and growled to life.

He glanced at the pile. It was underwear, a few bras and a pair of silk panties. He wondered if they were Karen's. A strange urge overtook him and he looked around to make sure no one was watching. He was alone.

He bent over the clothing and inhaled. He recognized the sweet scent of strawberries and tropical flowers. His mind flooded with images of her walking through her apartment with them on.

What was he doing? He felt embarrassed and backed away. Why was he fantasizing about Karen like this when he had Eileen?

Because she's a goddess.

Still, he knew he shouldn't be sniffing her panties like some pervert in a sitcom. What if someone walked in?

A noise startled him. It sounded like two hard footsteps in quick succession. He scanned the room. The door leading to the rest of the basement was open. He stuck his head through and looked around. The storage units were undisturbed and none of the shadows moved. Water dripped from a large pipe on the ceiling, splashing into a puddle below it. The other puddles were still.

He turned to the back of the laundry room to see a burgundy door covered in dust with the paint chipped around the edges. The doorknob was missing and two padlocks kept it closed. The locks were old and rusted, but when Dennis tugged on them they refused to budge.

He bent to peer through the hole where the knob should have been. It was dark. He couldn't make out much but a chair. A single shaft of sunlight leaked onto it. It was dark metal, thick and old, likely an antique. It looked like it had been painted over with a coat of dust. A pair of straps dangled from the arms. Another pair draped from the front legs onto the floor.

What was he looking at? He couldn't puzzle out what its significance was or why it was there. He wished he could see more, but the rest was black.

He left his basket on top of the machine and stepped back into the elevator. He was about to press his floor number, but pressed "1" instead. He thought he would look around for Mike.

He felt some guilt for snapping at him earlier, but Mike could be such a child. Dennis understood why and sympathized, but it didn't change the fact that it was frustrating. His self-absorption and refusal to take responsibility for himself were bad enough, but Dennis had never met someone so consumed with fear. He wasn't just afraid of his parents or afraid of school or afraid of being on his own—Mike was afraid of *life*.

But Mike was his friend and he had made a promise to watch out for him. He held out hope that with a little prodding the boy could grow into a man.

When he stepped from the elevator, laughter echoed down the hall. He followed it out the open double doors at the rear of the building and into the pool area. He was surprised to find Karen in the water, wet hair slicked back, arms propped on the sides of the pool and holding her just high enough to see the swell of her breasts. The sight froze him for a moment and he couldn't help but stare.

A tall black man sprawled out on a pool chair. He was lean but muscular, with a dark wave of a dozen or more braids falling from the back of the chair. He had a grin plastered across his face.

Margot sat next to him. She wore a blue bathing suit that fought to hold her inside of it and a pair of aviator style sunglasses. To Dennis' surprise Mike sat beside her. In contrast to how relaxed everyone else was, Mike was rigid. He sat upright, one hand tucked into the pocket of his jeans while the other played with a button on his shirt.

Karen noticed Dennis and waved. "Hey, Dennis. We

thought a little sun might help us take our minds off of the morning. Care to join us?"

He walked over and smiled. "Can I take a rain check? I haven't unpacked my swim trunks yet."

"You don't need them," Margot said. "Just go in the buff."

He laughed. "Yeah, I don't think so."

She patted Mike's knee. "That's what your roommate said too. Did you like the brownies?"

"Delicious."

"Glad you enjoyed them. I should have stuck around and helped finish them. Turns out my appointment got canceled."

"By you," the black man said.

"Well, that don't matter. Where are my manners? Dennis, this is Matthew."

Dennis shook his hand and turned in time to see Karen splash below the surface and swim off.

Margot grinned. "She's something, isn't she?"

He nodded. "Sure is."

"Why, if I were into women…"

Matthew smirked. "Aren't you?"

"Matt!" She slapped his leg.

He laughed. "You better watch it. I'll leave you out for the Blue Boy tonight."

"Blue Boy?" Dennis asked.

"It's nothing," she said. "Just one of this building's tall tales. Maybe I'll sit you boys down around the fire one night and tell them all to you over a glass of wine."

"Or three," Matt said.

"So," Dennis started. "Uh…this morning…"

"Poor Lloyd." Margot shook her head. "He just ain't been right for a long time. Ever since his girlfriend went missing."

"Went missing?"

"Yeah. He swore someone took her, but the police said she left him. She left a note about running off with her 'sweetie'—"

"Darling," Matt interrupted.

"'Darling.' That's right. Anyway, he just sorta went downhill ever since. Poor guy."

Matthew nodded. "Better off in an asylum."

Dennis turned to Mike. He had a forced and awkward smile on his face and Dennis could tell he didn't like hanging around so many new people. He probably got called over here by Margot and then couldn't figure out a way to leave. Probably better give him one. "When you gotta get home, pal?"

"Um…soon, I guess."

Margot took her sunglasses off and sat up. "Home? I thought you two were roommates?"

"Yeah. We are. But Mike's still got a month on his old lease, so he's taking his time moving in."

Mike nodded.

"Good," Margot said. "I was afraid I wasn't going to get to see you again." She patted Mike's knee.

"Oh, we'll be around," Dennis said. "We should probably get going."

"Yeah." Mike stood and straightened out his shirt. "It was nice talking to you guys."

Matthew grunted and closed his eyes.

"Anytime," Margot slid her sunglasses back on and

smiled. "Just knock when you wanna do it again."

Dennis took one last look at Karen swimming before dragging Mike off.

When they were on the elevator, Mike sighed. "Thanks for getting me out of there."

Dennis laughed. "Man, that Margot chick is all over you."

Mike's face was red. "No."

"Right."

"You think?"

"I think."

"Hmph."

Dennis almost warned him away from her, but thought better of it. Maybe it would do him good to get laid. Especially by an older woman. Maybe she could get him to grow up a little.

"I've got some laundry in the wash. You really need to get home soon?"

"Yeah. I guess…I mean…well, I'm definitely going to tell them tonight."

"Good." Dennis patted his friend's back. It seemed Margot's influence had started already.

★ ★ ★

Sweat dripped onto the table in a fast rhythm. *Tap-tap-taptap. Tap-tap-taptap.* Jack rubbed his hands and forearms dry with an oil-stained rag. The heat under the lights of his workroom made it difficult to focus on soldering the tiny board in his voltage meter. He wished he could do without two or three of them, but knew better. There could be no shadows here. Not in this room.

When he was done he slid the board back into place, reconnected wires, and tested it on some batteries. Satisfied that it worked, he pulled a notebook labeled "anomalies" from his shelf and committed the last several weeks of readings to memory. Then he pulled his regular notebook down and started his rounds.

He always started on the roof and worked his way down. There were no readings out of the ordinary this time (except for the elevator, but its being out of the ordinary was nothing out of the ordinary and required an entire notebook of its own). He kept his Maglite clicked on the entire way, dispelling any shadows he came across. He had never had a problem anywhere outside of the basement, but didn't want to take any chances.

When he finished, he grabbed the plastic grocery bag from his fridge, went outside, and trekked through the thick brush of the forest away from Raynham and the supermarket. He slid down a hill, dirt and leaves flying through the air, and came to rest against a small concrete rise. It was half covered with fallen limbs and rotting leaves. He swept enough of the debris away to see the series of padlocks holding the rusted gate in place. He tugged on them out of ritual. He knew they'd hold but needed to check for his own piece of mind.

The tunnel had been disconnected from the basement years ago. A large section of it had been hauled off and the makeshift grate installed as a cap on this piece in the woods. The tunnel had been used during the building's days as a hospital to haul the dead away in secrecy lest the living patients see what awaited them. The other end had been covered when the highway was built. This grate was the only way in or out.

Thank God.

He pulled the tubes of hamburger from the grocery bag, sliced them open with his pocketknife, and shoved the meat through the tiny squares of the grate.

"Dinner time, boys."

His voice echoed through the black tunnel.

Silence.

The fear that they'd already eaten shook his hands. Then he heard the familiar scratching and shuffling. Jack shoved the last bit through and scrambled up the hill. He hummed a tune as he jogged through the woods. He hated to hear them eat.

It gave him nightmares.

Chapter Six

A pile of clothes had devoured the room. Dennis leaned against the wall and stared at the mess, not sure if he could tell what was clean and what was dirty.

He decided to throw everything in boxes and use the sniff test when he unpacked. He thanked God their new place had onsite laundry. The low point of his week was lugging a basket of clothes to the nearest laundromat. Once he got there he would sit and wait for his clothes to finish, paranoid of laundry thieves in the same way old women clutched jewelry against their chests as they walked down certain streets. He felt like an idiot thinking someone would steal his sweaters or gym clothes, but the laundromat was not in a good area. Of course, he had met Eileen there, so he supposed it wasn't *all* bad.

He taped the last box of clothes shut, scribbled "Mo' clothes!" on the top, and sat on a milk crate. He glanced at his watch. *3:55pm.* He was giddy that he was finally leaving this place. It wasn't a bad apartment when he first moved in, but that was four years ago. It hadn't taken more than a year for the tiny efficiency to feel cramped. He could never relax for more than a few minutes inside before claustrophobia overtook him and he had to leave. In the end his need to get outside was probably good for him. He had been working a decent amount of overtime at the gym and hitting the weights more than usual. Both would come in good use in the fall when classes would cut into his work schedule and Coach Hatmaker would require a tortuous tryout to get his spot back on the wrestling team.

A different spot, he reminded himself. He had only been a hundred eighty five pounds when he last wrestled. Now he was hovering around two hundred. Not a heavyweight by any means, but still a weight class or two up. He remembered Hatmaker's disposition and knew the coach would put him through the wringer to make sure that all of that added weight was functional on the mat.

A knock at his door pulled his mind back to the present. He stood, walked across the room, and squinted into the peephole. It was pitch black.

"Eileen…"

He heard her giggle on the other side and unlocked the door. She always found it funny to press her thumb against the peephole. Dennis thought she must have watched too many Mafia movies as a kid. He swung the door open.

"What are you doing here?"

She faked a frown. "I can leave, if you want."

"Get in here." He tugged her arm and pulled her inside. She held a plastic grocery bag in one hand. He shut the door behind her.

"I went out for some food and thought you might need a little snack, too. Ya know, with all that packing you should be doing." She scanned the room and saw nothing but four boxes, a sleeping bag, and the milk crate. "Damn. You're fast."

"I practice a lot. So, what did you bring?"

She sat the bag on a box and pulled out a block of cheese and some crackers. She took a step to the side and smiled, doing her best Vanna White.

Dennis whistled. "That's a mighty fine spread there, miss."

"Why, thank you. The food's not bad either." She leaned in and kissed him.

He unrolled the sleeping bag onto the floor. She sliced the cheese with his pocketknife and joined him on the bag with a tube of crackers. He rattled off his list of reasons to be happy about moving and she laughed.

"And that's just me," he said and stuffed a cracker in his mouth. "Mike's gonna be a whole new man."

"Are you sure about this? What if Mike backs out again?"

"He won't."

"But what if he does? Can you afford the place on your own?"

He shrugged. "For a month or two. If he flakes—and he won't—I'll just post a flyer on campus. It won't be a problem."

"You have a lot of faith in that kid."

Dennis laughed. "Kid? He's only two years younger than you."

"Physically, yeah. Emotionally?"

"Yeah. I know." He leaned against the wall. "I have to push him like this, ya know? Everybody else in his life coddles him. That's why he's still—"

"Fucked up?"

He frowned.

"Sorry."

"What about me?" he asked. "Think I'm fucked up, too?"

'Oh, yeah. Definitely." She laughed and punched his thigh. "But now I'm in too deep."

"Laugh it up, Chuckles. Laugh it up."

She crawled across the sleeping bag and inched herself up until she straddled him. "Naw. Truth be told, I think you're just right."

"The porridge Goldilocks chose, huh?"

"Something like that." She kissed him, full and deep. One of her hands pressed against the wall above his head for support. The other traced small lines down the back of his neck.

His own hands drew her closer, pressing her small body against him. He slid a hand up the back of her shirt and rubbed the warm skin of her lower back. It didn't take long for her hips to grind against his pelvis.

They stayed on the sleeping bag for the next hour, exploring the contours of each other's bodies until they collapsed with exhaustion.

Eileen draped an arm over Dennis and rested her face against his chest. "You're in pretty good shape, pal."

"You ain't so bad yourself." He was quiet for a moment, thinking of what to say.

It was too long and she noticed. "What's wrong?"

"Nothing's wrong. I just...does this mean we're..."

"Exclusive? I don't know. Do you want to be?"

"Well, yeah."

"Good," she said and kissed him. "Me too."

"Good."

"That's settled. What took you so long?"

He ran his fingers through her hair. "I don't know. You just seemed like it wasn't something that you wanted."

"Really? How?"

"I…shit. I don't know, really. That's just what I thought."

"You sure you weren't just displacing your own fears and concerns onto me?"

He laughed. "Damn, girl. One psychology class and you think you're Freud."

"Seriously. After everything you've been through…I mean, have you been with anyone since Allison?"

"Honestly?"

"No, lie to me. Yes, honestly."

"Well, there were a couple of, um…"

"Fuck buddies?"

"Friends with benefits."

"Fuck buddies."

"Okay. Fuck buddies. Anyway, I've slept with a couple of girls—always using protection, of course."

"Of course."

"But I haven't been involved with anyone. Not seriously. Hadn't really wanted to, truth be told."

"Then you saw me playing *Donkey Kong* while my clothes dried and your whole world changed."

"What can I say? I love me some *Donkey Kong*."

She laughed and propped herself on one elbow. He looked up at her and smiled. She was beautiful. The smell of her was even better; it lingered over him like the sweat that sprinkled his body and smelled like spring. Her skin was soft and warm against his.

"Can I ask you something?"

He nodded. "I can deny you nothing at the moment."

"What was she like?"

"I don't really think…"

"I'm sorry." She turned and stood. "I shouldn't have pried. I—"

"Lie down," he said and pulled her back onto the sleeping bag. "What I mean is—do you really want to hear about it? It won't bother you?"

"That's why I asked."

"It's just that…it didn't end like a normal relationship, ya know? We didn't yell and cuss at each other. She didn't run off with some other guy and I didn't cheat on her. I never went through a phase where I hated her, or realized how bad we were for each other. She *died*."

Eileen took his hand. "I want to know everything about you and that means knowing about her. If you're okay with talking about her, I want to know."

He sighed and rolled onto his back. His eyes traced the cracks in his ceiling and he debated whether he should give her the whole truth or the edited version. He settled on the edited version. "She was…well, energetic. From doing gymnastics all her life, I guess. She would never get tired. I was an All-State wrestler and she would make me feel like I was out of shape half the time. She was always up on current events—politics, genocide in Africa, all of that. And she genuinely cared, too. Not like most people who just fake a cause to be cool or whatever. She loved her family, loved her brother, and helped out in the community with things. Ya know, bake sales and all that."

He took a deep breath and continued. "She had this short, rock star kind of haircut. Like an updated Pat Benatar or something. I know, sounds lame, but it looked great on her. Her hair was dark, too. Like the sky right before it rains. And she had these gorgeous blue eyes. I've never seen that color blue again.

"She used to laugh a lot, said it was what made life worth living. She...she had this pet turtle, named it Darwin. Her parents hated that. She used to come to all of my matches, and she would make these signs..." He laughed. "They were fucking retarded, really. All covered in glitter with my name written in big block letters, and she would hold them up high during my matches and scream like a banshee while I wrestled. My friends loved that.

"Then, she had a bad few months. Grades slipped, she quit gymnastics, started missing school. She was still there for me, but..." He couldn't bring himself to tell the truth and so skipped ahead in the story. "Her parents came down real hard on her. School nurse said she needed to be on anti-depressants, but her Dad was against her going to a psychiatrist. Then I get a call one day, from her mom. She's crying and...she starts cussing me and...They had found her. Earlier. In the bathtub."

Eileen sniffed. He kept his gaze on the ceiling. Inside he was a waterfall of tears, but he didn't let himself cry about Allison anymore. Not in front of other people, at least.

"We buried her that weekend, and then everyone's life went to shit."

She kissed his cheek. When she pulled away he was left with a hot wetness high on his jaw. It wasn't a surprise; he had learned long ago to never underestimate a woman's capacity for empathy. That was something else that Allison had taught him.

"I'm sorry," she said.

"It's okay. I've had a couple of years to deal with it."

"I mean I'm sorry I made you tell it."

He rolled over to face her. She had wiped her face dry, but her eyes were still puffy and red. "You didn't make me do anything. You asked and I obliged." He kissed her. "How does it make *you* feel?"

"Awful," she said, and gave a nervous laugh. "But I needed to know."

"Still want to be serious with me?"

"You bet." She pressed her lips against his.

"Hope you don't regret that."

She giggled. "I can't possibly think of how I could."

★ ★ ★

The Pritchett family ate dinner in silence. Mike stared at the vegetables on his plate drowning under a tide of gravy. His mother cut her food into tiny bites. His father chomped away.

"Why aren't you eating?" his mother asked.

His stomach turned. He'd felt like vomiting since taking his first bite. He wished he didn't have to do this. Wished he could keep things as they were. Wished he was okay still being a kid.

"Mike?"

The words formed in his mind, rolled down the back of his neck, and rested like a lead weight in his mouth. But, try as he might, he couldn't force his jaws apart. He was saying it, he was sure, positive the electro-chemical impulses were firing along his nerves, but nothing happened.

His father sat his fork on the plate. "Mike? Your mother's asking you a question."

Here it was. Now or never. Be a man for once, dammit.

"I'm moving." It leaked out and sapped all of his energy. His hands shook and a bead of sweat rolled down his nose. It fell from the tip and splashed into his gravy. His throat was tight and breathing was painful. *But I said it.* As scared as he was, he was also shocked. And proud.

"What was that?" His father's voice was soft. Questioning. *Back out. He didn't hear. You can go back. Pretend it didn't happen. Like a do-over in kickball or—*

"I'm moving," he repeated.

His parents stared at him. Neither moved or reacted, except to blink.

"Dennis got a place," he continued. "It's a two bedroom. Nice area. Rent's cheap." They stayed silent and he went on. "He's gonna teach me how to drive. His girlfriend's selling her car. It's a Saturn. Good condition. Low miles. She'll cut me a deal."

"Don't be silly, Mike." His mother went back to cutting her food.

His father stared at him from across the table, his face expressionless. "No," he said and shook his head.

Mike felt heat in his stomach. It rose all the way to his face. He ground his teeth together. "I wasn't asking permission. I was telling you."

"And I'm telling you 'no.' It's not open for discussion."

"Why would you want to leave here anyway?" His mother shook her head. "It doesn't make sense. You have free room and board, I do your laundry—"

"That's why." Mike fought hard to keep his anger in check. "I need to learn how to take care of myself."

"I have no faith you can do that," his father said. "Now keep quiet. You're upsetting your mother."

"I can't keep quiet."

"Mike—"

"I've already given Dennis my share of the deposit."

His father's face twisted. He rose from the table and stomped upstairs.

His mother shook her head again. "You shouldn't have, Michael. You shouldn't have."

After a moment, his father stormed back down. "You son of a bitch," he roared. "You snuck into my room and stole that goddamn card."

"I can't steal what's mine."

His father paced back and forth by the table. "How much did you give him?"

His mother continued eating.

"Half of the deposit."

"How much is that?"

He opened his mouth to answer, but somehow "That's none of your business" came out instead.

"How dare you…What has happened to you? Your sister never would have talked to us like that."

"I'm not her, though, am I?"

"You most certainly aren't. She'd be ashamed of you if she could see how you treat us. And what would she think of you moving in with the son-of-bitch that took her from us?"

Mike shook his head. "Dennis didn't take her, Dad. She killed herself."

His mother gasped. Her spoon fell from her hand and clattered onto her plate.

His father's eyes glistened. His jaw shook. "That bastard is why she did it."

"No, *you're* why she did it." Lights flashed in Mike's eyes and the world shifted. He blinked and found himself on the ground, his chair tipped over and his food spilled across the floor. He tasted pennies. His ears rang.

Fucking Christ, he punched me!

His mother stood over him, her hands pressed against his father's chest. The old man trembled, his fist clenched so tight that his fingernails bit into his palm and blood leaked out over his knuckles.

"YOU PIECE OF SHIT!" Spittle flew. "I'LL FUCKING KILL YOU!"

Mike crawled to the staircase, stood, ran to his room, and locked his door behind him. He sat on his bed and listened to his father scream, his mother try to calm him. Eventually the front door slammed and his father's car sped off.

He felt like crying. Yet a weight had been lifted from his shoulders. He felt guilty for what he had said to his father, but it was the truth.

His mother knocked on the door. He moved to it slowly, deliberately, like he waded through mounds of sand. He knew what was coming and watched it all from somewhere outside of himself. His world was ending.

Not ending. Changing. Everything would be different from here on out.

He wasn't sure how he felt about that.

She cried as she told him his father wanted him out of the house. They hugged and then she went to her room. Mike knew she was draining the contents of the whiskey bottle hidden in her underwear drawer.

He grabbed a bag and shoved clothes inside. When the bag was full he looked around for a suitcase. He thought one was in his closet, but then it hit him: it was in Allison's room.

They hadn't taken a trip since before she died. She had borrowed his suitcase for a gymnastics weekend in D.C. a few months earlier and hadn't given it back before everything happened.

He tiptoed across the hall and stopped in front of Allison's door. His mother cried behind her own door as he stared at the dusty outlines of old posters long ago pulled down from his sister's door and boxed away. He hadn't been inside in years. He wondered if it looked the same. He knew his mother cleaned it top to bottom every Friday, but he didn't know how many of his sister's things were still inside.

He took a deep breath and turned the knob.

A pale sliver of moonlight limped through the window and fell across the bed. He was startled by how much the room conformed to his memories. The brass bed with red sheets poking out from beneath a vanilla comforter. The scented candles lining the shelves and filling the room with a subtle hint of rose. The posters of Olympians, musicians, and poets.

It was like a dream of better days, a hazy memory fighting its way through the cold that had claimed the home and bringing a bit of warmth back. It was a fragile thing and Mike knew if he clutched at it that it would shatter.

He sat on his sister's bed. It *was* warm and comfortable. It felt like home.

He hoped he had made the right decision.

★ ★ ★

The bottle of wine slipped from Eileen's fingers and clanked onto the concrete.

"Shit."

It bounced once before rolling away. She sat the two bags of food on her trunk and bent to grab it, one hand holding her black dress down to avoid revealing herself. She snatched the bottle up and found a small space in one of the bags where she could shove the neck.

She checked everything one last time before heading up the stairs to Dennis' building. She had planned the evening when she first heard he was moving. She was making lasagna, followed by a chocolate and peanut butter pie. The bottle of wine was a favorite she had developed a taste for during a summer spent with her family in Tuscany and the black dress was slick and revealing.

"Need a hand?"

She hadn't heard anyone approach and jumped. She turned to see a tall, thin man in a black shirt and jeans. He had dark, wavy hair and wore a pair of stylish glasses. He smiled.

"Didn't mean to scare you," he said.

"Oh. It's all right. This place is just a little creepy. Especially at dusk."

"Sure is. Let me give you a hand."

She handed him one of the bags. "Thanks. I'm Eileen."

"Jason." He opened the front door and followed her in. "What floor do you live on?"

"Oh. I don't live here. Visiting someone on three."

Jason laughed. "Boyfriend?"

"Yeah. Why's that funny?"

"Just figures." He pressed the button for the elevator and smiled again.

"What does?"

"Pretty girl like you, I was hoping to get your number."

Eileen rolled her eyes, but still blushed. "Right."

He laughed again. "Sorry. Worth a try though, huh?" They stepped into the elevator. "Nice dress, by the way."

She glanced down to make sure the bottom hadn't come up too high. It was still down. *Just a compliment, Eileen. Take it.* "Thanks. How long have you lived here?"

"Three years. My whole band used to live here, but they've trickled off to other places."

"What kind of music do you guys play?"

"Rock. No 'emo' or 'metal' or anything. Just rock."

"Cool."

The doors opened and they walked to Dennis' apartment.

Jason's cell phone rang. He glanced at the caller ID and sighed. "Aw, shit. I've gotta take this. You okay the rest of the way?"

"I think I'll be fine. Thanks for your help."

He handed her the bag. "My pleasure. Maybe I'll see you around."

She just nodded. She was flattered that he flirted with her, but with things getting serious with Dennis, she wasn't going to encourage him.

He opened his phone and chatted as he climbed back into the elevator.

She knocked on Dennis' door. He answered in a towel, his hair dripping.

"Just get out of the shower?"

"What gave it away?" He kissed her on the cheek and grabbed a bag. They walked in and sat the bags on the table. "You look fantastic."

"I know," she winked.

"Now how did you get dressed up so fast after leaving my place and I'm still wet?"

"Secret female stuff. If I told you, I'd have to kill you."

He laughed. "So what's for dinner?"

She grabbed the towel and yanked it from him.

"Hey."

She threw it across the room. Dennis didn't bother covering himself; instead he put his hands on his hips and mock frowned.

"*I'm* for dinner," she said and slowly pulled her dress up to reveal a thin ribbon of white silk.

Later, after dinner and dessert, they cuddled in a chair by the window. Dennis had changed into a pair of pajama pants and Eileen sat in his lap wearing one of his oversized sweatshirts. They stared out the window at the field. Drops of moisture in the grass captured the moonlight like a thousand diamonds sparkling below them. It was beautiful.

Except for the boarded up supermarket and skeleton of a shopping mall lying dead at the edge.

"So did your uncle Gary say why they never tore that place down?"

"Never said."

"It's a pretty horrible sight. Gotta be some kind of safety hazard, too."

She shrugged. "Who knows? People in charge of that sort of thing are usually morons."

"True."

Eileen jumped to her feet. "Let's go down there."

"What?"

"Yeah. C'mon. Let's go explore." She grabbed his hands.

"Are you serious?"

"Yeah. Why not?"

"Um…I don't know. Snakes. Rusty nails. Spiders. Crazy homeless people."

"Chicken."

He laughed.

"I'll make it worth your while…"

He cocked an eyebrow. "How's that?"

She leaned close to his ear and whispered what she had planned.

"Let's go," he said.

He found an old pair of gym shorts that, while they didn't fit Eileen, they didn't fall off of her, either. He grabbed a T-shirt, his cell phone, and his keys, and they both slipped their shoes on and went downstairs.

"I think we can get there through the pool area," he said.

"Maybe we could skinny dip after…"

"I don't think that would be a good idea."

"Spoil sport."

They heard splashing as they headed for the pool. Dennis hoped it wasn't Karen swimming around out there. He was afraid his attraction to her would be too obvious. They opened the doors and stepped out onto the concrete.

The water was still and quiet. A slight breeze whispered through the brush.

He scanned the area. There was no sign of anyone. "I thought I heard someone out here."

"Well, whoever it was is awful fast."

The growth blocked the moonlight from the pool and the two floodlights positioned over it seemed to create more shadows than they dispelled. Dennis understood why the area was empty.

They walked around the pool and through the narrow walkway where he had glimpsed a fountain. When they approached Dennis finally had a clear view of it.

"Well, that's definitely not family friendly," Eileen said.

He nodded. The fountain wasn't very large. A statue carved in the same style as the ones lining the courtyard climbed from its center. Yet this one formed both shapes: the satyr and the nymph. The nymph stood, bare-breasted, her hands raised together over her head and her fingers intertwined. Her eyes were closed and she bit her lower lip, forever locked in a moment of ecstasy.

The satyr was behind her, one hand covering the space between the nymph's legs. The fingers disappeared between her stone thighs, the cause of the nymph's expression. The satyr's other hand was pressed against her abdomen below one of her breasts, the fingers pointing slightly upward, indicating their destination. The satyr's head rested on her shoulder, his eyes barely wider than slits staring down on Dennis and Eileen. A devilish grin stretched across his jaw.

"I don't know if that's supposed to be erotic or frightening." She shivered.

"Maybe both. C'mon." He tugged her along past the fountain to a little area with a grill, two tables, and plastic lawn furniture. It opened onto the field, the supermarket little more than shadow in the distance. The night was humid and Dennis wiped a trail of sweat from his brow.

"Well, there she is," he said.

"Let's Lewis and Clark this bitch." Eileen took off through the grass. Dennis laughed and ran behind her.

"Wait up."

"Catch up," she yelled back at him.

He pumped his legs faster and hoped he didn't catch his toe in a rodent's hole. He overtook her and spun around, running backwards the rest of the way. "Slow poke."

"Asshole," she said.

He spun around and slowed in the shadow of the supermarket. Eileen jogged up with her arms outstretched. He opened his own to accept her embrace.

He misjudged her and she shoved him instead. He stumbled backwards and fell hard on his ass.

"Ow."

She giggled. "Oops."

He jumped to his feet. "Ha, ha."

"Check out that graffiti."

The side of the building was covered in spray paint. Some was the standard multi-colored tagging expected on an abandoned building, but the rest was unique. Strange lines cut weird angles across the wall. Spirals and circles were placed in odd patterns. He thought he recognized Arabic painted in one area and something that looked like Chinese in another. There were other shapes that were obviously language, but he didn't know what they were.

"Dennis, is this Latin?"

He walked over and scanned the wall. "*Anapavo Eosphoros.*"

"Well, Mister Classical Antiquities, what's it mean?"

"I...I don't know. It's not Latin, though. Sounds like

Greek, but whoever painted it used the Roman alphabet instead."

"Why are there so many different languages on here?"

Dennis shook his head. "Beats me. I didn't know the average gang of teenagers was so multilingual."

"You sure moved into *The Twilight Zone*."

His cell phone rang. He pulled it out and frowned. "It's Mike."

"Aren't you going to answer it?"

"I should let it go to voicemail."

She shrugged. "Don't blow him off on my account."

"Alright." He flipped it open and Mike started babbling. "Whoa, slow down." Dennis walked a few feet away, his phone pressed against his ear.

When he hung up, he walked back over, laughing. "Well, Mike's moving in."

"Sure he is. When?"

He shook his head. "Tonight."

"What?"

"He tried to tell his parents and they got in a big fight. He was kicked out. He's hanging out at a coffee shop with some of his stuff. We gotta go pick him up."

"Right now?"

"Yeah. Why?"

She sauntered over and pressed a hand against his chest. "Because I still owe you something."

He looked around and laughed. "Here?"

"Why not? No one's around…"

He laughed. "We're like a couple of animals."

"Don't get stodgy on me, old man. This is what our college years are all about. What's the expression? Young, dumb, and full of…you know." She winked at him.

Dennis considered it for all of three seconds. "Who am I to ignore biological impulses *and* social norms? But afterward we have to go get Mike."

"Trust me. This won't take long."

★ ★ ★

He watched from inside the unfinished pharmacy as the girl went down on her boyfriend. He always thought of the shopping center with its open ceilings and exposed walls as an abortion, something that could have grown into a Blockbuster, a Subway, and a nail salon if it hadn't been snuffed out during gestation.

It excited him, watching her head move back and forth, and his hand moved to his crotch. He gripped tight and moved fast, his excitement mixed with anger that his hand wasn't her mouth. He grunted as he finished, even angrier now that he saw the boyfriend wasn't done.

He thumbed the top of the knife that hung at his side, wondering if he could make it to the lovebirds before they finished. As he calculated the distance, the man whispered something and she pulled away. He fixed his pants, she stood, and they walked back toward the apartment building hand in hand, giggling all the way.

He slammed his fist into a board, splitting it in two.

He stepped out and watched their shadows disappear through the field. When they were gone, he went back into the pharmacy and leaned over the girl.

"It's time," he said.

She squirmed, her wrists and ankles straining against

the ropes. She screamed something, but it was muffled against the duct tape. She couldn't have been more than thirteen and a part of him felt pity for her.

He grabbed her, threw her over his shoulder, and marched across the parking lot.

As he approached the supermarket, one of the lights flickered on overhead. A warm breeze tickled his face. He wondered if it was an acknowledgement.

"For you, my darling," he whispered.

★ ★ ★

Mike sat on the curb and stared into his coffee. Sipped it. Wished he added more sugar, more cinnamon, more *something*, to offset the bitterness.

Maybe it's not the coffee that's bitter.

Whatever. He never liked coffee much anyway. He just bought the thing as a way to kill time while he waited for Dennis. He took another sip, holding the giant plastic cup in both hands like a child's sipping cup. His bags and suit-case were crowded around him on the sidewalk and he re-arranged them as people filed into the shop. Not that it mattered; they were still obvious and everyone still stared.

So what? I got kicked out. Big deal. I was moving out anyway.

A group of teenagers came giggling toward the coffee shop, two young guys in stylish T-shirts with the forearms of baseball players, a petite bubbly girl on each arm. One of them kicked Mike's red duffel bag as he walked by. It wedged between his back and his suitcase.

"Watch where you put your shit, dude," the ballplayer said. One of the girls laughed.

Mike glared at his back as the group went inside.

Fuck him. He doesn't know who you are. Go in there, throw your hot coffee in his face, then break his nose.

He shook it off. As his Dad always said, "It's not a Smart Thing to do, Michael." He didn't know exactly what constituted a Smart Thing, but his father assured him he never did one, whether by accident or design.

Maybe it is a Smart Thing, maybe it isn't. But you need to stop getting pushed around.

He ground his teeth together and stared into his coffee.

It's what Dennis would do.

Is it? Would Dennis go in there and break that guy's face just to prove a point? Mike doubted it. Dennis knew what a Smart Thing was. Those guys never would have talked to Dennis like that, anyway. People didn't push Dennis around. They didn't laugh behind his back.

Why did he care what Dennis would do, anyway?

Headlights blinded him. He blinked. Turned his head. A green Saturn rolled up to a stop in front of him. The trunk popped open. Someone got out. Mike rubbed his eyes and stood.

"Hey, Mike." It was Eileen. "Thought you might want to take a ride in the Saturn, since Dennis said you were interested in it."

"Oh. Yeah. Sure."

"Hey, man." Dennis grabbed Mike's things and threw them into the trunk. "Wanna talk about it?"

"Maybe later. I'm just so goddamned pissed."

Dennis climbed into the backseat. "Take shotgun. Eileen can tell you about the car."

Mike nodded and climbed in.

"Buckle-up," she said. "We'll take back roads. Nice night for it."

"Sure," he said.

As she pulled away he glanced inside of the coffee shop and saw the ballplayers laughing.

Laughing at me behind my back.

No one's laughing at you, he told himself. Probably telling jokes. Calm down.

"So it's got eighty thousand miles on it. Air conditioner works. So does the CD player."

"Why are you selling it?"

Dennis leaned forward. "She's getting a hybrid."

She laughed. "It's silly, I know. But with gas prices and everything…besides, I want to do my part for the environment, ya know?"

He nodded agreement, but he didn't know. In fact, Mike didn't give two shits about the environment.

"It's an automatic, too," she went on. "Dennis said you've never driven before, so it'll be a lot easier to learn on."

Dennis said, huh? Does Dennis often talk about me when I'm not around?

Jesus, Mike. Get a hold of yourself. The world isn't out to get you, you know?

It sure feels like it.

"…and airbags." She patted her steering wheel.

"Cool," he said. He'd missed most of what she'd said, but didn't care. It had four wheels and would keep him from taking the bus or having his parents drive him everywhere. That's all he cared about. A little autonomy. A little solitude. A little control. Not a lot of these things, just a tiny amount. That wasn't too much to ask, was it?

His Dad's voice echoed in his ears: "A car's a big responsibility for a man." But everyone he knew had a car. How big of a responsibility could it be?

"How do I get insurance?"

Dennis leaned forward again, wedging himself between the seats so he could face Mike. "After you get the title and registration in your name, we'll call my insurance company. It's easy to set up."

Title and registration?

He opened his mouth to ask, and then thought better of it. He'd ask Dennis later, when Eileen wasn't around. No point in letting her know how unfamiliar he was with cars.

"So, twelve hundred, huh?"

"Yep." She turned the radio on and tuned through several stations until she found one she liked. She tapped her fingers against the steering wheel. "Twelve hundred."

"Deal," he said.

She looked at him, her eyebrows raised. "You sure?"

He smiled. "Yeah."

★ ★ ★

Dennis flicked on a lamp and tilted it to shine on Mike's face. "Oh, yeah. It's swelling."

"Great."

He moved the lamp back into place and walked into the kitchen. After Eileen had left, Mike told Dennis every detail of his fight with his parents. None of it had surprised him, especially the punch. He just hoped things weren't irreparable between Mike and his folks. He knew how bad that could feel.

He grabbed a bag of snap peas from the freezer and tossed it to Mike. "You should hold that against your face. It'll keep the swelling down."

Mike nodded and placed the bag against his jaw. He hissed at how cold it was, jerked it away. Grimaced. Reapplied it. "Burns."

"Yeah. Don't hold it there for more than thirty seconds, then reapply it every minute or so. There's a bag of broccoli up there, too, when that starts to thaw." Dennis slumped down in his brown leather chair, one of the few things he still had of his mother's. It always made him feel good, no matter what he was sick with or what problems bothered him. The chair soaked these worries up like it did his body heat.

Aside from the chair, all he owned of hers was a silver crucifix, an old rocking chair she used to scoot next to the fire and knit in, and a framed picture of her and his father on her prom night. He loved that picture most of all; she was so young and vibrant in it and he could almost hear the laugh that had been captured on her face every time he looked at it. Her long hair hung down over her green dress, tangling around the white corsage she wore. Her eyes were brilliant and smiled with the rest of her face. Behind her his father stood in his Marine dress blues, the lights glinting from his gold buttons and creating a thousand tiny lens flares. His hair was cropped close and his face gentle; smiling in response to her laugh, unable to hide while in her presence the way he would later in life, after she had gone and all he had were anger and tears. They were happy in that picture, before Dennis came along, and he cherished it.

He wondered if Mike's family was ever that happy? They weren't at any point he had known them. Even before Allison had died, the Pritchett family was...*off*. That was the best word he could think of to describe them. Just *off*. He knew they loved their children, and he assumed they loved each other, but there was always a stream of acid flowing through that home.

He was going to mention it to Mike, but thought better of it. "So," he said, "the car."

"Yep." Mike pulled the ice pack away and grinned.

"How does it feel? The car, the apartment, school...?"

"Good." He nodded, and then shrugged. "I don't know. A little scary, too."

"Yeah. I understand that. It's always a little frightening to take control for the first time."

"It's not just that. I mean, that's a big part of it and everything, but what if...never mind." He reapplied the ice pack.

Dennis leaned forward. "What?"

"Well...it's just...what if I fuck up?"

He laughed. "And how would you fuck up?"

"I don't know. Forget an insurance payment, fail a class, break a leg. Hell, get into a car accident. I don't know."

"You're not gonna fuck up."

"But what if I do?"

"Then you'll deal with it."

Mike shook his head. "But what if my parents never want to talk to me again? If I fuck up royally and need their help or have to move back home or—"

"Stop it. Okay? You'll be fine. And you're not going to have to move back home. Alright?"

"I guess."

Dennis sunk back into the chair. "Your parents aren't going to disown you, anyway. They love you. They're just…"

"Assholes?"

He smiled. "Yeah. Assholes."

Mike nodded and leaned his head back onto the arm of the couch. He closed his eyes. He was silent for a moment, long enough for Dennis to wonder if he'd fallen asleep. Then: "Do you think I'm an asshole?"

"You're not an asshole, Mike."

"Hmph."

"A dipshit, maybe. But not an asshole."

Mike threw the peas at him. Dennis plucked them out of the air with one hand and jumped from his chair. "These are thawing already? I'll get the broccoli."

As he passed he ruffled Mike's hair. Mike smoothed it back into place.

Dennis traded the bags of vegetables out. "Here. You want me to bring you a pillow and a blanket?"

"Huh?"

"You're sleeping on the couch, right?"

Mike looked around, confused. It reminded Dennis of Eileen's cat whenever it heard a strange noise. "I don't know."

"Well, it's that or the floor, because you sure as hell ain't sleeping with me." He turned and headed toward his bedroom. "I'll get you a pillow."

"And a blanket."

Dennis sighed. "And a blanket."

He pulled them out of a box labeled *Bed Stuff* and

brought them over. He dropped the pillow on Mike's face and tossed the blanket on top.

"Hey!"

"Good night. If you need anything…"

"I know, I know. Night."

That kid never thanks me. He went back into his room and shut the door. He shed his clothes, threw them into his mother's rocking chair, and changed into a pair of pajama pants. The room was hot and humid and he opened the window.

It stuck an inch from the bottom. He yanked it, but nothing happened. He examined the frame and noticed an excessive amount of paint built up on it. Little bubbles had dried here and there and blocked the window.

He grabbed his pocketknife from the dresser and scraped some of the paint away. He tried the window again and it slid right up.

He paused, thinking he saw something flash from the corner of his eye, and stuck his head out into the night air. He scanned the field, expecting to see kids with flashlights wandering around the abandoned buildings. But the night was empty.

It was almost like one of those parking lot lights flickered. Probably someone in another apartment turning a light on.

A cool breeze settled into the room. He fell onto his bed and clicked the light off.

Not long after, as he started to sink into sleep, he heard a soft sobbing from the living room. He almost went out to check, but stopped. That's what Mike's mother would do. Besides, it would embarrass him. What he's got to work through, those tears are probably the best way to do it.

Dennis ignored it and was soon asleep.

PART TWO
AUGUST

"All your renown is like the summer flower that blooms and dies; because the sunny glow which brings it forth, soon slays with parching power."

—*Dante*

The thick, oppressive heat of summer's end had settled in to the Tennessee Valley. Nestled between the Appalachians on one side and the Cumberland Plateau on the other, the area trapped humidity like a barrel left out to collect rainwater. As July grew old, withered, and made way for August, the air grew heavier. To some it was like a coat wrapped around their shoulders, even when wearing nothing but swimming trunks. It made them tired, and made it hard to think, but this didn't bother them much. Summer was not a time for introspection.

To others, it pulsed with malignancy, digging sharp fingers into each and every pore and crawling down their throats, gradually filling their lungs with balmy fluid, threatening to drown them with every breath.

Raynham Place itself lost a little color every summer. The sun leached a bit of vibrancy from its painted walls and the moisture gathering on its surface trickled ever downward, ripping bits of tint along with it, leaving pale streaks and deposits of rust behind. The inhabitants could always sense this change in weather the way a gambler senses that he's been dealt a bad hand. They stayed inside more and more during the day, only venturing out to their jobs if they could avoid all else. They ran their air conditioners, roaring wall units crammed into windows with duct tape and rotted boards, and prayed for the days to give way to night.

At night they swam in the pool (though never alone), or left for groceries or to sample the bars that were scattered along Emory Highway.

In Apartment 112, Cody Tate was sprawled out on his bed. Melissa Sweikow lay perpendicular to him across the bottom. Their fingers danced against one another's as they talked and laughed. They were naked and covered in sweat. They'd shower soon, but not yet. This was the part that they enjoyed the most. Like all new lovers, they found an intimacy after sex that was impossible to achieve under other circumstances. Naked, exposed, left out raw for the world to see, with no expectations or hesitations of what might come. There was a comfort in this kind of vulnerability that they relished and, though the night stretched on and they both had to work early, they didn't want the moment to end.

In 315, Sharon Newman drank a glass of Cabernet in her pajamas and flipped through television stations, searching for something to distract her. When her husband passed away she had been forced to learn the art of living alone. It was a difficult thing, much harder than she thought it would be, but she had done it. The most difficult times were before bed. These hours were heart wrenching and the ache of solitude pressed around her, pushing the walls of her apartment out to unimaginable lengths until she felt she was the only person in the entire state. He had always joked with her while she washed her face and brushed her teeth. Always tried to take her pajamas off as soon as she put them on. Always rolled up next to her and talked about their day as they flipped through the channels. Now it was only her and the television, the closest thing to company she had, as she lay in bed and prayed for sleep.

Margot Deschaine and Matt Reynolds swam in the pool, kicking around in the cool water and attempting to forget the troubles of their day. Carl Petrie nursed a bottle of beer as he watched them splash, dangling his feet in the pool but embarrassed to remove his shirt in front of a woman. He knew that he needed to lose weight. It was just so damn hard. They told him to come in and he laughed and shook his head. Glanced at his watch. Said something about it being well past pool hours. Matthew responded by grabbing his thighs and dragging him in with a loud splash, the beer bottle rolling away and spilling on the concrete. Carl put on an act of irritation, but was glad; he now had an excuse to stay hidden beneath his shirt as he swam.

Karen Donahue was in the laundry room, folding clothes she had forgotten had dried much, much earlier. She laughed at her frequent bouts of absentmindedness and wondered how many people had to maneuver around her bra and panties during the day. She stopped folding and shoved the rest of the clothes into her basket. It was far too late to be down here. She told herself the sudden nervousness was because she had to work early in the morning, but her mind cursed her for a superstitious little girl as she pounded her way up the steps. Once out of the basement she could laugh about it, about the stupid little feeling that eyes stared at her from the darkness down there, watching her every move.

In 228, Josh Torrance washed the dishes. He had to be at work in less than seven hours, but the place just wasn't clean enough for his wife. Morgan had come home from work late again, screaming and yelling, cursing him, calling him "lazy" and "stupid" and pointing out how fat he was letting himself get. They hadn't slept together much lately and every abuse she slung at him told him why. She pointed out the dishes, the dirty carpet (*I don't see a speck on it*, he had thought), and the tub. She wanted them clean and couldn't understand why they weren't. What do you do with your day, I work and slave and blah blah blah *you are worthless*. He had mouthed off at her, something about her acting like her mom, and she had thrown her cup of tea at him. It had bounced from his forehead and almost took him off of his feet. The pain was little more than a dull throb now and when she came up behind him and said she was sorry and her voice trembled and she sniffed back tears, he told her it hadn't hurt a bit. She smiled and kissed him and took his hand, walking him to the bedroom. That was the only thing he enjoyed about her bad moods. After some explosion of curses, she apologized to him the only way she knew how. It was that show of tenderness, that little glimpse of the woman he had married five years ago, that kept him from leaving in the middle of the night.

Little Peggy Wills sat in her bed, her Hannah Montana sheets pulled up to her chest, and thought of the hospital as she drifted off to sleep. She hated its white walls and sterile smells. She hated how the nurses were rude and how her mother would cry every time she went. She let these thoughts swirl around as she drifted off to sleep, unaware of her closet door creaking open. She would have screamed if she had known; like all children, she was afraid of closets and the spaces under beds. Like all children her age, she wanted nothing more than to go outside, go to school. Play. Have friends. But summer was no vacation for her, no break between grades. Summer meant treatments and vomiting and crying. She hated it all and the dark of her closet drank that in.

Jack Stark sat at a table in his workroom, soldering together a few bits of wire on an old pocket radio he had. He had thought about scrapping it, thought about getting one of them iPod things, but decided against it. The frequencies he picked up while in the building were unique and he was afraid the things he heard, the things he had recorded in the "Voices" section of his "Anomalies" book, couldn't be picked up if he used an iPod. Hell, they couldn't even get WIVK, could they? And what would he do without the country music that station played as he worked? So he soldered his radio under the hot lights of his workroom, bearing the heat as best he could in exchange for keeping the shadows away.

In 116, Tony Parker watched his daughter sleep. His time with her was so short these days. He felt her drifting from him and worried about how the divorce affected her. She seemed so young, but she was a junior in high school now; she could probably handle more than he thought. *I wonder if she's had sex yet? Or gone down on a boy in a movie theater, or given a handjob in the backseat of a car?* He shook those thoughts out of his head. She was his little girl and he had taught her better. She moaned and kicked the sheet off. He realized how hot she must be and turned the air conditioner up a notch. Then he kissed her forehead and left, shutting the door behind him. He went to his own room, shut and locked the door, and sat at his computer. He clicked through his "Favorites" folder until he found the site he was looking for. He grabbed a dirty towel from the laundry hamper and found a young girl that looked vaguely like his wife (*ex-wife*, he reminded himself). As the video played, he wondered if the girls were really "Nineteen and Wet" as advertised.

The walls of Raynham Place sweat as much as its tenants. It weathered the hot summer nights like an old tree, letting them batter against it and give it life. And like a tree, the worms inside of it went about their business and it paid them little attention. Summer was not a time for introspection, after all.

Chapter Seven

"Mike…Mike. MIKE!"

Mike slammed the brakes and Dennis jerked forward in his seat. The seatbelt slipped and bit him across the neck. He yanked it down.

"Sorry."

Dennis swallowed the string of curses barreling up his throat. Counted to three. Sighed. "It's okay, man. Just… let's just keep it under forty for now, okay?"

Mike nodded, but his irritation was obvious. Dennis knew the signs: crinkled brow, clenched jaw, refusal of eye contact. What he didn't know was whether Mike was irritated at him or himself.

This was the third weekend in a row Dennis had taken Mike out for driving lessons. The campus was empty, the summer mini-term having just ended and the fall semester not starting for a few weeks. The first weekend he'd let Mike drive the Saturn around a huge parking lot, getting a feel for the basics. The next weekend he had taken him inside one of the parking garages, letting him get used to steering and parking. He had been doing well, and Dennis thought it was time to get him on one of the empty streets twisting around the campus.

It wasn't going so well.

Mike's ubiquitous anxiety had taken hold and, when he didn't freeze up all together, he went much too fast. Worse, he had started to mix up the brake and gas pedals, jerking to sudden stops or jolting forward while parking. That would have been expected the first weekend, maybe even the second. But now it just frustrated Dennis. Mike knew better. He had proven that already.

They were parked at an odd angle a few feet from a telephone pole Mike had seemed intent on colliding with. Dennis saw a landscaping crew up on the hill. They had stopped what they were doing and stared down at the car, pointing and laughing. *Better get Mike out of here before he notices them. Otherwise it's all over for today.*

"Alright, let's just back her up, turn onto the street, and head back for the commons."

Mike looked down at the gear shifter, scowling at it like everything had been its fault. He fumbled with it, slid it into place. The car jerked backwards and then settled into a slow pace as his foot found the brake. He twisted around and stared out the back windshield, his gaze intense, biting his lower lip in concentration. When he was back on the road he took a deep breath and managed to turn the car around. He shifted into drive and inched down the road.

Dennis was glad Eileen hadn't been selling a manual transmission. "You can speed up a little. Just keep it under forty."

"Yeah, yeah."

Yeah, yeah? I'm giving up my Saturday for this. You could be a little more appreciative.

He realized he was getting angry with Mike and felt bad about it. He always felt bad about getting angry with Mike. It was like getting angry with a dog for pissing on the floor; he couldn't help it. Better call it a day.

He glanced at his watch. "What time you gotta be at work?"

"Four."

"Well, it's two-thirty now. Maybe we should head that way and grab some lunch, then I'll drop you off."

Mike shrugged and pulled the car over onto the side of the road. The stop was much smoother this time, as though the declaration that the lesson was over had removed whatever troubled him. They got out and switched seats. Dennis sped down the road and onto Cumberland Avenue, not saying a word until they came to the first string of shops on Kingston Pike.

He thought about asking Mike what bothered him, but didn't want to hear it. He was tired of the excuses. It would just be the same litany of accusations: his dad, his mom, his manager. Dennis. It was always someone else's fault. Never his. No, he was perfect. The only reason things didn't work out for him was because everyone else was out to get him.

Dennis said something about getting sushi. He knew Mike hated the stuff, but there was a hamburger place he loved next door. Mike mentioned it and Dennis was glad his plan had worked; he didn't want to eat with Mike. He wanted to be done with him for the day. At least until he picked him up from work at midnight.

The car slid into a parking spot in front of the restaurants and Mike leaped out and slammed his door without a word.

Good riddance.

Dennis went inside and ordered, then sat and called Eileen while he waited. It went to voicemail.

"Hey," he said. "It's me. Just wanted to see what you were doing later. Thought we could hang." He paused. Something paced across his tongue, hesitant about coming out. I'm not ready for *that*, he decided. Even if I were I'd like to think I'm a little more romantic than to leave it on her voicemail.

Realizing the pause had become awkward, he mumbled something about thinking his food was coming and hung up.

The moment left an imprint on him, a feeling of anxiety. Is that how he felt about her? Was that something that needed to be addressed? Was it too soon? Or was it too late? If he didn't say it, would she feel like they were going nowhere and head off to look for another man? Or would she—

Stop it. You sound like Mike.

Mike. He wondered if this was the kind of feeling his roommate walked around with. If so, it was no wonder he was so difficult to be around sometimes. Dennis hated being confused, hated being unsure of himself or his situation. He could see how that would make someone insufferable.

Pity washed over him and he dialed Mike's cell to apologize for the day. It rang twice and went to voicemail. Dennis had the same phone and knew what that meant: Mike had seen him calling and silenced him.

Asshole.

Dennis pounded off a quick text message:

SOMETHIN CAME UP. GOTTA GO.
CAN U WALK TO WORK? PICK U UP
@ MIDNITE.

He never received an answer, but didn't care; they need-ed a break from each other. The theater was only a block away from where they were. If Mike had trouble walking there, that was his problem.

He felt petty and childish, but shook it off. What else was he going to do? Fight it out with Mike? Like that would work. All Mike would do was blame everything on Den-nis, not just the driving but *everything*: moving out, the fight with his parents, the whole thing. Then he would try to avoid him for a week or so while he sulked and nursed his bruised ego. It was impossible to talk to him sometimes. Better just to let it blow over.

His phone vibrated to tell him he had a text. It was one word:

FINE.

Its tone was clear, blasting at him from the blue LCD screen like Mike had yelled it from across the room.

He asked if he could get his order to go and left. He pulled out of the parking lot before Mike could see him go.

When he stopped at a red light, Dennis deleted the text message and tried to pretend he'd never gotten it.

Eileen did come over that night and went with him to pick Mike up from work. Her presence worked wonders to set aside the day's tension and the three of them laughed and joked the entire way back to the apartment. She stayed over and, like the few times in the past month that she'd done so, Mike's behavior was stranger than normal. The mornings were the worst; she'd get up early and make all three of them breakfast, but Mike was unapproachable for the first few hours of the day. He'd get a plate of food, nod an awkward greeting, and retreat to his room. Once everyone had showered and changed and he could forget she had spent the night, everything was fine again.

She asked Dennis about it once and he shrugged. Deep down he suspected Mike felt it was a betrayal of his sister in some way, but never would have told Eileen that. He worried that she already felt like she was in Allison's shadow in some way and didn't want to add to that.

A storm blew in that morning, but had vanished by early afternoon. It left behind a cool breeze and the day's heat had difficulty fighting it. Eileen said they should all go swimming and Dennis jumped at the suggestion. To his surprise, Mike was excited about it too, and they all changed into swimsuits and hit the pool.

It seemed the entire building was out back. Usually everyone was so quiet and private, but the respite from humidity brought them out in droves. A cursory head count made Dennis estimate that nearly thirty people milled around on the concrete patio. They were introduced to a new face every foot or so.

Carl Petrie and Kurt Hagen roasted hot dogs and burgers on the grill. Carl wore an ill fitting T-shirt and blue jean shorts, while rolls of fat hung over Kurt's camouflage swim trunks. He smiled at them from under his ball cap. "Y'all hungry?"

Dennis laughed. "Man, I could eat that whole pack of

dogs."

"That's what I like to hear, brutha. Carl, throw some dogs on there."

"And why can't you?"

"Shit, man. You been eating three-fourths of everthang I cook. Throw some dogs on now, will ya?"

Carl sliced open a package. "Alright. You folks see what I put up with here?"

Kurt smacked his back and winked at Eileen. "Don't pay him no mind. He's just trying to impress a pretty lady, but everbody done knows I'm the sexy one here." Kurt patted his swollen belly.

"Whatever, Tubby." Carl positioned the dogs to sizzle on the grill.

Patty Malone dragged the trio over to her cooler, chatting the entire time about how much the recent humidity troubled her bad knee, and sent them away armed with beer. Jason Teague gave them flyers to a show his band was having; Dennis didn't like the long stares he gave Eileen from behind his black-framed glasses and filed him away in the mental Rolodex. Terry Crowley invited them to play cards with him, Jack the maintenance man, and Tony Parker. Tony's teenage daughter Sarah pulled up a chair and studied the men as they played.

A Golden Retriever came trotting up to Mike, panting and wagging its tail. It sniffed his hand and rubbed its snout into his leg. Mike knelt down and petted the dog. It licked his face. He turned his head and wiped a long string of spittle from his chin. Dennis and Eileen laughed.

"That's Lucy," a young boy said. He looked to be about twelve, shirtless and wearing "Transformers" swimming trunks. "She loves everybody."

Lucy turned her attention to Dennis, jumping onto her hind legs and placing her front paws on his chest. He scratched her behind the ears.

The boy patted his thighs. "Lucy."

Lucy jumped down and ran over to him.

"I'm Joey," he said. "Lemme know if you ever wanna play with Lucy." Then the two of them took off running towards the grill without another word.

"I want a dog," Eileen said.

Mike nodded. "Me too."

They made it to the pool and slid in, the cool water forcing sharp breaths. The air above it had the subtle, acrid tang of chlorine and sunscreen. Dennis and Eileen held their breath and submerged, popping back up and pulling their hair from their eyes, as Mike held onto the wall and kicked his feet around. A group of children splashed in the shallow end, but they had the deep end to themselves.

Margot swam over not long after and introduced herself to Eileen. She wore a red swimsuit that did a worse job of holding in her breasts than most of her clothing. She crept across the wall, hand over hand, until she floated next to Mike. Dennis nudged Eileen under the water and flashed a wink.

"How you been, Michael?"

Mike's face reddened and he looked down at the water. A grin tugged at the edges of his mouth. "I've been good. How about you?"

"Just so damn hot."

Eileen turned to Dennis and rolled her eyes.

"You must live down here, Margot," Dennis said. "I see

you here all the time."

"I love this pool," she said. "One of the reasons I moved in here eons ago."

"How long have you lived here?"

"Oh, well…guess I moved in here in the fall of ninety-five."

Dennis whistled.

"I just love this old place. There's a pulse to the building, you know. You may have felt it already. The people, the seclusion, the history…it all adds up to something special, I think."

Eileen tapped Dennis' shoulder. "I'm gonna do some laps."

"Okay."

She dove underwater and swam off.

Mike shook his head. "What about all those creepy statues?"

She laughed. "Honey, I'm the reason those things are still around." They gave her a puzzled look and she went on. "Rudy, God bless him, hates those damn things. Says they're tacky."

"I can see that," Dennis said.

"You hush up now. Those things are wonderful. Sure, they may be a little bohemian, but that's what makes them special. Anyway, Rudy has tried to get them removed about once every other year since he took over as manager in ninety-six. Every time he does, I get the tenants together and organize a letter writing campaign. Works like a charm. It's kinda become a fun little game, our tug of war. I look forward to it and suspect he does too."

"One man's trash…"

She shook her head. "It's not just that. It's the history behind them." She splashed a bit of water into Mike's face and giggled.

Dennis held his breath. *If ever there was a recipe for a historic Mike freak-out moment…*

Mike laughed and wiped it off.

Dennis smiled. *Man, has she gotten to him.* "What history?"

"Oh, no one's told you the story?" Her eyes grew wide and sparkled. She leaned forward. "Honey, this place is chock full of history. Back in, oh…I guess this had to be around 1922, when this was the Sanatorium—"

"Sanatorium?" Mike asked.

"Just a fancy word for 'tuberculosis hospital,' sweetie. Anyway, there was this doctor by the name of Whaley. More than a doctor, really. He married into money and sat on the Board. Back in those days the doctors would live at the hospital for weeks at a time, on account of how far out it was and all. So, getting lonely and needing to satisfy those needs a man often needs to satisfy—" She nudged Mike and he blushed. "—he set his eyes on a nurse, beautiful young octoroon girl named Calliope."

"What's an octoroon?" Mike asked.

She grinned. "I feel like a schoolmarm. *Octoroon* was a polite way of saying *mixed* in those days. Lot of the nurses came from a hospital in New Orleans and Calliope was one of them. Half-white, half-black, probably some Indian in there, too. She was a stunning creature, beautiful in every regard. Graceful and bright, too. They say her smile could light up an entire building. But what really attracted Whaley to her was her intellect. It was so rare for a woman to have a good education in those days, especially a non-white woman. But at some point in her short life she had learned to read and write and had taken an interest in poetry and the classics.

"Her and Whaley used to sit around on the porch and talk about Greek mythology or philosophy or what have you and his lust gave way to love. He finally convinced her to go to bed with him and they became, for all intents and purposes, husband and wife during Whaley's long stays here.

"Now Calliope lived in one of the bunk houses out behind the hospital, about where them old ratty stores are today, I guess. So when Whaley would go back down to town to spend time with his family, she was stuck up here on the hill. That didn't sit too well and they started fighting. Nothing too big, I reckon—their love was too strong for that—but enough to put a strain on them. She wanted him all to herself, you see, but for him to leave his wife would have been unheard of in those days. His money, his career, his status—POOF!

"But Calliope was a proud Catholic girl and didn't like living in sin. So when she became pregnant she didn't know what to do. She went to Whaley for help and he convinced her…well…"

"To have an abortion," Dennis said.

Margot nodded. "He did it himself, somewhere up on the third floor. Poor girl bled to death during it."

Dennis and Mike shared a look.

Margot didn't seem to notice. "Whaley never forgave himself. He spent more and more time up here, slept in her old room in the bunkhouses, stopped eating. Just wasted away without her. His wife took the children and moved

123

back to New York. They didn't divorce—people didn't do that back then—but the marriage was over. He still had access to the money, though, and hired an artist to come up here, a Creole fella from New Orleans, Calliope's cousin as some stories say, and a renowned sculptor. Other stories say he was also a Voodoo priest, but who knows? What all the stories do agree on is that Whaley had him sculpt each and every one of them statues as a monument to the passion he and Calliope shared."

Dennis realized he had drifted closer during the story and pushed back a foot or two. "That's why they represent Greek mythology, huh?"

"Mmm-hmm. Those statues over there?" She pointed to the hedges that hid benches and the near-obscene satyr and nymph in the fountain. "That's supposed to be exact images of the doctor and his octoroon. Minus the horns, of course."

"So," Mike said, "they've stood here all these years?"

"God, no. Whaley committed suicide after they were carved—slit his own throat at the foot of the fountain, they say—and the Board had the statues removed. They sat in the basement all these years until this place was turned into apartments. Rudy's father put them back in their original spots, God only knows why. I'm glad he did, though. Wish his son appreciated them as much."

"This is a weird building," Mike said.

Margot laughed. "Yes, I reckon it is. Full of stories. But that's why I love it."

Dennis nodded. "What about the 'Blue Boy' I heard you guys talking about the other day? What's that story?"

A jagged grin ripped across Margot's face. It reminded

him of the smiles carved into the nymphs' faces and he shuddered.

"The Blue Boy," Margot began, "is another sad tale. Back in, oh, I guess this was eighty-two or eighty-three, about a year or two after the Crossroads Killer was caught—oh, don't tell me you boys don't know about the Crossroads Killer? I swear I oughta write a book. The Crossroads Killer was a sick, twisted young man who killed young ladies in the late seventies and early eighties. He'd leave their bodies, all tortured and defiled in the most grotesque ways, tied to trees at crossroads all around here. Killed about thirteen or fourteen girls before they caught him. Bastard lived up here, though now he's rotting in hell I dare say—hung himself in prison. Police thought he tortured the women somewhere in this building, but could never find any evidence.

"But I'm rolling off the rails, as my daddy used to say—he was a railroad man, of course. Anyway, the Blue Boy. He was six or seven. Smart boy. Cute too. His momma was teaching him to swim. She'd bring him down here every afternoon in the summer after his father had gone to work. Well, one day he was in the midst of a swimming lesson when he asked his momma if he could try the deep end. She of course said that he could not. But just as she was getting outta the pool to dry off, one of her neighbors comes out and asks her to help with a broken faucet or something—or maybe she had a phone call—whatever it was, his momma went inside for just a moment and left him to dry off.

"But the boy, being such a smart and driven child, knew that he could swim from the shallow end to the deep end and back. He thought his momma would have been so proud of him when she saw he could do it on his own. So he dove in."

"And drowned," Dennis said.

Margot nodded. "His momma had told him to meet her back up in their apartment. By the time she was done with whatever had called her away and had scoured every inch of her apartment for her son, she came back down here to find him floating face down, right about here." Margot swirled her hand around the water in front of her. "They pulled his pale, blue body from the water, all swollen and bloated. Some folks say he was in there for hours before she realized he was missing."

"Poor kid," Mike said.

"Well, story don't end there. See, on some nights, when there's no one out here, you can hear the boy splashing around in the pool, crying for his momma."

Dennis recalled the splashing he and Eileen had heard when they'd gone out to examine the supermarket. He looked around the deep end of the pool, imagining that poor boy thrashing around as he drowned.

"Some folks even claim they've *seen* him swimming under the surface, his face as blue as the night. That's why they call him the Blue Boy."

Mike glanced around the water and shivered.

Eileen emerged with a splash next to Dennis. She pulled her hair back and blinked. "What'd I miss?"

"Long story," he said. "I'll tell you later."

Margot had wedged closer to Mike and shifted her torso, her breasts within inches of him. His face was as red as her swimsuit.

Dennis turned to Eileen. "Hey, wanna get a hot dog?"

She glanced over at them. "Uh…yeah. A hot dog sounds great."

"I'm hungry, too," Mike said.

"You stay put. I'll bring you one." Dennis swam over to the edge and climbed out. He lowered a hand and helped Eileen over the side and they walked toward the grill.

"What," she asked, "is *that* all about?"

"I'm pretty sure that Margot chick has got the hots for our little Mikey."

"No? You think? I mean, why is an attractive older woman after Mike?"

"Beats me."

"I'm not trying to sound like a bitch or anything. He's not a bad looking guy. He's just so—"

"Childish?"

She shrugged.

"Maybe she's just horny. Ya know, likes them young and virginal."

Eileen laughed.

"That way she can teach them what she likes."

"I don't want to think about it."

"Well, I hope he sleeps with her."

She raised her eyebrows.

"I think it'll be good for him. Help him grow up."

"Hmmm…we'll see…"

They had reached the grill. Carl was nowhere to be seen, but Kurt sang *Burning Love* to himself while he grilled. He smiled, threw some dogs on buns, squirted an ocean of mustard onto them, and handed the plate away. Dennis looked around for a good place to sit, but didn't see one.

"Where should we eat?"

"How about in your bedroom?"

"Oh, yeah?"

"Oh, yeah."

Dennis took her hand. He was happy to still be in that early stage of a relationship where making love was paramount to everything else.

They went inside.

★ ★ ★

Mike arched his neck back to look for Dennis and Eileen. He didn't see them.

Bet they went upstairs to screw.

"What are you studying in school?" Margot asked.

She was close and he could smell the coconut-scented sunblock she used. He fought not to stare at her breasts, but her eyes and mouth were just as enticing. His erection ached against the rough fabric of his swim trunks and he hoped she didn't look into the water and see it.

He rotated his hips so his thigh blocked the view. "Um…I don't know yet. Just kinda getting started, I guess."

"What I wouldn't give to be back at college."

"What…uh…what did you study?"

"Political Science."

"That's…um…that's cool. You work in the Mayor's office or something?"

She laughed and shook her head, her hair swishing back and forth around her shoulders. "Lord, no. I'm a regional buyer for Victoria's Secret." She winked.

He swallowed.

"I'm kidding," she continued. "Just Sears. It really has nothing to do with my degree, I know, but what do you do?" She shrugged.

Mike looked around again for Dennis.

"I don't see your friends."

"No…"

"They've been gone about twenty minutes. Must have gone upstairs, huh?"

"Probably."

"You hungry? They never brought you a dog."

A way out, he thought. Then: Why do I want a way out? "Yeah, a little."

"I'm not much for hot dogs. Why don't you come upstairs and I'll whip something up for us?"

Mike's breath caught in his throat. Here it was, he thought. This was like one of his fantasies staring him in the eye, smiling, inviting him upstairs. But he was so nervous he couldn't say anything. Would he have to make a move, or would she? Would she ridicule him for his lack of experience? What should he do?

The moment stretched out. Her eyes bored into his, twinkling at the edges, her tongue barely visible behind her thick lips. Mike breathed out. Inhaled. Caught a whiff of coconut, of lavender shampoo, of chlorine. Felt light headed.

Someone screamed.

He whipped around to see a woman running toward them. She wore a yellow swimsuit tucked into a pair of blue jean shorts. Her stringy blond hair was pulled into a ponytail, her face covered with streaks of mascara.

"It's Bobby," she cried. "Somebody help him!" She

pointed to the field behind her.

A handful of people rushed that way, but the rest stayed where they were, rooted to their spots by confusion and panic. Mike swam over to the other side of the pool and pulled himself out. Curiosity nudged him into the field, following the woman as she ran toward a group of young boys. They stood in a circle and stared at the ground. The men that had made their way over (*What were their names? Kurt? Jack? I don't remember the others*) were kneeling in the middle. Someone shouted: "He's not breathing!"

"Someone call 911."

"Oh, dear God, oh Jesus…"

"Does anybody know CPR?

"…my baby, oh, Bobby, oh, Jesus…"

"Hello? We need an ambulance at—"

"Bobby. Wake up, Bobby. Wake up."

Mike shuffled into the circle. He glanced over his shoulder at the others running up, then down at the boy. He was shirtless, probably around eight years old. He had sandy blond hair that hung into his blue-tinted face. He was an apparition of the Blue Boy, called into existence by Margot's story.

"Does anybody know CPR?"

Mike hesitated. He knew it; Allison had made Mike and Dennis go with her to CPR classes at their church. But he had never used it on anyone. What if he fucked up and the kid died? Would everybody blame him for it?

But what if he didn't try? Wouldn't the kid be dead by the time the ambulance got here?

What if CPR doesn't even help?

This is your chance to be a hero. All your life you've never done anything worthwhile. You can save this kid and everyone will pat you on the back and tell you what a great person you are. You can get Margot. Hell, you can probably get Karen, even.

He was shoved to the side. He spun and saw Dennis crouched over the boy.

"I know CPR," he said. He took the boy and checked his mouth, then pressed his lips against him and pushed on his chest.

Everyone watched. Silent. Hopeful.

Mike seethed. *That son of a bitch. Your chance for glory and he steals it out from under you.*

It wasn't long until the boy coughed once, sucked in a breath, and then launched into a full blown coughing attack. Spittle, blood, and mucus flecked out into the air. But he was breathing and the color came back into his cheeks. Everyone applauded.

That should have been for me.

The ambulance came and went, taking Bobby and his mother (who Mike learned was named Marie Callahan—they lived in 109) to the hospital. The other boys were snatched by their parents to explain what had happened. Marie had wrapped Dennis in a huge embrace and kissed him on the cheek before they went and everyone kept coming up and congratulating him. Patting him on the back. Praising him.

That should have been for me.

Eileen called him "hero" and gave him a big kiss. Kurt brought him a beer. Karen sauntered over, more beautiful than Mike had ever seen her, and told Dennis how fantastic he was as she shook his hand. Her fingers lingered on his and Mike noticed how their eyes locked on each other. He thought about grabbing Eileen and showing her what was happening, but then Karen left for a beer.

He couldn't watch such a gross display of aggrandizement any longer. He walked over to the edge of the field, where one of the boys was being grilled by his father. Mike pretended to stare out at the supermarket as he eavesdropped on their conversation, curious as to what had happened.

"I don't know, Dad."

"Rusty. Tell me what you boys did. The doctors are gonna want to know and it may save Bobby's life."

"We didn't do nothing."

"*Rusty…*"

"We were just playing, Dad. And then Pete dared Bobby to go into that grocery store—"

"What did I tell you boys about playing in those buildings?"

"I know, Dad. Honest. I swear I told him he shouldn't go in there. But then Pete called him a sissy and he said he'd go inside and bring something out. He walked up to the doors and they opened—"

"Bullshit."

"They did!"

"That building doesn't have any electricity running to it."

"I dunno, that's what I saw."

"More like Bobby pried them open."

"I dunno."

"Well, then what?"

"Bobby went inside. Just a few feet. The doors started to close behind him—"

"Rusty…"

"They did! And then Bobby came rushing back out, scared shi— scared real bad. And then we all ran back for the pool and then Bobby started grabbing at his neck and coughing real hard. Then he fell down and Pete went and grabbed Mrs. Callahan."

"You ain't telling me everything, boy. We gotta get to the hospital. You got till then to tell me the truth, else I'm gonna tan your hide."

"It *is* the truth."

"C'mon."

Rusty's father grabbed him by the arm and dragged him off.

Mike shook his head. *Stupid kids.*

He looked over at the supermarket. The sun shimmered against the closed doors. It looked like a massive jaw clenched shut. He didn't like to look at the place; it gave him cold chills and he wasn't sure why. It was the same feeling he had when he looked over the edge of a bridge, or when pressing the gas pedal in the Saturn—some instinctual dread that crept through him.

A hand fell on his shoulder. "Hey, buddy," Dennis said. "Crazy day, huh?"

"Hmmm? Oh. Yeah. Guess so." Mike shrugged the hand from his shoulder and walked back toward the building.

Dennis ran up next to him. "Is something wrong?"

Mike whipped his head toward him. "Yeah. I…" What was he going to say? He was mad that Dennis saved that kid's life? How petty would that sound? "I'm just sick, that's all. I need to lay down for a bit."

"Well…get to feeling better, I guess."

Carl came up and slammed one hand on Dennis' back, shoving a beer at him with the other.

Mike could tell he didn't believe him, but he didn't care. He turned away and went inside, leaving Dennis to his praise.

As he walked through the halls of the building, he wondered what was wrong with him. He should have acted faster instead of being seized by anxiety. He should have been happy that the kid was alive, instead of being angry that he wasn't responsible for it. But that was his life, wasn't it? Just one long string of "should haves."

The hallways were deserted. Anyone who wasn't outside was huddled up near their air conditioners, trying to wait out the day like a rodent in a hole listening for its predators to scamper off. His footsteps echoed through the halls, the green flip-flops he wore earning their name with every pair of sounds. Something about the noise unnerved him; it was like the building itself told him he had no one, that he was in this by himself.

Rather than listen to *that*, he took the elevator.

It groaned and creaked up the shaft and Mike couldn't shake the feeling that he wasn't alone. He turned to make sure he hadn't missed someone while daydreaming, but the tiny box was empty. Seeing that didn't erase the sensation. He felt pressed against the doors, felt like an entire horde of people shifted back and forth against each other, trying to fit inside. His breath quickened and he thought he could feel the air warm around him like the heat bodies gave off when crammed into such a small space.

A rough fabric brushed against his shoulder and he jumped. He bit off a scream and whirled around again. It was just him, alone.

The doors *dinged* open and he shuffled out, turning sideways to avoid the other passengers that weren't there.

The doors closed and the elevator made its way down again. Mike calmed a little. Don't be an idiot, he told himself. You've stressed yourself out. Probably some psychological residue from feeling so crowded out by the pool. He nodded; that's what it was, of course. What else could it be?

He walked to his apartment, passing Margot's door on the way. He hadn't seen where she had gone after Bobby's mother screamed, but now her door was cracked

—inviting you in—

and he could hear a soft singing inside. He paused, peeking through the crack long enough to see Margot in her kitchen slathering mayonnaise on a slice of bread. He thought about knocking, but didn't; he'd had enough of other people for one day.

When he entered his own apartment, the heat was stifling. Why had they left the windows shut *and* the air conditioning off? He poured himself a cold glass of Coke and went into his bedroom, shutting himself in and cranking up his wall unit full blast. He grimaced at the boxes still lining his room. He hadn't finished unpacking, even after five weeks here, and wasn't quite sure why. He just couldn't bring himself to. Maybe it was because he was lazy or maybe it was because he kept waiting for his parents to call and invite him back.

He hadn't talked to them since the night they kicked him out. His mother had shoved two hundred dollars in twenties into his palm and kissed his forehead and that was the last he had spoken to her. He could imagine her jumping every time the phone rang, hoping it was him, but she wouldn't call. Not yet. Not until his father's anger cooled enough to allow her to.

He hadn't tried to call her either. His father's hold over him, too, he supposed.

He glanced out the window and wished he hadn't. The only view from his room was the supermarket. The damned thing seemed to fill his entire window. He usually tried not to look at it, but it drew his gaze in, the way drivers' eyes are drawn to car accidents on the side of the road. He tried to read the graffiti, but it was too far. Dennis and Eileen had gone down there once and Mike thought he might go with them to get a closer look if they ever asked. But they never had and he wouldn't go down there alone.

He pressed his face against the glass and tried to get a better look. Something was different. He couldn't quite place it, but there was something off from this view. Something had changed since he was outside. What was it? Nothing was obvious; no one milled around the thing, it still had four walls, its doors were—

The light no longer reflected from the doors.

They're open, his inner voice whispered and he shuddered. *They're open, waiting for you to enter. Won't you go, Mike?*

He was being silly again, like in the elevator, letting his imagination run wild. They weren't open. He was just seeing them from a different angle. That's why he couldn't see the light reflect from them.

He laughed, but even that didn't keep him from closing the blinds and turning away from the window. Some things are better left unseen, he thought.

Chapter Eight

Weeks had passed since the incident at the pool, but Eileen found her thoughts going back there over and over again. Even here at work, a hundred customers shuffling in and out of J. Crew, all of the teenage employees needing her watchful eye as manager, she kept picturing that poor boy being hauled into the ambulance.

It was unnerving, and not just because of its near-tragic nature. No, more than anything, it was the dream she had had the next few nights while tossing and turning in Dennis' bed. She had come up with reasons why not to spend the night since. Those reasons were wearing thin, though, and she had made plans with Dennis to stay over tonight. The dream kept trying to come back to haunt her, but she refused to let herself think about it. Her mind was a traitor though, and a masochist at that, choosing to at least dwell on the boy's mysterious seizure.

She and Dennis had been making dinner a few nights after the incident when Marie and Bobby came over with a cake as thanks. Bobby had seemed healthy, happy even, and his mother said that no one knew what happened.

"The doctors couldn't find a reason for it. They said

they thought he might be epileptic, but I could tell they were just grasping at straws. None of the tests showed anything wrong."

"They didn't even want to hear about my dreams," the boy said.

His mother assured him the dreams came from the comic books he always read before bedtime, but Eileen wasn't so sure. Her own dreams were in their infancy and she hadn't pried, but she thought she might have to knock on the Callahan's door one day before Bobby started school again.

"Eileen?"

She looked up from her desk. A quarterly sales report sat in front of her, but she hadn't been reading it. Even if she wasn't distracted, she would have avoided it; she refused to let J. Crew suck her in any deeper than it already had.

Erik stood in the doorway, his scruffy Amish-looking beard and sideburns doing little to hide the fatness that had crept into his cheeks during the past year. He was twenty and had been gaining pounds since his marriage. His wife was the first girl he had ever slept with. He snatched her up so fast that a joke amongst the staff was that she told him she possessed the world's only vagina. Eileen had seen the same thing time and time again. They'd be divorced in ten years, just like her brother, or be cursed with children and stuck in an ever-devolving marriage of spite and resentment, just like her sister.

If Erik had asked for her opinion before the marriage, she would have told him to sleep around first. She knew full well that what a man thinks of as love was often lust.

No matter how much they think you hung the moon, no matter what sweet poetries they whisper to you at night, once they slide inside of another woman they realize how much of their feelings are an illusion.

Maybe it's a good thing he never did *ask my opinion.*

"What's up, Erik?"

"I've got a lady out here wants a refund on a sweater."

"And?"

"Well, she bought it from the Christmas sale last year and I didn't—"

"She can't have a refund, but we can exchange it or give her store credit.'

"Okay. Just making sure. Thanks."

He ducked out of the tiny office and she wheeled her chair over a few inches until she could nudge the door shut with her foot. It swung a little too hard and slammed louder than she intended. She jumped up, opened the door to apologize, and saw that Erik and the two teenage girls behind the counter were staring her way, eyes wide, faces white with fear. A giggle escaped her lips. "Sorry. Ignore that slam. No one did anything wrong."

She shut the door and sat back down. The district manager had made a habit of using the office door as a way to communicate how happy he was with his employees. She laughed thinking of how they'd all become Pavlov's dogs, salivating or whimpering based on the sound of the door.

Her mother talked like that. Not with the door so much as with pots and pans. Whenever she was angry at Eileen's stepfather she would go off into the kitchen and beat around, uttering coded messages through a series of metallic bangs and clunks, until he finally deciphered them and left the comfort of the couch to go apologize. If only her brother and sister had come to such agreements with their spouses.

Contrasting her mother's marriage, normal even in the frequency of its fights, to the botched attempts by her siblings had been a favorite mental exercise of hers. Dennis always accused her of playing pop-psychologist and, in many ways, he was right. She had already diagnosed her siblings with an acute desire to be their mother and stepfather. They had married too quickly, not to mention too young, and had paid the price. And for what? A vain attempt at becoming one of their progenitors while denying the other, that's what. Her sister had never had a sense of her own identity, while her brother was emotionally crippled from middle-child syndrome. Eileen looked on them as examples of how not to live and acted accordingly.

Not that all of her relationships had been golden. Quite the opposite, in fact. If she were honest with herself (which, while rare, did happen from time to time) she could pin it all on her absentee father, whom no one had seen since he went out to get a beer after a football game fifteen years ago. But it was those mistakes that made her appreciate what she had with Dennis so much.

And what did she have? They had grown close, but she still felt a wall between them. Sometimes that wall was a thin, porous thing and they almost felt like the same person. Other times it was carved from marble and she had to strain to even hear his voice. She knew he cared for her—his actions made that clear, even if he never said as much—but he had gone through so much in the past few years. She didn't know how much more serious he could allow himself to get.

Not that she wanted marriage or anything, especially at this point in her life (she had school and a career to think about, after all), but a girl still had to have something on the horizon. Once a relationship stopped barreling towards the future and reached a destination, it usually died. At least that was her experience. Hope and expectation kept love alive as much as any other feelings.

She shook off her doubts. Things were great with Dennis and she had no indication that they wouldn't continue to be great. They were in—

No. She wasn't going to use *that* word. Not yet. She had whipped out that word far too quickly in the past, and like a gunfighter whose timing was off with his draw, had taken her fair share of shots for it.

Closing time approached and she stepped out onto the floor to make sure everyone knew their duties. She closed down one of the registers and took the drawer back into the office. She sat it on the safe and began filling out her paperwork. She had being doing this since high school and a part of her mind was able to do the calculations by rote. She used the rest of her brain to call Dennis at work.

The girl at the front desk, an aspiring model with a bubbly, high-pitched voice, answered.

"Oh, hey, girl. He's with a client right now."

Her real name was Shelley, but she called herself Angel (*a stripper name if ever I heard one*) and flirted with Dennis every time Eileen came to join him for lunch. She was barely into her twenties and was already saving for breast implants. To Eileen, Angel summed up everything that was wrong with women today. Eileen was far from being a bra-burning feminist, but she still felt that women like this squandered everything the suffrage movement and the feminists of the sixties fought for. She ground her teeth together as Angel pretended to be some close friend, bitching about how she had three guys she was seeing right now but didn't really like any of them.

Eileen, for her part, at least feigned a chuckle. "You're like the female Rodolphe."

"Who?"

"He's from *Madame Bovary* by Flaubert. It's really good, you might like—"

"I don't really read."

You don't say? I never would have guessed. "Well, they made a movie out of it. I think it was called—"

"Oh, speaking of movies, I saw a great one on Lifetime last night."

Christ, I can't listen to this. She's literally *killing my brain cells.* "Hey, I hate to cut this short, but I'm closing up here. Could you get Dennis? It'll only take a second and then he can get back to benching or whatever."

"Of course, girl. You and I should hit the clubs together one night."

"Mmm-hmm."

Then she was on hold, listening to the Beatles tell her to let it be. She finished counting out the cash, made her deductions, and slid the drawer into the safe.

Dennis came onto the line, breathing heavy.

"Hey, babe. What's up?"

She giggled. "Out of breath, huh? Angel must have come back and gotten you herself."

"Well, now that you mention it, she did."

"Mmm-hmm. Anyway, I was just seeing if we were still on for tonight. I already picked up *Dog Day Afternoon* and some wine on my way into work."

"Awesome. I've been dying to see it."

She had been introducing him to all of her favorite books and films and had been surprised by how similar their tastes were. There had been a short point at the beginning where she had been afraid he would reveal himself to be a dumb jock, but those fears were quickly crushed. Dennis had turned out to be anything but typical and discussed literature and movies with her like a seasoned critic.

"You coming straight over?" he asked.

"As soon as I'm done here."

"Cool. Well, I gotta get back—"

"Yeah, yeah. I'm sure she's all worked up by now."

"Of course she is. I do have the touch, you know."

She laughed. "You're touched all right."

She hung up and finished her closing duties. When she was done she dismissed the staff, set the alarm, and locked up for the night. Something about closing the chained gate reminded her of the dream

—*the slobbering, tearing sounds*—

but she shrugged it off.

The mall was empty as she walked through its white halls. The fluorescent lights washed the color from everything and she had the distinct impression that she walked through a hospital,

—*a tuberculosis hospital*—

the only nurse on the night shift. Her steps echoed from the walls like shotgun blasts in the otherwise silent mall. She felt tense and wasn't quite sure why. The echoing footsteps increased the feeling tenfold as the noise made its way down the hall and doubled back, sounding like another set of feet trotting behind her.

She stopped and turned, but all she saw was a long line of closed chain gates and locked up kiosks. She continued on toward the parking deck, but couldn't shrug off the impression she wasn't alone.

She finally came to the two glass doors that opened onto the parking deck. She gave one last glance over her shoulder, half-expecting to see someone behind her

—behind her,
callused hands trailing up her abdomen—

but it just confirmed she was alone.

The night clawed its way into the parking structure and added an otherworldliness to the yellow lamps sunk every few feet into concrete supports. Her footsteps here still echoed, but it was a dull, flat sound compared to the booms of the shopping mall. She jumped when she heard an engine roar to life somewhere on a floor below her and then burst out laughing. She was being silly, she knew. Her old superstitions coming into play.

Old superstitions my ass. It was that goddamned dream.

She tried to shake it off, but the images danced around the corners of her mind. She attempted to replace them with thoughts of Dennis or the time spent with her girlfriends at the lake the past weekend, but it was no use.

They kept flooding back, like

—a river of blood and offal,
a tide of every foul thing that ever was,
rushing to drown her,
to drag her to the depths,
where hands grasp her and fingers dig into—

if you tried not to think of someone naked; your mind forced itself to do so.

She didn't understand what was wrong with her. She usually didn't allow herself to get this wound up and, unlike most of her girlfriends, fear wasn't a common emotion for her. She had mace on her keychain, right next to a small nail file that could double as a knife if need be, and her cell phone was in easy reach. With her head high, eyes alert, and shoulders straight, she knew she didn't look like a target.

Her uncle Gary, the notorious drifter, had taken her aside as a teenager and told her that criminals only looked for easy targets. "If you look like you'll scream or put up a fight," he'd said, "they'll pick on someone else. The reason they fuck with folks like you and me, pardon my French, is because they're looking for easy money. Don't look like that's you, and they'll move on to some twerp who shoves his hands in his pockets and stares at his feet while he walks around." The advice had stuck and Eileen never felt vulnerable the way some women seemed to.

So why was she so worked up now?

As she slid her keys into the Prius' lock, she realized it was the idea of staying at Dennis'. Her mother and grandmother had filled her head with Appalachian folklore growing up and it had obviously taken a far deeper root than her love for an occasional horror movie. She had joked with Dennis that his building was haunted, but never really believed it. Her nightmare, though…it made her shiver. It felt so *real*, so tangible. Worst of all, it hadn't felt like it had sprung from her thoughts like the usual garbage that floated through her mind as she slept.

It felt like it had come from the building.

That's absurd. It was just a dream.

But even sitting in the comfort of her new car, turning onto Kingston Pike with its multitude of streetlights and throngs of traffic, some upbeat, happy sounding pop song blaring from her speakers, the feeling settled in her stomach like an invading army and refused to leave. The building had created that dream, those awful images. No matter how much she chastised herself, how much she knew the idea was beyond impossibility, the feeling refused to leave.

She rolled down her window and let the warm, night breeze whip her ponytail around behind her. Her hand felt around for the radio's volume button and she cranked it up, singing along to the pop song, substituting similar syllables where she didn't know the lyrics just to keep singing. Soon her trick had worked and she felt at ease. Carefree. Excited.

That was the thing she loved—that she *liked* about Dennis the most. The prospect of being with him still excited her in every way. Talking to him, holding him, sleeping together—it all sent a delicious thrill along the outside of her skin, raising goose bumps on her arms and the back of her neck.

She turned onto the interstate and sped north, past the

Papermill exit where she would have needed to get off if she was going to take the back roads home, and smiled. She was committed now and she liked that.

Ten minutes later she was taking the Emory Highway exit and it wasn't long before the gas stations, bars, and restaurants gave way to great, dark fields and thick woods. She turned her radio down and slowed to a crawl, careful now that she navigated the tiny, twisting country roads. It was quiet out, the only noise an occasional cricket or barking dog, and she thought of *The Legend of Sleepy Hollow*. It had been one of her favorite books growing up, though she never really understood it until she reread it as a teenager.

But out here in the dark, everything black and formless outside of the influence of her headlights, she thought she understood how Ichabod must have felt. Anything could be going on in those dark fields and darker woods, all kinds of unnamed blasphemies occurring inside the black shapes that rose up at the end of driveways, any number of horrors far worse than the Headless Horseman and—

Stop it.

Why was she doing this to herself tonight?

She was relieved when she came upon the single streetlight marking the steep hillside road to Raynham Place. She frowned as her phone rang, clutching for it as her eyes fixed on the curves ahead of her.

"Hello?"

"Hey, babe."

"Hey. I'm just pulling up."

"Ah, shit. I'm sorry. I'm gonna be late."

"Late?" She pulled into the parking lot but left the car running. She stared up at the face of the building illuminated from underneath by a series of tall lamps. It gave her the impression of someone standing in the dark, shining a flashlight onto their face from below, shadowing their features and whispering, "Boo."

"Yeah. Our network went down so I have to enter all of my sales and training logs by hand."

"How late will you be?"

"Shouldn't be much longer. Maybe forty minutes."

"Oh."

"Mike can let you in."

She sighed.

"I know, I know. I'm sorry. Can't be helped."

"Great. Me and Mike. What will we talk about?"

"Sports? Politics? Religion?"

They both laughed.

"I don't know. Pretend you have an interest in video games or anime and you guys might hit it off. I gotta go. See ya in a few."

"See ya."

She hung up. Her and Mike, alone together for almost an hour? She couldn't think of a more awkward evening. She didn't have anything against Mike; she liked him sometimes, in a kid brother sort of way, but she had nothing in common with him. And she had never spent any time with him without Dennis around.

She sometimes had the impression that Mike didn't care for her. It went beyond his usual weirdness, beyond the cold shoulder he would give her at breakfast when she stayed over. It was almost like jealousy. Could that be it? Was Mike jealous of her time with Dennis?

Or was he jealous that Dennis had found a replacement

for Allison and he hadn't?

Whoa. Where did that come from?

She shut the engine off and went inside.

★ ★ ★

The first thing Dennis heard when the elevator opened was laughter. It was muffled behind some closed door and he couldn't tell which apartment it came from.

He walked down the hall, fumbling with his keys, and stopped when he was outside his door.

It came from his apartment.

He looked around, made sure he was on the right floor. The television must be up too loud.

He opened the door and stepped inside. He paused, confused, staring at Eileen on the floor. She sat with her back against a chair, her knees tucked into her chest and her face red. A deck of cards was spread out in front of her and she cackled like a hyena. Mike sat on the couch across from her, a can of Coke in his hand, chuckling. They looked up at Dennis standing there, shocked, and then looked to each other and busted out with more laughter.

"Alright," Dennis said. "What did I miss?"

Eileen jumped up and gave him a kiss. "Mike just told this story...Oh, you gotta hear it. Mike. Tell it to Dennis."

Mike laughed again and shook his head. "He won't get it. You have to know the guy."

Eileen winked at Dennis. "I'll get you some wine."

She darted into the kitchen and Dennis followed. She poured them both a glass and yelled "Mikey. You need another Coke?"

"No. I'm good."

Dennis raised an eyebrow. "Mikey? Did I just step into *The Twilight Zone*?"

She smiled. "I guess you did, because we've been having a blast. Turns out we know some of the same people. A couple of his old classmates work under me at the mall and his manager is a guy I dated in high school."

"Oh, yeah?"

"Yeah. Wait until you hear this story. It's great." She shoved a glass into his hand and scampered back into the living room.

Dennis shrugged. Thank God for that. If they had found some common ground, that was one more worry off of his shoulders. Maybe breakfast wouldn't be so awkward from now on.

He saw a box of pizza open on the table. It was still warm and he piled a few slices onto a plate and went out to join them. He sat on the couch next to Mike and took a huge bite.

"So," he said, through a mouthful of cheese and pepperoni, "what's this story that's so funny?"

Eileen threw a card at Mike. He grabbed it and tossed it back. They laughed. "It's just something stupid my manager did."

"Is this Eileen's ex-boyfriend?"

"Uh-huh," she said. "And he's just as asinine as ever."

"Well, go on."

Mike shook his head. "We built it up too much. You're not gonna think it's funny."

"Look, if Eileen was about to keel over, I'm sure it's hilarious. Tell the damn story already."

"Okay. So Beau decides one night that he'd play a practical joke on the customers."

"Go on."

"So he changes out the Coke with Pepsi and serves everyone Pepsi all night."

Eileen and Mike giggled.

"I don't get why that's so funny."

"Because," Mike went on, "he thought he was being badass, like that was some kind of genius *Punk'd* stunt or something."

Eileen laughed.

Dennis shrugged; he still didn't get it. "Okay. Did anyone call him on it?"

"This big guy came up at the end of the night and said 'Hey, man, this is clearly not Coke.' And then he started cussing."

"Really?"

Mike lowered his head and smiled. "No, I made that up."

"I think," Eileen interrupted, "you do have to know him. Beau always thought he was badass, like Mike said, but never had the guts to go through with anything serious."

Dennis took another bite of pizza. "I guess I'll take your word for it."

Mike and Eileen burst into laughter again.

★ ★ ★

Right before the movie ended, they heard Mike snoring on the couch. When the credits started to roll, they turned off the lights and left him sleeping.

They crept into Dennis' room and Eileen changed into her nightshirt. He followed her to the bathroom, sliding his hand up her shirt while she brushed her teeth. She smacked it away, smiled, and finished her nightly routine. Then they made love and, though neither of them would admit that's what they were doing, deep down they both knew.

Afterward, as Eileen lay on her stomach and Dennis ran his fingers along her back, they both felt like talking about where they were. Instead they talked about Mike.

"I'm just surprised I had such a fun time with him tonight," she said.

"Now you see why I keep him around. Mike's a social retard sometimes, but he's a good guy at heart. I'm just glad you two finally hit it off."

"Tell me about it." She rolled over onto her back. Dennis' fingers continued their motion on her stomach. "Has Mike ever had a girlfriend?"

He thought for a moment and shook his head. "I don't think so. He's been on a date or two, and I know there was this girl he went to high school with that he was head over heels for, but I don't think he's ever had anything serious."

"So he's still a virgin, right?"

"As far as I know. Why?"

She shrugged. "I was just thinking of that woman across the hall from you guys."

"Margot."

"Yeah. Her."

"Did Mike mention her?"

"Not in so many words…"

"It's never 'in so many words' with him."

"Well, I'm starting to see your line of thinking. Maybe it would be good for him to just experience a woman, ya know? Help him grow up a little."

"That's what I've been saying."

"Yeah, but it sounds smarter coming from me."

He pinched her hip and she yelped and twisted away.

"Has he talked to his parents since moving out?"

"Not that I know of."

"They've really done a number on him, haven't they?"

"A few numbers, I'd say. Like six digits."

She nodded. "I forget sometimes how lucky I am to have good parents. Aside from my dad, that is, but we don't really count him."

"Good? Shit. You might as well have sprang from the loins of Ward and June Cleaver."

She laughed. "If June's first husband ran off, then yeah. No, Mom and Steve, they fight, and we disagree on things, but they've always been good to me. I turned out okay."

"Well, I don't know about *that*..."

"Shut up."

"What about your brother and sister?"

She shrugged. "They didn't turn out *bad*, they just have messed up ideas about relationships."

"I'd say."

She propped herself up on one elbow and turned toward him. "You know, you never talk about your folks."

"No. I guess I don't."

"I mean, I know your mom is...gone, and that you and your dad aren't too friendly, but..." She trailed off.

He was quiet for a long while. "I don't like..."

"Talking about it? I kind of figured."

"*Thinking* about it."

"I'm sorry. I always feel like I'm digging too deep with you."

"It's okay. I guess I've got a bit more dirt to sift through than most of the guys you've dated."

"I just ask because I..." She paused and he hoped she would say it, that she'd be the one to open the door. "I care," she finished, and he was equally as glad that she had left the door closed.

"I know. You have a right to know some of my secrets, I guess."

"*Some?*"

He laughed. "If you knew all my secrets, the mystery would be gone."

"Whatever. You've tap-danced around this enough. It's okay if you don't tell me."

"No, I...I want to, I think." His hand found hers and gripped it tight. She gave him a little squeeze. "I need to, maybe."

"I'm here."

Thoughts flashed through his mind in rapid succession. A crib. Bouquet of flowers. Beer cans rolling around on the floorboards. Clenched fist dripping blood. Bits of hair and scalp stuck to shattered glass.

He decided, once again, to give her the condensed version. "It's nothing interesting. Just a car accident when I was little. Mom's birthday, of all days. They had been talking about having another kid. Dad was pretty messed up about it. Started drinking a lot. I guess that's hereditary. Anyway, he never really recovered. Took a lot of it out on me. That's why I moved out the day I graduated high school."

"Do you guys talk?"

"Rarely."

She kissed his cheek. "You've been really lonely, haven't you?"

She hit something, touched some deep part of him that he hadn't even known existed. His lips quivered and he could feel tears forming. He sucked in a sharp breath and held them back. "I don't know."

She kissed him. "You don't have to be."

They locked eyes and, not for the first time since they started seeing each other, Dennis lost himself staring into her. His stomach twisted, hair stood up on his arms. He screamed at himself to stop, but his tongue ignored him.

"I love you," he said.

It was quiet. To Dennis the moment stretched out for eons. Eileen stared at him like he was a stranger. He had the horrible thought she would stand up, say she didn't feel the same, get dressed, and sprint out the door.

She reached up and kissed him. "I think I love you, too," she said.

They made love again and this time they allowed themselves to recognize it as what it was. It made them feel whole and they fell asleep in each other's arms.

Chapter Nine

Eileen screamed. Dennis jolted awake, rolled over, clicked on the light. The alarm clock read *3:36 a.m.*

She sat up, covers tucked to her chin, scanning the room. Her breath was labored. Her brow glistened.

"Babe? Eileen? What is it?"

Her eyes found his face and she cried. She cuddled close to him, burying her head into his shoulder as she wept. He wrapped his arms around her and held her tight, rocking her back and forth, one hand running through her hair as he whispered that everything would be okay.

After a few minutes she calmed down and pulled away.

"I'm okay," she said and wiped the tears from her face.

"Wanna talk about it?"

She stared at him, eyes wide, shoulders trembling, and chewed her lower lip. She shook her head, lay back down, and rolled away. He turned off the lights and cuddled under the sheet.

The soft hum of the air conditioner lulled him back to the edge of sleep. He thought he felt the first stirrings of a dream himself when her hand fell on his shoulder.

"I think maybe I do need to talk about it."

He clicked the lamp back on. It stung his eyes. He tilted the shade away, aiming the light onto the wall. It created a giant yellow circle and cast the rest of the room in an odd array of dim light and weak shadows. Eileen's pale, shaken face was faded in such an environment, as if she were an actress being projected from a faded print of an old movie.

"Nightmare, huh?"

"Not just one. I've had...*been* having these dreams for a while."

"How long?"

"For a few weeks. Only when I stay here." He raised an eyebrow and she took his hand again. "It's not you. It's this building."

"The building?"

She nodded.

"It *is* kind of creepy."

She shook her head. "That's not it."

"What is it?"

"I don't know."

"Well, what are the nightmares?"

She pulled her knees to her chest and wrapped her arms around her shins. She looked down at her hands and he followed her eyes. She played with the ring on her pinky, spinning it around, moving it up and down. She suddenly looked like a little girl; young, weak, vulnerable. More than anything, she looked innocent, and the fact that something had shaken and disturbed her worried him to his core. He wanted nothing more than to take her into his arms and protect her.

This is *love,* he thought. If he had any doubts about having said it to her, they were swept away.

Eileen smiled weakly and he smiled back.

She stood. "I need a glass of water." She slid on one of his long white T-shirts. It hung to her knees, swallowing her completely and hiding her shape. It made her look even more childlike as she tiptoed out into the apartment.

Dennis sat up and peeked out the door. The couch was empty and Mike's door was shut. He was grateful; the last thing Eileen needed right now was Mike saying something moronic.

He heard her rummage through the cabinets and then the high-pitched whistle of the kitchen sink. Her bare feet smacked their way across the wooden floor and he thought she was coming back, but then the bathroom light clicked on. It spilled out onto the sofa and reflected off of several empty Coke cans. Mike was such a pig sometimes. *Used to his mother cleaning up after him.*

He heard water running again, and then the *rush-whoosh-rush* of a toothbrush scrubbing in her mouth. Didn't she already brush her teeth? He heard her gargle and spit, then the light went off and she walked back into the room.

She shut the door behind her and sat her glass of water on the dresser. Leaned against the wall. Closed her eyes. Grimaced. "I can still taste him."

Dennis felt a surge of jealousy and almost asked *Who?* but stopped himself. She was obviously shaken by the dream; he doubted it was some kind of sexual fantasy. And even if it was, he couldn't exactly accuse her of infidelity based on a dream.

She sighed. Took a deep breath. She opened her eyes, took her glass in both hands, and drank. Sat it back down. She crossed her arms across her chest, hugging herself and staring at her feet.

"It's the same dream, but it...it gets worse every time. Keeps going. Like a...a...soap opera. I get a little bit each time and it plays out a little further."

Dennis realized that she had avoided spending the night lately. All of the early work shifts, the car problems, the invitations to cook for him at her place—it was all her way to keep the dream from coming.

And he talked her into coming over tonight.

"It, uh, it starts with me wandering through the woods. It's dusk and I know I have to get out of here before night falls. I come across this concrete tube, like some kind of drainage thing, but big. Almost big enough to fit my car into. And there's this rusted grate locked shut over it. I hear something inside and bend down to get a closer look. My finger gets cut on the grate, and a bit of blood drops down into the darkness. It's quiet at first, but then there are these sounds. This horrible growling, and then these tearing sounds, like animals ripping into meat. And suddenly, there's a flood coming out of the thing. This foul smelling tide of, I don't know, *sewage*, I guess. And I run and run, until my heart's about to burst. But this river of shit crashes over me, dragging me under, and there are other people trapped in it, I can feel their bodies bounce off of mine. I fight to the surface but hands grab my calves and ankles and try to drag me under.

"Then suddenly you and I are walking up the driveway. It's night and we're holding hands. There are these dim lights along the driveway, like...um...like gaslights. Ya know? Like outside of Scrooge's shop in 'A Christmas Carol,' those Victorian lights."

"Yeah."

"We're alone, but I can feel people lined up along both sides of the drive. Just, I don't know, standing. Watching us walk. But for whatever reason I never look to the sides, just straight ahead, watching the building grow as we move toward it. It kind of…kind of *breathes*. I really don't know how to describe it.

"Then we're walking through the courtyard, but it's sudden. Like, we're in the driveway then suddenly the courtyard. Ya know, typical dream logic. The courtyard is lit with the same gaslights, but they're not as strong. All of the statues are completely in the dark but they seem to be moving. Undulating. Dancing. Touching each other. There's faint moaning coming from the dark. Heavy breathing. The air is hot. Thick and humid. It smells like jasmine and…*sex*."

"Sounds hot," Dennis said and smiled.

She stared at him, confused.

"I'm sorry," he said.

She took another breath and ran her hand across her face. "So we get to the door, except it doesn't open onto the lobby. It opens onto the pool area, like the front of the building isn't a building at all, just some kind of facade. The gaslights aren't here, just the normal dim light bulbs. But there's even more people, still in the dark, watching. They're excited. You can feel it all around you. The air is hungry. Lustful.

"And the pool…God. It's filled with *bodies*, floating lifelessly. Bloated. Blue."

"Blue?"

"Yeah. From drowning, I guess. And there's something

else in there with them. It swims around under them, bumping them every now and then and causing them to splash around. And you can see that goddamned supermarket past the pool, all lit up. The parking lot, the supermarket itself, the other stores—all of it. But the graffiti's still there and the grass is still waist high, so it's not open. It's more like it's…it's…"

She shook her head. "So you and I walk past the pool over to that grotesque fountain. The water sprays out like usual, but the color's different. It's red, blood red, and there are bits of white and…" She shivered. "It's disgusting. But the worst part is the statues. They're moving. The satyr's hand is fondling the woman's breast and she's pushing back against him, moaning. Her eyes are closed, but he's looking right at us."

Dennis shivered. The statues unnerved him under normal circumstances in broad daylight. But this…No wonder she was so upset.

"And their skin. It's the same color as the stone they're made from, but it looks like human skin. It's got the right texture, and flexibility, and there's even a pulse underneath it as blood pumps. And you step up to the fountain and he looks at you and I scream for you to get away but he says… he says…"

"What's he say?"

She closed her eyes. "He says that his woman is for you and yours is for him. And you just nod your head. I'm screaming at you, angry, hurt, but more afraid than anything. Then the woman opens her eyes and steps down onto the edge of the fountain. She takes your hand and whispers 'darling,' and squats down until she's sitting, and her legs are spread, and she grabs your face and pushes it down.

"Then she's moaning and clutching at the back of your head. I want to run, but I can't. I can feel all of those people just waiting in the dark and if I run I know, somehow I just *know* that they'll tear into me. And the satyr is watching you and his nymph fuck and he's stroking himself."

"God damn, Eileen."

"Oh, it's not over. That's where it ended last time. To-night…dear Christ, tonight *he stepped down.*"

Dennis felt the sudden urge to tell her to stop, that he couldn't listen anymore. But deep down he was consumed by a morbid curiosity and, though he refused to admit it even to himself, her dream not only horrified him but also turned him on.

"He steps over you right as you yell and give one last thrust. Then he gives you a knife and you…you…" She sniffed and her lips quivered. He thought she was going to cry again, but she took a deep breath and sucked it all in. It looked like it took a tremendous amount of will, but she pulled herself together.

Her eyes focused on a point on the ceiling and she rattled off the rest of the dream matter-of-factly, as though she recited a series of statistics for one of her classes.

"You open your throat and slump over into the bloody water. The nymph grabs your body and tosses it completely in and then she mounts your dead face and grinds back and forth, moaning, as she laps up the blood coming out of the fountain. Then the satyr is behind me, running his calloused fingers along my abdomen. He whispers to me, I don't remember what, and his erection presses against my back.

"Then he spins me, pushes me to my knees, and presses his fucking dick against my lips. I don't want to open for him, but it's like my jaw and teeth are mush and he pushes himself inside my mouth. And then he's thrusting. Not gently, God no. He's fucking my mouth so rough that his pelvis busts my nose open and the blood runs down onto my lips and all I can taste is my blood and this sweaty, diseased *thing* that's in my mouth, and it tastes like rotten hamburger…and sour milk…and…"

She broke down and started gagging. She ran to the bathroom and Dennis heard her vomit. His first thought was to rush after her, see if she was okay, but he was rooted to the bed. He was a jumble of emotions—fear, distress, disgust, jealousy, anger, and lust.

What could cause a dream like that?

He heard the toilet flush and she came back into the room. He stood and took her into his arms. He held her for a long while.

He kissed her forehead. "What do you think caused it? Are you taking some allergy medication or maybe ate something that—"

"It's this building," she whispered, gesturing with her finger to the floor. She looked conspiratorial and Dennis had to stifle a laugh.

"The building…"

"That sounds crazy, but I just know it. It doesn't feel like something from my own mind. It's like…like…like a movie or something, like it's been given to me, and I have no control over how it happens or…or…"

"But the fountain. The slitting of the throat. The statues."

She crossed her arms over her chest. "What about them?"

"Well, I mean, it's like that story I told you. The one Margot told us that day at the pool when the Callahan kid had a seizure. That doctor built those statues for him and his mistress and then slit his own throat in that fountain."

"And?"

"I'm just saying, maybe that's kicking around in your subconscious somewhere. It's a little coincidental, isn't it?"

She shrugged. "I don't know. Maybe. It just seems like…"

"Like what?"

"Nothing." She threw her arms up into the air and laughed. "You're right. I'm being silly."

"No you're not. That's a fucking scary dream. You have every right to be upset. But I seriously doubt the building is feeding you these images. That's just not possible."

She shrugged again and slumped down on the foot of his bed. "You're right."

He kissed her cheek.

"I don't know if I can get back to sleep now."

He stood, grabbed her clothes off of the floor, and tossed them at her. He grabbed his own jeans and slid them on.

"What are you doing?"

He zipped his pants and smiled. "We're staying the rest of the night at your place."

She stood. "No, no. That's ridiculous. I'm already—"

He grabbed her around the waist and kissed her. "It's okay. We'll spend the rest of the night there. And tomorrow night, too. And the next. We'll stay there every night, if we have to, until you stop having this dream."

She smiled, her eyes filling with tears. "Thank you."

"No thanks necessary. You have satellite TV, it's that simple."

She laughed and hugged him. He rubbed his hand up and down her back, trying to comfort her, but a question kept nagging at him.

What if the dream never stopped?

★ ★ ★

Mike pulled off of the interstate exit and onto Emory Highway. He stopped a little too hard at the red light and his seatbelt pinched the skin on his neck. He readjusted it and, making sure that the road was still clear, turned right.

He was nervous driving, but happy to be able to. He thought that Dennis wasn't going to take him out again after the last time, but he did. Eileen even took him out one day while Dennis was at work. She had been much more fun than his roommate, laughing and joking the whole time, and he had felt more comfortable with her. After that he was confident enough to get his license and start taking himself to work. And right on schedule, he thought. It was the end of the month and school would be starting up before he knew it.

The thought of school sent a wave of nausea blasting through him. He wanted to go, was excited to, but had never been more nervous about anything in his life. This wasn't like high school; he would have to sign up for his own classes, buy his own books, find his own way around campus. The thought made him want to run home, not to the apartment but to his parents' house, bang on the door, and beg to be let back in.

But his parents hadn't even called to see how he was doing. To Hell with them. He didn't need them anymore. At least, he didn't think so. He worried sometimes that he did, especially when thinking of school, but he had some money saved up and had received letters notifying him that he was approved for a student loan, so he was fine. Independent. Grown up.

Was he?

Sure. He set his own curfew, didn't he? He had control over his checking account for once. He cashed his own paychecks. He paid his own bills. He even drank. What else did adults do?

They dated, that's what.

He had been feeling particularly lonely since moving out, and he had to admit, *horny*. One of the reasons he wanted his own place was to bring a girl home, but he hadn't been on a date in over a year. The last girl he had gone out with was a seventeen-year-old named Kyrie who worked at the theater over the summer. Mike had gone out with her six times, kissing her on the fourth and fifth dates, and making out with her on the sixth. He had even felt her tiny breasts that night while sitting on a bench in the park. He had thought that this was it, he had a girlfriend finally, he was going to get *laid*, but then she canceled their next two dates. She had bullshit excuses, something about helping her dad fix the garage. Then summer was over and she had gone off to college. He had tried calling and e-mailing a few times that fall, but she never called or wrote back.

He didn't understand it. Why would she have gone out with him so many times if she didn't like him? Why would she have let him grope her? It didn't make any sense and filled him with bitterness and resentment when he thought about it. The only conclusion he could come to was that she really didn't like him that much, that she just passed the time with him. Used him. Maybe to make her feel better about herself, maybe to make some guy jealous. Who knows? Whatever the reason, the experience left him with less confidence to speak to women than he had ever had (which was never much) and he hadn't so much as asked for a phone number since.

As he drove down Emory Highway, picking up as much speed as he could before the road twisted and curved out of control, he wondered if all women were like that. He reasoned that most probably were, but not all. Look at his mother, or his sister, or Eileen, for that matter. He wished he could find a girl like Eileen.

She was great. Funny, laid back, beautiful. She didn't talk down to him or treat him like he was retarded. And she didn't want to go out and party all the time, wasn't into the bar scene and the club scene and taking ecstasy and drinking beer until she passed out. No, she was too classy for that. She liked to do the same things he did: watch movies, play cards and board games, hang out at coffee shops. After his driving lesson they had spent the afternoon in a coffee shop, talking about their favorite movies. He remembered how the sun shined in the back window and lit up her hair from behind, like something out of a Spielberg film or—

Do I have a crush on her?

He noticed how sweaty his palms had become on the

steering wheel, how dry his mouth was. He wiped his hands on his lap, one at a time, and swallowed.

It made him sick to his stomach. What was he doing with a crush on Eileen? She was dating his best friend, his roommate for Christ's sake. Did Dennis know? Oh, shit. Could he tell? Did he know before Mike even realized it himself?

Could Eileen tell?

He felt nauseous again and rolled down the window. A cold breeze had settled into the valley for the past few days and made him feel somewhat better. It wouldn't last, he knew; the weather report said that the weekend was going to be another scorcher. But he was glad it was here now.

He took a curve a little too fast and lurched back into his seat. *Get your mind off of Eileen and onto the road.* This was ridiculous, this stupid little crush of his. It was juvenile and childish. He was an adult now, damn it. Why couldn't he act like one?

He chastised himself for how predictable it all was. He was usually jealous of Dennis. His physical ability, his charisma, his sheer will and determination to tackle things head on instead of cowering away from them. Why wouldn't he be jealous of his friend's girl, too? It fit perfectly with the part that he ended up playing, didn't it? He was the side-kick, the comic relief, the surrogate little brother, the ward. A Hollywood screenwriter couldn't have done a better job of mapping out his life, creating a neurotic, anxiety-ridden geek who couldn't grow up and get a handle on his life.

Even the building he lived in. Look at it there, rising out of the hill like some kind of giant mental ward. That's where he belonged, wasn't it? Would that make these winding roads symbolic of some kind of twisting in his mind? Would that mean—

A shape darted in front of him. He slammed on his brakes, his tires squealed, something went *thump*. Then an awful series of sounds in quick succession—*crackcrack-crack*—and he felt something under his tires. He came to a stop and sat there, breathing hard, replaying it in his mind.

What just happened? Something *had* run out in front of him. Maybe it was just a possum. Yeah, a possum, that's all. They keep coming out of the woods and wandering around down here, that's probably all it was. It couldn't be one of the kids that lived in the building, chasing a ball across the driveway at night, not noticing the headlights until they came around the curve and—

Why wasn't he paying more attention?

He put the car in park and opened the door. His seat-belt unclipped and whipped back into place on the seat. He leaned out and twisted around, afraid he would see a shoe or a ball cap or—

Nothing.

He sighed. Maybe he didn't hit anything after all. But that thought didn't have any weight; he knew he had hit something. He had felt it. He had heard it.

He stepped out of the car.

The breeze kicked up around him, blowing his hair, sneaking into the creases between his work vest and his thin T-shirt. He shivered and looked around. He didn't see anyone and the night was quiet. Grass and leaves rustled as the wind blew through the yard, a faint electric hum issued from the streetlights positioned every few yards up the drive, the Saturn's engine whirred, but he couldn't hear anything else. No crickets chirped, no dogs barked, no one whispered about seeing a car hit someone.

He glanced up the drive, wondering if he would see lights coming on, if someone would scream and run down the path. The only lights were the ones he had seen when first glancing at the building and the doors stayed shut.

His headlights shot up the drive and onto two trees growing close to the path. He had never noticed them before and was glad; they were gnarled and twisted, growing together toward the top, their limbs intertwined and covered in the strange webbing that caterpillars left behind when devouring plants. They were sentinels sent out to watch for this kind of tragedy, to witness when an inevitable accident like this occurred and report it, to indict the responsible party.

But tell who?

The building.

He looked away from the trees and tried to get a grip on himself. He took a few steps toward the back of his car and gasped when he saw a pool of red liquid.

He laughed when he recognized it as his brake lights reflecting off of an oil stain. The laughter gave him confidence and nearly erased the dread that he had been feeling since stepping out into the night. He strode to the back of his car—

And threw up onto the pavement.

Under his back tire was Lucy, her torso crushed, her back broken. It inverted at an odd V shape along the spine, bending in a direction that backs weren't meant to bend. Her hind legs had disappeared in a pool of red and black mush spotted with reddish-blond fur. Her gore-covered snout hung open, her tongue dangling limply onto the pavement, and her glassy eyes stared off into the sky, searching for whatever star her soul planned on traveling to.

What had made him vomit was the point of the V, her abdomen, which had burst open and spilled her insides all over the driveway.

He stumbled backwards and collapsed onto the curb. His muscles trembled. He realized he was crying. He had never killed anything larger than a fly before, especially not a sweet dog like Lucy. He loved dogs. And Lucy had never done any harm; all she ever did was wag her tail and rub her wet nose on the back of your hand until you petted her. She'd whine and nuzzle closer to you, just wanting to be loved. That was all she ever wanted, was to be loved.

And he killed her.

He didn't know how long he sat there crying. Finally he heard a car engine and he jumped up, knowing that the car was going to be speeding up the driveway, knowing that it was going to be the Turners returning home and that little Joey would jump out of the backseat and scream and call him a murderer and—

Headlights zoomed by the driveway and disappeared around a bend.

He wiped his eyes with the back of his hands. He had to do something. If he sat here much longer he would be found, and then how would he explain it?

Accidents happen.

Yeah, they do. But people still get blamed for them. People still get beaten up by angry fathers, sued by distraught mothers, ostracized by a building that thinks you're a *dog killer*, while your roommate is a *hero*. Dennis saves one kid; he kills another's dog. How's that going to look?

He could hear people whispering around the pool already. *There goes that Mike kid. Killed poor Joey Turner's dog, he did. The Turner kid just hasn't been the same since. He loved that dog more than anything. His parents are going to have to put him in an institution because of it. Too bad that Mike kid isn't more like his roommate; Dennis is a stand-up guy. You'd think some of that would have rubbed off on him by now.*

He had to get rid of the dog. He stepped around her, popped open his trunk, and tugged at an old sheet that Eileen had left in there. A giant metal gas can pinned it to a corner and he struggled to yank it out. He also had a few bags of groceries; he had stopped on his way home to buy his share of things. He pulled out a box of garbage bags, ripped the top open, and jerked one out. It stuck to the roll and he had a hard time breaking it off. It didn't help matters that his hands were shaking and his palms slick. He finally got it off and ripped it in two. He wrapped his hands with it and bent to pull the dog out.

What was he thinking? His tire was still on it.

He jumped into his car and shifted gears. The car slipped into neutral and rolled back over Lucy's body. He slammed on the brakes, cursed, and put it into drive. He pulled forward, driving over her again, and stopped a couple of yards up the driveway.

He jumped out and readjusted the garbage bags on his hands. He raced over to Lucy and, with the car gone, could now see the full extent of the damage. He started crying again, whimpering like he imagined she would have done if he was a second faster with his brakes and just clipped her, just broke her leg and could have taken her to the vet and gotten a cast put on. He saw the extra damage caused by slipping out of gear and almost vomited again. There was a slick tire track of black, red, and green about three feet long going over and through Lucy.

He heard another car going by and froze. He had to act fast. He spread the sheet out next to her and bent over to pull her body onto it. He grabbed her hind legs and tugged, trying not to look, and heard another series of cracking sounds followed by a *squish* as he pulled what was left of her onto the sheet.

He glanced down and her eyes stared straight into his. Accusing him.

"I'm sorry," he said.

The smell hit him and he turned away and gagged. He took a big breath, held it, and went back to scooping the larger bits onto the sheet. When he was finished he wrapped her up in it, grabbed another garbage bag, and shoved her inside. His makeshift gloves went in after her. The top barely tied together and he had to fight it so hard he thought it was going to split open. Finally he tied it closed and hefted it into his backseat. He glanced back at where she had been.

The ground was covered in her insides.

He looked around, wishing he had a rake or a shovel or a water hose. He glanced into his trunk and saw the carton of Cokes that he had bought. He took one out, shook it up, and aimed it toward the spot as he opened it. It fizzed for a second and then exploded out of the can, spraying into the mess on the ground and scattering some of it.

He remembered an experiment done with cola in a chemistry glass he had in high school. They had dropped a corroded penny in a glass and marveled as the soda ate away at the corrosion. He didn't know if that would work with organic material, or even with this much material, but he was running out of options. He emptied the can onto it and grabbed another, and another. He went through six cans before he gave up.

The soda had spread the bulk of the gore around, and trails of fizzy, bloody gunk ran down the driveway. It didn't clean the mess, and he doubted the Coke would magically eat it away to nothing, but it was getting difficult to tell what the mess was.

If I can't get rid of it, maybe I can hide it.

He grabbed a jar of spaghetti sauce from one of the bags. He fumbled in his panic, dropped it, and it shattered onto the concrete where Lucy had been.

Good enough.

He took a small tube of hamburger meat and ripped it open along the seam. He squeezed it out and spread it around the drive.

He stepped back. Hamburger meat, spaghetti sauce, cola. A pinkish-green pool of his vomit to the right. It looked like someone had gotten sick, maybe spilled a box of leftovers. But it didn't look like a dog was killed. Not anymore.

He thought back to the possums and realized that most of this would be gone by the morning, anyway.

He jumped back into his car and tried to catch his breath. He calmed a little with the evidence covered up. But then he thought of little Joey wandering around yelling for his dog and was overwhelmed by guilt.

Mikey, you did the right thing. That kid will just think she ran off, probably ended up on a farm somewhere where she can run and frolic and someone is taking care of her. He'll be sad, sure, but not as sad as if he knew she was dead.

He nodded. That felt right.

But what was he going to do with her?

He couldn't throw her into the trash. What if a garbage man found her, said something to someone, and they came looking for who was responsible?

What about burying her? No, that wouldn't work, either. He didn't have a shovel and, even if he did, where the hell would he bury her? Even if he found a place, it could take hours to dig a hole and fill it back in.

What he needed was an isolated, secluded spot he could dump her, someplace no one had any reason to go to. Someplace she'd never be found.

The supermarket.

It made perfect sense. It came to him in a flash; he could sneak back there, wedge the doors open, and toss the bag inside. No one ever went up there, especially not after that Callahan kid's seizure. No one would even think to look for her behind those closed doors. The place unnerved him, but he didn't even have to go inside. Just open the doors, leave the bag like some kind of

—offering—

delivery, and go back to his apartment. No one would ever know.

This was what his father would call a *Smart Thing*.

He put his car in gear and drove up the hill.

After scouting out the lobby and the pool area to make

sure no one was out, he went back to the car and grabbed the bag. It was heavier than he thought it would be and the sudden fear that the bottom would split open in the hallway, spilling its contents all over the floor, took hold of him. He grabbed another bag from his trunk and slid the first one inside of it. He had a slightly easier time tying this one and he lugged it up the steps into the courtyard.

With both hands on it, it still strained his grip and pulled at his shoulders. He felt like his tendons would rip before he even made it out back. He stopped, tried to catch his breath, and lamented what horrible shape he was in.

He heaved the bag up, trying to get it over his shoulder, but it only made it to waist level. It swung back down and crashed into his shins. The momentum from the swing toppled him over onto his ass, the bag coming to rest in his lap.

"Fuck."

He squirmed out from under it and stood. He gripped it again, gritted his teeth, and gave it everything he had. This time it swung up and over his shoulder, smacking into his back hard enough to make him stumble forward a few feet. He felt a sharp pain in his lower back that leaked around his hip into his thigh. He sucked a breath and took an awkward step forward. The pain confirmed his fear; he had pulled something.

Nothing to do about it now. He couldn't leave the bag there. Just suck it up and get it over with.

He limped forward, past the statues smiling down at him, and into the lobby. He heard the elevator whirring and froze, unsure what to do. He panicked and rushed for the back doors.

He stumbled into the pool area. It was empty. The breeze blew a little harder, chilling the sweat on his brow and his arms. He inched past the pool and out into the field. If anyone saw him now, hunched over with a bag on his back, he knew he would look like Quasimodo, or Igor bringing his master fresh parts.

He made his way through the grass, slipping here and there on loose rocks and dirt, but never completely lost his footing. Each slip sent new waves of pain through his hip and back, and he yelped once, but kept pushing on. Twigs and nettles stuck to the bag, grabbed at it, tore little holes into it, as though the field itself tried to wrest a prize from him.

The moon was little more than a sliver in the sky and he could barely see the supermarket against the blackness of the woods ahead. He slowed a little, wondering where the concrete started, when his foot came down on something hard and raised. A curb. He almost lost his balance, the weight of the bag trying to drag him backwards into the stinging grip of the field, but he stayed upright.

He took a step onto the parking lot.

The busted lamp above him flickered to life.

He froze. Was someone here? He looked around, couldn't see anyone, couldn't hear anyone.

He was alone. The light must be on a motion sensor, like the one over his dad's garage.

Still, he couldn't shake the feeling that eyes were on him. The light was far from comforting, even considering how dark it had been before. Now he was exposed. He whirled around and looked back at the pool area, certain someone watched him.

He didn't see a soul. He chalked it up to nerves and approached the double doors leading into the store. The glass was clouded over and filthy with dirt. All he could see was a blurry darkness behind them. He stepped up to them and almost screamed when they opened.

Why did the building still have power?

He shook his head. It didn't matter. He needed to throw the bag in and get the hell out of there.

He walked up to the edge of the doorway and peeked inside. It was black, blacker than any black he had ever seen. Cold seeped out from inside, colder than the breeze blowing around him. It reminded him of the chilly dampness of deep caves, like when his parents took them to Mammoth Cave eight or nine years ago. Deep, dark, icy, and impenetrable.

He tossed the bag inside. He thought he would hear it slap against the floor, see its shadow topple over, but he didn't. There was no sound, no visual.

It was like the shadows swallowed the bag whole.

It didn't feel right. He should grab the bag and get the hell out of there. Toss it into the woods, take it to some fast food restaurant's dumpster, anywhere, just not there.

But he couldn't bring himself to. If he had seen where it landed, maybe, but…

But what?

Maybe there are spiders, he told himself, trying to give a name to the fear he felt. Snakes. Rats. Crazy homeless people. Hell, even boards with rusty nails through them. It's done. Leave. *Now.*

He took two steps back. Three. Not able to take his eyes off of the darkness, as though he were expecting…

Expecting what?

When he was off of the sidewalk, the double doors slid together.

He turned and tried to run back through the field, but his back was little more than a knotted ball and agony shot through every nerve. He slowed to a fast limp and pushed his way through the grass. He didn't look back until he was by the pool.

The light in the parking lot was still on.

He went in, climbed into the elevator, and rode up to his apartment. Once inside, he went straight to his room and shut the door. The place was dark and quiet. Dennis was either asleep or at Eileen's again.

He remembered that he had left groceries in the trunk of his car, but didn't care. Nothing he had bought would go bad by morning and he could bring it all in then. He just needed to lie down for a short while. He was tense and stressed and in pain and needed to rest.

He glanced out his window at the supermarket. The light was alive in the parking lot and he wondered what was wrong with it.

He closed his blinds and slunk down into his bed. Sleep enveloped him and he pushed all thoughts of Lucy and the supermarket from his mind. His utter exhaustion allowed him to rest without dreams until sunrise.

He would have had nightmares if he knew what he had done.

★ ★ ★

In the dark, it moved.

It had slept for so long, the comfort of oblivion too sweet a seduction to resist. It was so much easier to dream than to be.

Dreams were such powerful things.

And yet now, after such a long while, the consciousness stirred, the slumber threatening to fall away.

Sacrifice is sweet, as the Old Testament states in gory detail, but no sacrifice as sweet as that given freely, without demand or request.

It dreamed of simpler times, of light and beauty. It had destroyed that peace itself, by its own vain hand. Consumed by self-loathing, buried away in the dark to forget and be forgotten, this horrid dream of what was and what could have been made it cry out in its sleep, a cry that tore wide a hole its dreams had first whittled so long ago.

It calmed and sleep claimed it fully again.

But holes were funny things. Stab a hole in a water hose, for instance, and the pressure of the water over time will stretch the hole, carve it ever wider, until more and more water flows through, out of its protective barrier, spilling on the ground around it. Such a flood always starts with a single *drip*.

Drip.

Drip.

Drip.

Chapter Ten

A cold breeze tickled his feet. Dennis stirred, pulled them back inside the comfort of his sheets. His thoughts fought through the strange wilderness between awake and asleep.

He knew he had closed that window. His bladder ached and urged him to the bathroom. But Dennis was a stubborn sleeper, and instead rolled over onto his side to relieve the pressure.

He heard a low creak. It must be Mike, going to the toilet.

The thought barely formed before his consciousness sunk back down into the sleep. He tucked the sheet up to his neck and wiped a small bit of drool from his chin. The cotton was cool against his skin.

The breeze picked up, softly ruffling the sheet like caressing fingers.

Something creaked again.

The sound nudged him. Something in the room had changed, some subtle shift in the air pressure or the temperature. It gave him the distinct impression that someone else was in the room.

His limbs were heavy, his lids heavier, and so he told himself it was a remnant of a dream and resolved to go back to sleep. But the feeling itching the back of his skull was stubborn, a horrible feeling of violation telling him that someone's eyes were on him while he slept.

Was he still dreaming?

That creak again.

This time he recognized it and his heartbeat tripled. His eyes were still closed but he was fully awake now.

It's nothing, he told himself. The wind. He had forgotten and left the window open and the wind was blowing his mother's rocking chair back and forth, back and forth, slowly, the way his mother used to rock while knitting or—

But he had closed the window. He was positive.

Another creak.

He rolled over onto his back and opened his eyes. Aside from a single stripe of pale blue light that streaked across the ceiling, the room was almost as black as the back of his eyelids.

He rubbed his palms into his eyes. His bladder beat like a heart inside his pelvis. He fought himself up onto one elbow and yawned, scanned his room, saw nothing but dark. It took his eyes a moment to adjust.

When they did, he sucked in a sharp breath.

Someone was in the rocking chair.

He froze.

A part of him wanted to roll over, flip on the light, dispel the dark. But the signals died somewhere along the nerves between brain and muscles.

The chair was in shadow, its dark outline barely visible. The outline rose slightly on one of the arms, the shape of an elbow resting over the side. A head shaped lump of blackness leaned forward at the top with what had to be hair draping down the back of it.

His jacket. He always threw it on the back of the chair. That was what he was seeing. He almost laughed out loud. He had read in a psychology textbook that the human brain tried to make familiar shapes out of the unfamiliar, like seeing animals in clouds or faces in the natural contours of a rocky cliff.

The chair rocked forward. He looked to the window, knowing that seeing the drapes gently blowing would completely calm his nerves. They hung flat against the wall, still, like they were glued there. He waited for them to move.

And waited.

And waited.

The chair creaked as it rocked back.

Dennis pressed himself against his headboard. His breath died in his throat and a cold bead of sweat rolled down his nose. It hung from the tip for what seemed an eternity before plummeting into the dark.

"Who…who's there?" Was that his voice? How did he force that out?

"I don't know how I got here," what should have been his jacket whispered. It was a low, raspy sound, the voice hollow and filled with static, like a vinyl recording of a depression-era radio program played through blown speakers. It sent chills rippling across his flesh like thousands of tiny spider legs scrambling over him. His bladder let go, flooding his pajama pants in warmth and soaking through into the sheets.

The dark shape rocked forward again and for the first

time in his life he knew blind, unreasoning fear. It built in his gut and spread through his limbs and into the lump of matter at the base of his skull. He thought he knew how roaches must feel when the lights came on, or deer when a truck barreled down on them on a dark highway, or a mouse feeling the drip of warm saliva from a cat's mouth.

His skin was cold, his sweat colder. His breath was short and turned to mist as it leaked from between his lips. The room was thick and malicious with silence, punctuated by the occasional creak of the rocking chair.

"I've missed you," it said. Something in the pitch sounded vaguely feminine.

"...Mom?" He wasn't sure what made him say it, but uttering it solidified his fear. A part of him thought of her funeral, of the way she had laid so peaceful in her coffin. She didn't look like she was sleeping; no matter how many times people said that, there was no mistaking the unnatural stillness of her body or the brightness of the stage make-up painted on her face.

The shape in the rocking chair had the same stillness and, even though it lacked the brightness of the make-up, he was certain it was her.

"Mom?" he asked again.

The chair stopped.

The panic coursing through him took over. It forced his arm across the bed to tug on the little brass chain that hung below the shade. The lamp clicked to life and the room was flooded with warm, white light.

The rocking chair was empty except for the jacket draped over its back.

He blinked a few times. Rubbed his knuckles into his

eyes. Yawned. He *had* been sleeping still. It was a nightmare. A powerful, vivid nightmare, but nothing more. With the lights on and the shadows gone, his mind found the idea of ghosts and creaking rocking chairs to be ridiculous.

He thought of Eileen's nightmare and vowed to never tell her about his.

He stood and the wet leg of his pants stuck to his thigh. He hadn't pissed the bed since he was five. He pressed his hand against the sheets and found that they were warm and damp as well. He ripped them off and threw them into the clothes hamper. His pajama pants and boxers followed.

He grabbed his bathrobe from the closet and slid it on. The belt was missing, probably wrapped up in the leg of a pair of jeans he washed it with, and so he clutched it closed with one hand. He opened his bedroom door and peered out into the darkness of the living room. He paused, struck with the idea that someone was out there, sitting on the couch or standing in the corner, the shadows draped over them like a cloak, hiding them until Dennis stepped out and then—

He was being ridiculous.

He stepped through the living room and to the bathroom slowly and with purpose, as though sheer defiance was enough to expel his fears. He clicked on the light and shut the door behind him. The faucet handle squeaked as he turned the shower on and waited for the water to warm. Then he stepped underneath it and rinsed the warm urine and cold sweat from his body.

When he finished he toweled off, slid the robe back on, and went back to his room. He was tempted to leave the bathroom light on and the door open behind him, but fought the urge. What was next? A nightlight?

> —*And when the nightlight goes dim,*
> *the closet creaks open and fingers crawl out,*
> *long and spindly,*
> *and it tells me what wonders are in store for me*—

What was that from? A story he had read? A movie? He didn't recognize it and shook it off. He had worked himself up and his brain was sifting through its catalog of frightening imagery. If he kept this up he'd never sleep. He'd just lie in bed all night and listen to Regan MacNeil curse at her mother or tap his feet in time to the beat of the heart hidden under the floorboards.

> —*Deep under the floorboards,*
> *so far into the earth,*
> *sleeping where it had burrowed,*
> *thousands of tons of earth packed in above it,*
> *tossing and turning*
> *and unleashing its nightmares on*—

He shut the bedroom door behind him and chastised himself. He was being idiotic, letting a fear of the dark overwhelm him. It was a child's fear, a little boy's overactive imagination taking root in a man's mind. He ignored it, pushed it away as he rummaged for a clean pair of boxer shorts and clean sheets. He struggled to fit the sheets around the corners of the bed and then slid under them. He was about to turn the light off when his eyes caught the rocking chair again, and the jacket that his mind had made into his mother.

He hung the jacket in his closet and went back to bed.

He gave the room one last look before turning off the light. Everything was normal.

Of course it was normal.

He reached over and clicked the light off. Darkness poured in. Even the pale strip of moonlight was gone from his ceiling. He wondered if a cloud had passed in front of it, and then wondered if it was going to rain tomorrow. He put the thoughts of ghosts and demons from his mind and drifted off.

He rested, but never fully slept. He always found it difficult to sleep when he wasn't alone.

★ ★ ★

Carl Petrie, Kurt Hagen, and Terry Crowley sat out by the pool and watched the rain. They were sheltered underneath an umbrella as they sipped on their beers. Carl and Kurt worked construction, and Terry worked in landscaping, so the weather had given them all a day off. It was only ten after ten in the morning, but a day off was a day off and the three of them were well on their way to that glorious state of being that which was referred to as "bein' soused."

They stared across the field and drank.

"Rain's pretty warm."

"Yep."

"Breeze is gone, too."

"Mmm-hmm."

"You'd think rain like this would cool things off, not heat them up."

The other men shrugged.

One of them yawned.

"What you yawning for?"

"Didn't sleep much. Bad dreams."

They all nodded in understanding. None of them had slept much.

"You fellas see that light over there?"

They leaned forward and looked out through the field. It was faint and, if not for the dark clouds overhead, they probably would have missed it. But there it was, shining like a lighthouse in the storm.

"I'll be damned."

"I didn't think they had electricity over there?"

"Not supposed to."

They all drank in silence for a few minutes.

"Why you reckon that light's on?"

"Hell if I know."

"Maybe they're planning on finishing it up?"

"Naw. All them lights would be on, then."

"Hmmm…"

They drank some more.

"That place weirds me out."

They were all quiet.

A boy in a blue poncho walked through the field. A man in a green poncho was behind him. The boy looked like he was yelling, but the men couldn't hear what over the rain and thunder.

"What are they doing?"

"That's that Turner kid. Lost his dog."

"Lucy?"

"Yep."

"That's a damn shame."

"Sure is."

They drank some more. Lit cigarettes. Puffed away. The boy and the man made their way across the field and disappeared around the apartment building. They never so much as glanced at the supermarket, or the light shining from its parking lot.

"That place weirds me out."

"You done said that already."

"Yeah. Reckon I did."

They drank, puffed on their cigarettes, and listened to the falling rain.

Chapter Eleven

When the alarm sounded, Dennis almost punched it. He clicked it off, rolled out of bed, and stumbled to the bathroom. He felt like he hadn't slept in days. Part of it was the

—visitor—

dream he had had last night, but the other part was the storm. It was so difficult to get out of bed on a rainy day. The gloomy sky, the soft *patter-patter-patter* of the rain—it all worked together to keep him feeling sluggish and lethargic. His limbs barely moved as he struggled to wash his face and brush his teeth. It was like lead pumped through muscles made of concrete.

He heard Mike in the kitchen rummaging around and wondered if some dream had kept him up, too. Mike never got up before Dennis, was rarely up before noon if he could help it.

Dennis shuffled into the kitchen and for a moment thought he must still be dreaming. Mike rushed around, cracking eggs into a bowl, frying bacon on the stove, pouring orange juice. He seemed bright and happy and, aside from a slight limp and an odd bow in his back, moved like a pro.

"What's the special occasion?"

Mike turned around and grinned. "Thought I'd make us some breakfast."

Dennis grabbed a glass of orange juice and sat down. "I can see that. Why are you limping?"

"Oh, just pulled a muscle in my back at work. Lifting some boxes around in the back. It's okay, though. I took some Aleve this morning and can barely feel it."

"You should ice it."

"Not heat it?"

Dennis shook his head. "Lower back gets inflamed easy and heat just makes it worse. Ice it every couple of hours and you'll be fine in a couple of days."

"Good to know." Mike slid some bacon and scrambled eggs onto a plate and sat it in front of Dennis. He made his own plate and joined him.

Dennis laughed. "What, no toast?"

"Shit. I knew I forgot something."

"Sit down. I was joking. Thanks for breakfast. Beats the protein shake I was gonna have."

They ate, laughing and joking the entire time, and Dennis marveled at what a great mood his friend was in. Mike even cleaned up and washed the dishes afterward. He wondered for a moment if his roommate might be manic-depressive and this was one of his mania stages.

Stop it. You sound like Eileen.

"You work today?"

Mike shook his head. "Nope."

"Well, I was gonna go into town. Get some new shirts, maybe some notebooks and stuff for school. I have to meet Eileen for lunch at two, but other than that I'm clear. You wanna hang out? Maybe catch that John Carpenter triple-feature at Downtown West?"

Mike's eyes lit up. "What's playing?"

"The Kurt Russell flicks. *Escape From New York, Big Trouble in Little China,* and *The Thing.*"

"Let me change clothes. You mind driving?"

"Not at all."

Twenty minutes later they were heading down the driveway. The rain flowed along the curbs in tiny rivers, washing dirt, leaves, and litter along with it. Mike kept his face glued to the window.

"What are you doing?"

"Nothing."

"Hey, look at that." Dennis pointed to a family of possums making their way across the yard away from the driveway.

Mike smiled. "Huh…"

"What?"

"Nothing."

That night, after the movies, Dennis dropped Mike off at home and grabbed a change of clothes to take over to Eileen's. He had a shirt of hers she had wanted him to bring that she had left, a green cotton thing that clung to her in a way he enjoyed looking at. He had washed it and thrown it into the dryer with his things the day before, but when he dumped it out of his laundry basket onto his bed, noticed that it was wrapped inside of a still-damp towel. Sure enough, it was wet.

He grabbed some quarters from his nightstand and a paperback he was reading and headed downstairs. He took the elevator to the basement, but felt strange doing so. He felt claustrophobic all of a sudden, like he was stuck standing in his little two feet by two feet space and couldn't move around the car. He had never felt like that before; tight spaces rarely bothered him. He shrugged it off when the car reached the bottom and stepped out.

The basement was dimly lit at night. During the day an ample amount of sun shined through the windows, but at night the tenants were forced to rely on the sparse bulbs that hung from the ceiling. The maze of fenced-off storage areas that wound its way past pipes and water heaters cast long and deep shadows across the floor. His footsteps were loud and he had the odd sensation he disturbed someone, intruded on some private moment. When he reached the laundry room, he opened the door and went inside.

It was dark. He flicked the light switch, but nothing happened. He tried it again and again, but the bulb must have been busted.

Great.

He took his cell phone from the pocket of his jeans and held it open into the black. Its dull, blue light faintly lit the area and reminded him of the night vision goggles he had seen used in espionage films. He scanned the light across the cracked slate floor, making sure there wasn't the too-common puddle of water in front of the machines, and then over to the machines themselves. Pipes burst out of the brick above them, snaking up the wall before disappearing into the ceiling. They were thick with cobwebs and spots of red rust. The doors to the machines themselves hung open, the blackness inside them even thicker than what nested in the rest of the room. Dennis thought they looked like mouths hanging open, waiting for someone to come along and feed them socks and underwear.

He swung his arm around, about to close his phone and put it back into his pocket, when the light reflected off of something in the corner.

Eyes.

The light had only settled on them for a fraction of a second, but he couldn't mistake the inverted reflection of that pale light on a pair of small eyes, like the way a cat's eyes look in the dark. But this was too tall for a cat. He swung the light back over to the corner of the machines.

A small wisp of hair shot behind them.

He took a deep breath. It was just a kid. One of the neighbor's kids, some child playing around in the building, probably hide and go seek, ducking behind a washing machine to continue the game. Still, the basement was no place for a kid to play.

"Hey, kid." Dennis walked over to the machine. "Kid, you shouldn't be—"

There was no one there. The washing machine was pushed up against the wall only three feet from the other wall with its padlocked, knobless door.

He spun around. Did he miss the kid? Did he shoot past him or…or…

No. That was impossible. The path between the machines and the folding table was too narrow. The kid would have had to go right through him.

A chill tickled up his spine, slowly, until it reached the back of his neck. All of the hairs on his neck and arms stood straight and he took a few steps toward the door. He had the sudden urge to dart out, run to the elevator, and get the hell out of here.

Those eyes…

A child's eyes reflecting light back, the child peeking out from around the side of a washing machine, watching him, the face round and pale, hiding when he came close, and then disappearing, leaving him with the cold, unnatural memory of eyes.

Like a cat's eyes.

Or a rat's eyes.

A rat's eyes. That's what it was. He saw a rat.

He chuckled once he realized it, but backed out anyway. A rat wasn't something he needed to mess with, either. Not in the dark down here.

He looked at the shirt clutched in his hand and frowned. He threw it into a machine, popped his quarters into the tray, and hit the button. Then he grabbed a chair by the folding table and slid it out into the basement. He pulled it under a light bulb and sat, grabbing the paperback from his back pocket and opening it to the dog-eared page where he had last left off. It was *Lord Jim* by Joseph Conrad and, though the language weighed him down in spots, the story was engrossing. He finished the chapter and started another before he heard the noise.

It was faint at first, barely discernible, and he thought he had imagined it. He continued reading, but he heard it again.

A scraping sound.

He put his book down and stood, taking a few steps out into the room to try and hear where it came from.

Scrape.

The laundry room.

He took his phone out and shined it in again, half-expecting to see

—*a young boy*—

the rat perched on the edge of one of the machines, but there was nothing there. The dryer rumbled and shook, the soft *clack-clack-clack* of the shirt's buttons smacking against the sides as it tumbled around, and he again thought he had imagined the noise.

Scrape.

From behind the door.

He felt a little fear again; a holdover from the rat mixed with that innate fear of dark places that enters you as a child and never leaves. But his curiosity was stronger. He walked to the door and dropped to one knee, peering into the hole where the knob should have been.

A thin strand of webbing stretched from one side of the hole to the other. It was littered with the tiny desiccated carcasses of gnats. Past that was more ink, a room full of it, and his cell phone light could barely penetrate it.

Scrape.

This time he thought he recognized the sound. There was weight behind it. It had the resonance of three, no *four* tiny scrapes occurring simultaneously to combine into one half-discernible noise. It was a chair scooting across the floor. An occupied chair.

He tried to wedge his phone into the hole, but found it difficult to maneuver it in such a way that he could still see.

He thought he caught a glimpse of the light reflecting off of metal in the far corner. He repositioned and wiggled the phone around again.

Something passed in front of the hole.

He stood and stumbled back. Was someone in there?

"Hello?" He waited for a moment. No answer.

He knocked on the door, three loud knocks, and waited. Nothing.

A light shined into the room behind him, casting his shadow onto the wall. He turned and had to shield his eyes.

"Dennis?"

The flashlight clicked off. He heard the scrape of metal twisting into metal and then the room filled with yellow light.

Karen stood under the bulb. She wore green silk pajama pants and a light blue spaghetti strap undershirt. It hung on her crookedly and his eyes were instantly drawn to the side of a round, creamy breast that attempted an escape. Her hair was damp, darkening it to a deep shade of red, and tied behind her in a ponytail. She had a small basket of laundry tucked under one arm, the flashlight resting on top. Like usual, she took his breath away.

"What are you doing down here in the dark?" she asked.

He glanced over his shoulder, nervous. He couldn't figure out *why*, exactly, but he felt like he was caught doing something he shouldn't have been.

"Um, just drying some clothes."

She laughed and sat her basket on a washing machine. "I can see that. I mean, why are you just hanging out in the corner with no light? A little Norman Bates, isn't it?" She smiled and the room grew brighter.

"Yeah. Must look weird. I thought I heard a noise. Do you know what's in here?" He motioned to the door with his thumb.

She shrugged. "Think it's just a general storage area for the building. Fuse box, lawn tools, that kind of thing."

He almost told her he had peeked into there, that all he had ever seen was a chair, but stopped. It seemed oddly confrontational, not to mention obsessive, and he didn't want to make her feel uncomfortable. Even though he was perfectly happy with Eileen, a guy's first instinct with a beautiful woman was to impress her.

She sat her basket down and pulled out a small bottle of detergent. She glanced at him, smiled, and poured some into the machine. She slid some change into the tray and started it up. She waited for it to fill and then opened the door again. She held up a wad of blue cotton and looked to Dennis.

"You just going to stand in the corner and watch me drop my panties?"

"Oh. Sorry."

He passed her, purposely timing his breath to inhale as he walked by, and sat back in his chair. He opened his book and tried to read, but his eyes couldn't help traveling over the top of the book and resting on her.

When she was done loading the wash, she dropped the door and turned. "I didn't mean you had to wait out there. The light's back on." She pulled a small rectangle from the basket and held it up. "*And* I've got a deck of cards. Always plan on playing solitaire while waiting, but never do. It's creepy down here by yourself. So I go upstairs and forget I have laundry going."

He slid the book back into his pocket and grabbed his chair. "You play poker?"

She sat at the table and pulled the cards out. Her hands moved quickly, her fingers dancing through the cards as she shuffled. "Five-Card or Texas Hold-'em?"

He sat. "Dealer's call."

She dealt the cards and they played a few hands. She was far more experienced than he was and won most of them. They talked the entire time and she explained that she used to be a cocktail waitress in Biloxi. She'd caught the eye of one of the pit bosses and they dated for a few months. She had only been nineteen at the time while he was thirty. He had taught her how to play every game in the casino.

"When we broke up, after I caught him with another waitress, I turned fifty dollars into a thousand on his watch and quit. Son of a bitch."

"What were you in Mississippi for?"

She shook her head and smiled. "Just sowing my oats, as it were. Had this stupid idea in my head that I would travel the country, like Kerouac or something, eventually going to California. Farthest I got from here was New Orleans before deciding that I hated being a vagabond. Came back, got my degree, and here we are."

He felt her foot against his. She didn't move, and neither did he. Even such a small touch, felt through the confines of shoe leather, sent electric shockwaves up his leg. "What's your degree in?"

"Promise you won't laugh?"

"Well, I can't *promise*, but I'll try not to. Gimme three." He tossed three cards onto the table.

She took them and dealt three more. "Art History."

"Why would I laugh at that?"

"Well, what the hell do you do with it?"

He smiled. "I don't know. You tell me."

"I never figured it out. Two pair." She showed her cards, two eights, two tens, and an ace. "I'm working at a home shopping network now. Doing graphic arts work, making crap products look pretty."

He threw his cards down, an assortment of nothing worthwhile, and she snatched them up to deal again. "There's nothing wrong with that."

"No, but it's a far cry from Caravaggio and Brunelleschi. What about you? You're in college now, right?"

"Yeah, should have been out already, but…"

"We all got our 'buts.' What are you studying?"

"Classical Civilization."

"Really? The foundation of Western Art."

"The foundation of everything."

She nodded and dealt their cards. They picked them up, spread them shallowly in their hands, and examined them. "What drew you to that?"

"My mom. She used to read me Greek myths growing up. It eventually led to *The Iliad*, *The Odyssey,* and *The Aeneid.* Then I got into the histories as a teen, reading everything from Herodotus and Suetonius to Cicero."

"Pretty geeky for a teen, huh?"

"Probably. But I stayed pretty balanced, I guess. Mostly because of wrestling, I think."

"You wrestled?"

"Still do. I was All-State my senior year of high school. Hope to make the team this fall."

"The Greeks invented wrestling, right?"

He laughed. "Yep. Another influence from the Classical world on my life. I'm a bit of an anachronism, I guess. I feel more comfortable on the mat or with my head in a book than I do with the rest of the world, I think."

Why was he telling her all of this?

She smiled. There was something about it, about how she couldn't contain the expression on just her lips, about how it spread to her cheeks and her brow and the corners of her eyes that made the hairs on his arm stand up.

That's why he was telling her all of this.

"The warrior-scholar, huh? Another ancient ideal."

He shrugged.

"I think it's admirable, especially with this self-centered world we live in." She locked her eyes on his and he couldn't look away. It was like staring into a sunset, the colors more beautiful than anything seen during day or night, and he was transfixed in the fragile, temporary moment of her stare.

The dryer's buzzer went off.

He stood, shifting his legs as he became aware that more than the hair on his arms stood up. "Well, that's me."

She sat her cards down and stood, stretching her arms above her head. Her shirt rose, revealing her flat abdomen and the top of her hips. A tattoo was painted on her left hip, something blue and yellow that peeked out above her low waistline. He wondered what it was and how far down it went.

He bent, opened the door, and grabbed the shirt. He quickly folded it over and hugged it to his chest, suddenly self-conscious about washing another woman's clothing.

Another woman?

When he stood, Karen was little more than a foot from him. Her scent, that heady aroma of strawberries and something else, something exotic and alluring, brushed his face.

"Well," she said. "Thanks for playing cards with me."

"Sure thing. Anytime. I'd stay and keep you company, but…" He trailed off, unsure of what to say.

She just nodded. "Have a good night, then." Her eyes were still on his and, even though she had just said her goodbye, she didn't move to sit. In fact, she shuffled slightly forward, almost imperceptibly so.

Dennis was light-headed. He felt claustrophobic, as though the room had sealed itself off behind him and he was forever confined to this small space with her. He found her emerald eyes and couldn't look away. His mouth dried and he swallowed. Licked his lips. His stomach twisted and his groin was incredibly warm, so warm that he felt if he didn't open his pants soon he would blister.

Before he even knew what he was doing, he took a step forward. A voice inside screamed *Stop! Eileen!* But his body refused to listen. There were instincts at work, millions of years of evolution responding to full lips and pheromones in the air, and he could fight it no more than he could fight the urge to eat when hungry or sleep when tired.

One hand found her cheek, the other her lower back. Touching her skin was like touching warm silk and every nerve ending in his body came alive. Her own fingers found the back of his head, her nails pressing into the skin at a delicious depth, and guided his lips onto hers. They were soft. Thick. Moist. Warm. He trembled as her tongue ran over the inside of his own lips, tracing half-whispered promises inside his mouth.

206

Her other hand pressed against the thick muscle in the middle of his back, drawing him closer, closer, until he melted into her, no longer aware of where he ended and she began.

She pulled away, her cheeks bursting with red. She looked to her feet and tucked her hair behind her ears. Crossed her arms across her breasts. "I'm sorry. I shouldn't have done that. You have a girlfriend and—"

"No. I should apologize. I…um…" Warmth flooded his own cheeks and nervously laughed.

"Well," she said. "It was just one of those things. A momentary indiscretion."

He nodded and took a step back. They locked eyes again and he knew that she was wrong, that it was something more. "Um, I should be going, I guess."

"Yeah." She looked like she was going to say something else, move toward him again, but she turned back to the machine. "Good night."

He felt the urge to walk up behind her, slide his hands around her waist, kiss her neck.

He hurried back to the elevator before his willpower faded.

★ ★ ★

The light cutting through the drapes cast strange shadows across the room. Some of them looked liked snakes slithering across her walls, while others were more like long fingers reaching across her room towards her. The tiny bits of mid-afternoon light wedged between them stung her eyes.

Peggy crawled out of bed, still weak from the morning's treatments, and stumbled to the window. She squinted hard as she approached to pull the drapes tighter, and then returned to the soft, cool space between her mattress and her "Justin Bieber" sheets. Her computer speakers crackled next to her, faintly playing some iTunes selection about boys and horses, and she rolled back onto her side.

The treatments were awful. She felt worse after every one. Sicker, really, even though the doctors and her mother claimed it made her better. She had a vague idea of what was wrong with her, but had heard so many new words tossed around recently, words like "chemo" and "cancer" and "remission," (that last whispered with the same wishful tones that she sometimes spoke of Santa Claus and the Easter Bunny), that she couldn't decide how sick she really was.

Her door was cracked and she could see dark blue shadows dance in the hallway. She tried to listen to what her mother watched on television, but only heard dull murmuring. Her head throbbed, her stomach felt twisted and abused. She prayed she wouldn't vomit again. She hated the way it tasted and how her mouth burned after. Her eyes were heavy and they fluttered closed.

The phone rang, pulling her back. The blue shadows clicked off and she heard her mother say, "Hello?"

A pause, and then: "No, she's sleeping."

Peggy rolled over and exited iTunes. She rolled back and listened.

"As good as can be expected, I guess. Hmmm? I've lost count, really. Yes, yes it is. It's just…hard, you know?"

She heard her mother sniff and recognized it as the

forerunner to a wave of tears. Peggy had become very familiar with her mother's sounds lately.

"I mean, after Derrick left I…yeah. Well, Charlie isn't even out of diapers yet, and it's just me, and my insurance doesn't cover all of Peggy's…oh, Mom, I can't ask you to do that."

Peggy had to bite her lip to keep from yelling *Let her do it, Mommy! Please!* But she knew how it would go. Her grandmother lived in Florida and her mother had too much pride to ask for help. It was killing her. Peggy hated to see her mother's face so pale and puffy and the dark circles that lined her eyes. The worst part of it all was that Peggy knew it was her fault and the guilt kept her up at nights.

"Yes, Mom. I know." Her voice quivered. Another sniff. "Thank you. Yeah. I love you, too. Tell Dad I said 'hi.' Later."

A click, then silence. It was long and drawn out and Peggy wondered what her mother was doing. Then she heard the soft shuffle of feet moving through carpet and the bathroom door closed. A few moments later the metallic hum of water moving through pipes passed through her room. Her mother always did her best crying in the tub.

She rolled over and stared at the ceiling. The weak light struggling into the room barely lit up the constellations that her mother had painted over her bed. She stuck her arm up over her face and closed one eye. With her index finger she traced the lines of the Big Dipper, Cassiopeia, Orion the Hunter. As she did she whispered into the dark of her room, "God, please send my Mommy the remission. I don't want her to cry no more."

The water stopped running at the other end of the

apartment. Peggy rolled over and clicked "Sleep" on her computer. The screen went black and the white light in the lower corner pulsed slowly. It served as a nightlight, casting a small bit of light every few seconds while allowing enough darkness to take root in the room for Peggy to sleep.

The faint rhythm of her mother's sobbing drifted down the hall. She tried to ignore it, but couldn't. It made the muscles around her eyes quiver. She rolled over and stretched her hand toward the door. Her fingertips just barely touched the edge and she gave it a hard push. It swung closed with a soft click.

She shut her eyes again. The image of her on the scale in the doctor's office came into her mind. She stood on the cold, black thing as Dr. Brady slid the metal block back and forth, frowning. Her white gown with pink dots was open in the back and the skin of her thighs and butt was covered in goose bumps. *Why is there a mirror here? That's just mean, making me look at myself.* Her skin was sallow and clung close to her bones. There were bruises here and there, purple splotches like spilled finger paint. She could easily see the bones of her elbows and knees jutting out, and pockets of loose skin flapped from her arms.

She shook the memory away. *At least no one could call me Porky Peggy anymore.* The thought almost made her smile. That was one torture she would never have to deal with again. Now she had others.

She stole a quick glance at her closet and shut her eyes again.

Her brother let out a short, sleepy cry from her mother's bedroom. It was the prelude to a full-blown fit. The way that sound carried in the apartment, it was like Charlie was at the foot of her bed every time he cried.

Shut up, she thought, and then felt guilty. She loved her brother.

She heard the bathroom door open and close and her mother stomp down the hall. A few moments later and Charlie had quieted.

The silence was far from comforting. Peggy tried to sleep, tried to will it to come to her, but every tiny noise in her room was amplified. The wind whistled past her window, rustling the leaves of the magnolia trees that grew against the walls of the building. A horn honked somewhere. Kids yelled and laughed in the distance, their words little more than murmuring. The pulse of the white light from her sleeping computer shined against her lids and her brain manufactured a low rhythm to accompany it.

Drum-drum-drum.

Stop it. That computer don't make no noise when it's sleeping.

She envied it suddenly, its ability to sleep at the push of a button.

She rolled over again and winced at the loud crinkle of her sheets.

The closet door cracked open.

Her breath caught in her throat.

She had heard that, right? Of course she did. It was unmistakable.

She thought that maybe she should turn on the light, or open the door, or yell for Mommy, or even just hide under her covers. But she couldn't move. She just lay there like a rock, her eyes clamped shut, her breath held inside her so long that her lungs ached.

There was a soft thump and Peggy opened one eye half-way to peek. A doll had rolled out of the closet and onto the floor. It lay there face down, its pink dress hiked up in the back like it was mooning her.

The door creaked open a little farther.

She yanked the covers over her head.

She listened, hoping she wouldn't hear the rustle of feet through carpet. Her breath was warm underneath the blankets and she was already damp with sweat.

After a long silence, she slowly lowered the covers.

The room was empty.

She took a deep breath and exhaled. It turned to a soft, white mist as it left her mouth. She realized how cold the room had become. She looked over to the closet—

—and saw that the door was open completely.

She held her breath and dove back under the covers. She laid there, motionless, quiet, hoping that it thought she was still in the hospital.

A faint rustle. Tiny feet moving slowly through carpet.

A creak from her bedsprings as something pressed down on the edge. It had never come out this far before.

And then the mattress pressed down farther and she felt it above her. She could feel its steaming hot breath against the outside of the sheet as it leaned close to her.

"Peggy."

I'm not here. If I don't move and don't make no noise it won't know I'm here. It will think I'm still at the hospital or—

"I can hear you thinking," it said. Its voice was playful and gravelly. It was always like that, the voice of a child who wanted to play and an adult who wanted nothing more than to hurt you all rolled into one melodious sound. It made

Peggy's bones tingle.

"Leave me alone," she said.

"I didn't mean to make your brother cry," it whispered. "Not this time, anyway."

Please, God and Jesus who are in Heaven, hollow be thy name, thy Kingdom come—

It laughed, a sound like brittle twigs snapping. "Their names *are* hollow, aren't they? Hollow, meaningless things."

She shook her head furiously beneath the sheet as it leaned closer. She could feel its cheek press against hers through the sheet and her bladder let go.

It whispered to her the way her father used to when tucking her in for the night. Its hot breath pressed the sheet tight against her face and she could feel little flicks of spittle splatter against it.

"Come with me, Peggy. Step into the closet with me. There are wonders in there, dark and bloody, that will stay with you for years."

She screamed louder than she ever had in her entire life. It made her temples ache and flashed stars in front of her eyes she screamed so hard. Her throat felt raw and bloody and her stomach lurched forward with the first stirrings of vomit, but she kept screaming. She heard its feet rustle through the carpet and back to the closet.

The closet door slammed shut.

Her bedroom door swung open, her light came on, and she pulled the covers from over head. Her stomach jerked hard to the right, then the left, and she leaned over and vomited into the trashcan that her mother had placed next to her bed.

Her mother was at her side, pulling her hair out of the

way and rubbing her back.

"It's okay," she said. "Shhh…it's okay."

Peggy collapsed into her, let those great, comforting arms envelope her, and tried to cry. She shook and moaned and snot poured from her nose, but no tears came from her eyes. After a few moments, she pulled away.

"I think I need some water," she said.

Her mother nodded and left the room. Peggy stared at the closet door.

It was closed. For now, anyway.

Was that thing still behind it?

She was more afraid of it now than ever. It had never ventured more than a foot or two from the closet. It never seemed like it was able to before, like something kept it tied to the darkness in there. But if it could get to her bed now, what was next?

She placed one foot onto the floor, then the other. She had to hold the bedpost to get a sense of her balance but, once she did, she was moving to the door.

Her heart pounded in her chest so loud that it sounded like drums, like the ones they played at the football games she used to go to before she was sick, when Mommy and Daddy still loved each other. The carpet was moist and clammy against her bare feet. She knew she was in its trail, its wet, cold feet leaving a little something inbetween the threads of carpeting.

She reached a hand for the doorknob. Gripped it. It, too, was cold. She turned it and opened the door.

It was dark, darker than it should have been with her bedroom lights on. It was like the closet refused to let the light into it. She could see the vague outline of her clothes hanging on the rod, her toys and shoes piled up in the base, boxes on the top shelf. And somewhere behind everything, between it all, lying in the spaces between spaces, was a shifting, white shape. It moved around slowly in the cracks between those boxes, in the crevices of her toys, in the creases of her shirts. It watched her, studied her, but refused to come out into the light.

"Honey?" Her mother was behind her with a glass.

She took it and sipped it slowly. It was cool and refreshing, trickling over her chapped lips, across her dry tongue, and down her cracked throat.

"Thank you."

Her mother patted her head. "You're welcome, sweetheart. Did you have a bad dream?"

She glanced back over her shoulder into the closet and nodded.

"Wanna sleep in my room?"

Peggy shook her head. It didn't matter where she was. It had already been in her mother's room, anyway. Had already made Charlie cry.

"Okay. Do you want me to leave a light on for you, then?"

She nodded.

"Okay." Her mother clicked on a small lamp in the corner. "Let me know if you need anything else." She gave Peggy another hug and left.

Peggy stared into the black, watching the pale shape move away from the light, and wondered if things wouldn't be better if she just gave in, if she just stepped inside.

The thing in her closet laughed.

★ ★ ★

The shower's cool spray massaged the back of Eileen's neck. It rinsed the sweat away and relaxed her, as it always did after she exerted herself.

Things had always been sweet with Dennis. Tender. But the last two nights he had been an animal. They hadn't made love or even had sex; they had *fucked*. She had sweat more than usual, and her calves, thighs, and upper back were sore. The shower helped that some, but she knew she'd need to make Dennis give her a massage before she could sleep.

He opened the curtain and peeked inside. "Hey. I was heating up some of that casserole. Thought you might have worked up an appetite." He grinned. "You want some?"

"Good timing. I'm starving."

He reached in and tweaked her nipple.

She smacked his hand away. "Don't even think about it. I'm too sore."

"Fine." He mock pouted. "I'll go heat the food."

"I'll be out in a minute."

After she toweled off and put on her robe, she joined him on the couch. He had some History Channel documentary on and a bowl of casserole sat on the coffee table. He scooted a glass over to her.

"Diet Coke," he said. "We finished off the last bottle of wine."

"Damn. I'll have to pick up some more." She grabbed the bowl and stirred its contents. "Someday I'll have a wine rack. Or a cellar."

"Mmm-hmm." He chewed a giant bite, his eyes glued

215

to the screen.

She glanced at the television. It was some Civil War documentary. It didn't really interest her. Dennis was the history buff. She grabbed the remote and flicked a button, bringing up the onscreen programming guide. It covered a small portion of the screen and Dennis continued watching the documentary as she looked for something else.

She sighed. "500 channels and nothing on. Look at this: Food Network, Golf Channel, Home Shopping, Telemundo. Why am I paying for this? I don't want these things. Just let me choose what I want to watch."

"Mmm-hmm."

She pulled her feet up onto the couch and kicked his thigh. "You're really quite the conversationalist tonight."

"Sorry. This thing just sucked me in."

"What's it about?"

"Civil War prisons."

"Yeah. Real exciting."

"Haha."

The screen showed grainy black and white photos of Confederate prisoners being marched around a muddy campsite by Union guards on horseback with rifles. This was followed by a photograph of a gallows with scores of men lined up in front of it.

"Do we have to watch this?"

He wiped his mouth. "No. But you said yourself: there's nothing else on."

"Can't we just, I don't know, *talk* or something?"

"What do you want to talk about?"

"I don't know. Anything."

A photo came on to the screen of a large hill with a

216

crude wooden fort atop it and a series of gnarled trees lining the dirt road that weaved up to it. The narrator's monotone voice droned on over a bed of somber music. "Another tragedy occurred at Camp Opey, Tennessee."

Eileen leaned forward. "That looks like the hill where Raynham Place is."

Dennis shrugged. "Yeah. Maybe."

The photograph switched to one of a group of Union soldiers standing over a giant ditch. The ditch was filled with corpses. The Narrator continued: "Built over an old school house, Camp Opey became a prison in the last year of the war. Though its existence was short, its infamy lived on for many years. The atrocities at Camp Opey were only overshadowed by the tragedies committed in the notorious Andersonville prison."

The photograph switched again, this time to Andersonville.

Eileen pulled her knees to her chest and scratched her cheek. "I think that was where your apartment building is."

"I don't know," Dennis said. "Kind of hard to tell."

"Have you ever heard of Camp Opey?"

He shook his head.

"It could have been there before the sanatorium. Right?"

"Yeah. I guess."

She tapped his thigh with her foot. "Doesn't this interest you at all?"

"I don't know. It's a bit of a jump, isn't it? To see that photograph and think it's Raynham."

"I'm sure it is. The slope of the hill, the trees, the road running up to the prison. It's Raynham. I'd swear it is."

He sat his bowl down and turned toward her. "And

what if it is?"

She shrugged. "I just think it's interesting. It might…" She trailed off.

Dennis smiled. "Might what?"

"Nothing."

"No. C'mon. Might what?"

She shook her head. "You'll think I'm being silly."

"I already think you're being silly. Might what?"

"It might, I don't know, explain my dreams."

"Ah. There's the rub."

She kicked his thigh, a little harder this time. He didn't seem to notice. "Listen, asshat. If a bunch of Civil War soldiers were tortured and executed in your basement, don't you think there might be some kind of energy left over?"

He laughed. "Here we go with another 'haunted house' story, huh?"

She grabbed a pillow and hugged it to her chest and scowled. "You are in rare form tonight."

"What do you mean?"

"You don't think you're being a tad dismissive? A tad condescending?"

His brow furrowed. She could feel the tension building in the air like static electricity. A fight was coming. They had never fought before, but she knew the feeling well from old boyfriends, from her Dad and brother. She wished that the conversation hadn't gone down this road, that tonight wasn't going to be their first fight, but it was too late. Her hackles were raised and, as much as she didn't want it, she *needed* to fight.

"Dismissive, huh?" He laughed again. It wasn't a pleasant sound. "Because you're trying to pin some fucked up dream of yours on a Civil War graveyard under my apartment building? Excuse me if I don't merrily follow that train of thought to its predictable conclusion."

Where did this come from? Why were they fighting over something so trivial? So stupid? But even as those thoughts ran through her mind, her hands clenched the pillow tight enough for her knuckles to go white.

"You're a bastard." She threw the pillow at him and jumped to her feet. "You know how much that dream bothers me. You know!"

Dennis was on his feet in a flash. "Yeah, I know. But c'mon, Eileen!"

They stared at each other, eyes red with fury, hands trembling. But the phrase brought a smile to Eileen's face. Then Dennis laughed, and she laughed too, and the tension was broken.

"C'mon Eileen?" She asked and playfully shoved him. "Should I get you some overalls and a banjo?"

He laughed again. "I didn't even think of that. Bet you've heard that your whole life, huh?"

She nodded. "Yep."

He smiled again and then looked to his feet. "Listen. I'm sorry. I didn't mean—"

"Shhh." She kissed him. "We've both been under a lot of stress. Let's just forget about it."

"Deal." He held out his hand and they shook.

"I think I'm going to head off to bed."

He cocked an eyebrow. "Oh, yeah?"

"None of that. You can give me a backrub, though."

He glanced at his watch. "You know, actually, I think I'm going to head home."

Her stomach sank. "Home?"

"Yeah. I just…I feel a little antsy now and I haven't been spending a lot of time at home lately. I thought maybe I'd see if Mike wanted to go grab a drink or watch a movie or something."

"Okay. That's cool. I didn't need you waking me at three in the morning with your hand on my breast anyway." She smiled.

He smiled back and kissed her. He sat and slipped on his shoes. "What are you doing tomorrow?"

"Umm…not sure yet. Give me a call."

"Alright." He stood and kissed her again. It was short and felt like a formality. Had she said something wrong? No. The fight (if she could even call it that) was over before it had begun.

"Love you." He headed for the door.

"Love you, too."

But he was gone already. Eileen sat on the couch, pulled her knees to her chest, and twirled a finger in her hair. This was her thinking ritual. She twirled and untwirled, wondering what all of that could have been about. Dennis had seemed distracted the past two days. Even when they had been in bed, he hadn't seemed present. They didn't make love *with* one another. He had *fucked* her. The more she thought about it, the more she realized it had been done *to* her instead of *with* her and it made her feel sick. What could cause that?

She thought back to past relationships and how things had gone wrong. The signs had been the same with all of them and a thought rushed into her head.

Was there another woman?

She banished it as soon as it appeared. Don't be paranoid, she told herself. That's silly. He just had a bad week. Probably work. School starts soon. Just let it go.

But as she laid down in the dark of her room and drifted off to sleep, the thought danced through her brain, taunting her, reminding her of past failures and past abuses. She slept fitfully.

★ ★ ★

A hot puddle of sweat pulled Jack from his dream. He shook his head, wiped his face dry with an oil-stained rag, and glanced at his watch. It was ten at night. How long had he been asleep? It had still been light outside when he had come down here.

He climbed from his stool and yawned. Stretched. He looked around his workshop. Everything seemed in order. He had the nagging suspicion that something was off, though. He couldn't shake it. All of his tools were there and in place. None of the lamps had gone out. His notebooks were in order. What was it?

Probably nothing. Maybe the dream.

What was he dreaming?

He couldn't quite remember. It had something to do with the supermarket, the forest, and the grate.

The grate.

He snatched his keys and a flashlight. He paused for a second, trying to piece together the dream. All he remembered was the grate and a sense of something gone horribly wrong. He had always lived by the adage "better to be safe than sorry," and so unlocked the old Army issued footlocker in the corner. He pulled his gun out, checked it, loaded it, and clicked the safety on.

One of the bulbs overhead flickered.

Cold trickled down his back. He grabbed a rag and checked the bulb. Something had shaken it loose, probably the kids in the apartment overhead wrestling around or playing that dancing video game of theirs. He sighed and tightened it.

He left his workshop, fastening each of the locks behind him.

The basement was alive with shadows. They spilled out from every corner, from under every box, and seemed to writhe in irritation under the dim lights. He erratically moved his flashlight around, dispelling one patch before moving on to the next. He hated it down here after dark. Why had he let himself fall asleep like that? He hadn't been outside of his apartment after nightfall in almost ten years.

Something had changed.

That was exactly the problem. He wasn't sure what it was, but could feel it in the air. The pressure was different, the feel of it against his skin. Something itched inside of his skull and no matter how hard he scratched he couldn't get rid of it. It made him feel anxious and…

And afraid.

He clenched his jaw and went outside. The swollen moon draped pale blue light across the grounds, but he wasn't sure if he liked that or not. Yes, he had light, but sometimes light just created more shadows. Shadows were not the same thing as the dark. Not in his experience.

He made his way through the woods by rote. Twigs snapped under his boots and he heard tiny feet scurry away from him every now and then. Probably possums, he reminded himself. No reason to let that bother him.

More than once his light reflected back from a spider's web hung between two trees and he had to change his path. One belonged to a giant black widow that perched in the center, its sleek body almost as reflective as the webbing it rested on. The red hourglass on its underside shined like a neon warning sign as its front legs tapped against the cocooned body of a cicada. The insect writhed in the web, a futile struggle, as the spider's feet kept their rhythm, drumming away like fingers while waiting for the thing to die.

He didn't like the sight of it. The feeling that it was an omen gripped him. The Cherokee and Creek Indians that used to inhabit the area strongly believed in animal signs. He had always been interested in the indigenous people here, in their culture and beliefs, but couldn't quite remember what spiders signified. It couldn't be anything good, though. Of that much he was certain.

All of this area used to belong to those people. In his study of the history of this place, a study that tried and failed to shed some light on the countless entries in his "Anomalies" binder, he had traced it back to their occupation. Unfortunately they kept no written records.

What little he did know about that time was something scratched down in a land grant to Ms. Miriam Stowe, the Irish schoolteacher who had built her little schoolhouse on the hill where the apartment complex now sat. It was written by the land's previous owner, a minor British aristocrat turned American land surveyor named Virgil Tiberius Lawson, in 1815. He had sold off most of his properties after the War of 1812, when Americans eyed everything

British with suspicion. The only mention of the land prior to that time was found in the third paragraph, which he had copied by hand from a microfiche of the document at the University's library in Knoxville. He had read over it a thousand times, trying to decipher a meaning he knew lay hidden between the lines of perfectly scrawled words. He had read it so many times that he couldn't help but commit it to memory. As he neared the downward slope toward the concrete tube, those words ran through his mind:

God grant that Ms. Stowe find fresh air and calm and quiet environs for her teachings and her wish to Enlighten and Educate the young ones of these poor farming communities. The savages at one time revered this land until some time before the Good Christian farmers moved in when, in the barbaric ways of their people, two groups of them slaughtered one another in its fields. Christian folk came upon their remains still lying in the grasses after so many years and having rotted away to bones. A Learned fellow amongst them thus took to calling the place Ex Campus Osses Pulchri-flori, *a crude and likely inaccurate Latin that can be translated to "The Field of Beautifully Flowered Bones" and referring to both the carnage and the wild array of flowers that had found nourishment and sprouted from the dead. This has since been shortened by locals to* Camp O.P., *or* Camp Opie *as they are prone to pronounce it. I do not wish to distress you with this tale but thought it prudent to tell you, both for your love of History and to prepare you for the superstitions that you will most assuredly encounter from the locals regarding the place, those pious yet unlearned folk who will refuse to allow their children 'round after night falls and will undoubtedly try to frighten you with absurd tales of Haints and Will O' the Wisps and Black Hounds scouring the area, despite any and all evidence to the contrary.*

The rest of the document was pure and boring legalese, but this long paragraph had stuck in Jack's mind since he had first read it six years ago. Yes, there were the legends of the locals with their "Haints" and "Black Hounds," but what intrigued him the most was the "Field of Beautifully Flowered Bones." Why did those two groups of people, likely Creek or Cherokee warriors, decide to slaughter one another *here*? Were they drawn here by the strangeness of the place, or did their slaughter cause it? There was no way to know.

He crested a small rise and made his way slowly and carefully down the other side and through the ditch. He clicked the gun's safety to the "off" position and crept toward the tube.

He raised his light and almost screamed.

The grate was thrown wide, gaping at him like a hungry mouth.

He rushed down and slammed it shut. A loud *bang* echoed through the tunnel and he regretted letting the fear take hold of him like that. The way the sound carried inside there, they would be coming soon. He glanced to the locks and saw that they were intact. In fact, they hadn't even been unlocked. The grate showed absolutely no sign of being tampered with.

Yet there it was gaping open like the cave Ulysses took to the Underworld.

He fumbled with his keys. Dropped them. Cursed. Snatched them up, undoing the locks and re-securing them as fast as he could. When they were all in place he tugged on them one by one. They held.

Then how was the grate open?

His instincts told him to rush back to his apartment, lock his door, and hide in bed with the gun in his lap until dawn. But he couldn't. He had to know if they had gotten out.

He heard scratching along the inside of the tube as something made its way up. He shined his light down, seeing nothing but black for a long time, before he caught a glimpse of eyes and gnashing teeth barreling toward the grate. He wished he had brought meat for them so they wouldn't focus on him. But he didn't, and before long they were all there, scrambling over each other, throwing their weight against the grating, drooling and growling. He counted them, recounted them, and counted them again. They were all there.

Then how did the grate open?

Something was very wrong here.

He did the only thing he could think of to ensure they didn't get out again. He raised the gun and opened fire. The shots were like great thunderclaps echoing through the tube. They tore through the ones that pressed against the grate and the rest of them scurried back into the dark. He hated killing them like this, knew somewhere deep down that he wasn't supposed to, but the instinct was too strong. If they ever got out...well, that was too horrible to consider.

One of the ones he shot whimpered and limped back into the black. The other one was dead, part of its face split open down the center and leaking blood and brain matter onto the concrete. The shots still echoed in his ears and all he could hear was a high pitched humming.

He jumped when the dead one moved.

He raised his gun, his finger quivering over the trigger,

but stopped. It *was* dead. Its glassy stare was proof of that. But still it moved, sliding slowly backwards down the tube. He heard growling and realized they were dragging it back down.

Did they have that much compassion?

No. His aching eardrums were soon hit with the sounds of meat tearing. They were hungry.

They were always hungry.

He backed away. When he reached the hill, he turned and scrambled up it. At the top he paused, worried about his locks. He spun around and shined his light back down onto the grating.

One of them stood at the top, its face pressed so hard against the grate that it bled. Its eyes were twin balls of green fire, its face twisted into a mask of pure rage. He thought for a moment that it was going to speak, to taunt him, to threaten him, but almost laughed at the idea. They had never spoken. They *couldn't* speak. The idea was ridiculous.

"We'll taste you yet, Jack."

He ran back to the building and locked his door behind him. He couldn't sleep and so drank and thought about Haints, and Fields of Beautifully Flowered Bones, and Black Hounds.

Black Hounds that spoke.

He waited for dawn.

★ ★ ★

The image of Sam and Dean Winchester roaring down the road in their black Impala flickered across the television screen. Mike turned the volume up and sprawled out on the sofa like a king. The feast spread out around him was certainly a royal one: pizza, hot wings, breadsticks, cola, and brownies. He shoved a slice of pizza halfway into his mouth and scratched his abdomen. Dennis was at Eileen's tonight and, as long as Mike cleaned up afterward, he could lounge around in just his boxers and eat junk until he burst.

He felt good today, incredibly good. He hadn't felt this comfortable in the apartment until tonight, but he finally had the sense that this place was his. It was a good feeling, an empowering feeling, and he relished it. He felt independent, as independent as when he drove his car

—and hit that poor dog—

where he wanted, when he wanted. But this feeling was even better; he was home. He belonged here. That was a feeling worth everything he had gone through with his parents.

There was a knock on the door. He wondered if Dennis had forgotten his keys again and stood. He sat his slice of pizza down, wiped his mouth with the back of his hand, and opened the door.

Margot stood in the hallway, wearing a snug black T-shirt tucked into the waistband of a skintight pair of jeans.

"Hey," she said and smiled.

Mike was suddenly very aware of the fact that he was in his boxers.

"Umm...come on in." He spun quickly and rushed toward his room. "Let me just throw some clothes on."

He heard her giggle. "No need to get dressed on my account."

He zipped his jeans up and slid on a T-shirt. When he walked back out into the living room, Margot stood over his food with her nose scrunched up.

"Well, I was gonna see if you boys wanted to join me for dinner, but it looks like the two of you already chowed down."

"Um...yeah." Mike didn't want to admit that he had devoured all of the food by himself. "Dennis just left." Margot smiled. "Up to no good with his lady friend, no doubt. Those two can barely keep their hands off of one another."

"Tell me about it."

She headed back for the door. "Well, I've gotta get something in me, or I'm gonna starve to death."

Mike followed her. Before he knew it, his mouth was open and words were streaming out. "Gotta get something in you, huh?" What the hell was he saying? Since when did he flirt? He meant it to be playful and desperately hoped she took it that way.

She smiled and slapped his arm. "Mike..."

"Ya know, I've already eaten, but maybe we can have some drinks later."

Did he say that? He had definitely surprised himself. He didn't know why he said it, or how, but there it was. It hung there, floating in the air between them, building tension as it waited for her to reject it. Reject *him*.

She leaned in and kissed him on the cheek. It was slow, lingering, and incredibly sensual. His nostrils filled with her scent and he had to fight to keep from quivering.

"Forty-five minutes?" she asked.

"Um...yeah. Sure. Forty-five minutes sounds great."

She opened the door and walked back across the hall.

"I'll have the place ready for you then." She waved back over her shoulder as she nudged her door shut behind her with her foot.

Mike shut his own door and collapsed back onto the couch. A smile overtook him, transforming into a giggle. Had he just made a date? How did he do that? He wasn't the kind of guy that just asked girls if he could come over for a drink. And she had said yes. What did that mean?

He knew what it meant and his pants grew tighter. He jumped to his feet, shed his clothes, and ran to the bathroom. He started the shower running as he squirted some toothpaste onto his brush and went about his usual grooming ritual.

When he finished he glanced at the Felix the Cat clock he had hung over the toilet. Dennis hated the thing, but conceded to Mike's point that it was funny to have a cat staring at you as you pissed. It read 9:22. What time had Margot come over? Maybe half an hour earlier? He rushed to dry off. He rubbed on deodorant, splashed on a little too much aftershave, washed it off, reapplied it, and went looking through his closet for something to wear.

He had never had much in the way of clothing and was now regretting that fact. He thought about borrowing one of Dennis' shirts, but anything Dennis had would swallow him whole. So he opted for a blue dress shirt with a clean pair of jeans and his one pair of nice, brown loafers.

He looked at himself in the mirror and, while the outfit looked fine, *he* looked awkward. Of course, that was nothing new for him. He had never looked at himself without feeling that he looked awkward. But tonight that feeling was more analytical than instinctual and, while it hovered around his thoughts, it never sank into the pit of his stomach like it usually did. He still felt good.

It was a strange feeling and he didn't know how to deal with it. It took him a long while before he realized that what he felt was confidence. It was such a foreign situation that he wasn't quite sure what to make of it. He had never felt confident about anything his entire life.

You felt confident about dumping that dog's body.

He shook it off. Why think about that? What's done is done.

You felt confident that no one would ever discover it. Ever find out it was you.

Shut up.

What if that's why Margot came over? She was going to tell Dennis. That fucking bitch, she was going to say "Hey, Dennis. Your piece of shit roommate killed the Turner kid's dog and dragged its body to the supermarket. He really thinks he can get away with it, that's how stupid he is. Look at his awkward little face with his ratlike nose and—"

"Shut up!"

He took a deep breath and looked around the room, embarrassed at his outburst. He was alone, of course. Nothing to be embarrassed about, he reminded himself. The feeling of confidence wavered, threatened to flee, but he grabbed hold of it and pulled it tight like armor against his usual onslaught of self-doubt. Forget about the dog. Margot doesn't know, Dennis doesn't know, no one knows. Margot came over for one thing.

He locked his door behind him and crossed the hall.

Chapter Twelve

The bar rose and fell with the mechanical precision of well-oiled pistons. It slowed toward the end, his muscles finally protesting the strain.

He ground out another rep, sucked in a full breath, and squatted deep one final time. His hamstrings and glutes were on fire, his knees shook like they were going to dislodge from his legs, and for a moment he was afraid that he would be stuck in that bottom position. The thought of four hundred twenty-five pounds across his back pinning him to the ground sent a jolt of adrenaline through him. He pulled the cold iron tight against the back of his neck, pressed his head back into it hard enough to form stars at the edge of his vision, and grunted out of the hole. The movement lasted an eternity and he wasn't entirely confident that he could get more than half way.

So this is how I die.

It wasn't a thought so much as an animal's instinctual sense of its own end. He was in a place where words and logic no longer came to him. He was purely physical at that moment and glad for it. Another grunt and he stood upright, re-racking the weight onto the hooks and stepping back. The rack shook from side to side and he wondered how much weight it would take to rock it to pieces. He took a deep breath, took another step back, and nearly toppled over.

He waddled like a drunk to a nearby bench and collapsed. His legs felt more imagination than flesh, strange ephemeral limbs that he could *almost* feel, and then only if he concentrated. What had come over him? He never doubted himself like that, especially when he was under the bar. That was dangerous. Your mind had to be fully committed to lift that kind of weight. He had never had a problem before, but today...

Shit. Not just today. The past week or so. Ever since he had kissed Karen in the laundry room. That brief moment spent with her had stolen his equilibrium. He was no longer sure where he stood or what he desired anymore. He had avoided Eileen since then. Sure, he spoke to her on the phone and exchanged e-mails. They had even had lunch yesterday. But his hectic schedule became a handy reason for avoiding any kind of intimacy. She didn't notice anything wrong, or at least she wore a good poker face.

He had planned to devote the week to catching up with Mike, but his roommate had become a ghost. Signs of Mike's passing littered the apartment—dirty dishes, toothpaste on the sink, a note about groceries or the bills—but no sign of Mike himself. Dennis hadn't bothered calling him. Something felt off and he didn't want to push his own insecurities onto his roommate.

Loneliness had settled in after a few days. Dennis found himself doing exceedingly smaller loads of laundry almost daily, grasping onto any excuse to walk by the pool when he could, but he had failed to see Karen. He knew he shouldn't wait for serendipity, should simply knock on her door, but what would he say?

He chided himself for the thought. Life wasn't a romantic comedy. And what about Eileen? He loved Eileen. She loved him. But is love exclusive? Should all relationships be meant to last forever, or are some short bursts of passion that remind you of life and reconnect you with the world?

The way that he saw it, it was a Catch-22: either destroy the love between him and Eileen for what could end up being a meaningless fling, or never explore what he could have with Karen and damn the entirety of his life by hanging that "what if?" around his neck like an albatross. Why couldn't there be a better way?

He stood to remove the plates from the bar. He could imagine Karen bringing it up over a load of laundry (he found that most of his fantasies with her occurred in the laundry room): "Well, Dennis, I have a perfect idea. The last thing I want is to come between what you and Eileen have. But I don't see why that should stop us from exploring what could possibly be the greatest thing that ever happened to either of us. So we'll take it for a trial run, a test drive, and see how it goes."

He took the last plate down and slid it back onto the rack. His fantasies were taking hold of him and, after his performance with that last set of squats, he decided to call it a day and force his head back into reality. He took a shower, changed clothes, and drove home. During the drive he found his fingers tapping against his cell phone. He didn't want to go home alone. Should he call Mike? Or Eileen?

He hated that his choices were so limited these days. All of his old friends had moved away after college and he hadn't gone out of his way to make new ones. Why was that? He wasn't sure. He was personable enough and comfortably traded jokes with coworkers, but had never bridged the gulf between superficialities and actually forming any type of lasting, meaningful bond with anyone.

There was nothing he hated more than people who were consumed with self-loathing and pity and here he was barreling down that road. He had always fought hard to avoid those feelings. It had consumed him after his mother's death, and certainly after Allison's. He wasn't going to allow himself to plunge back into that depression just because he felt confused and lonely.

He grabbed his phone and dialed Eileen's number. Maybe spending the night with her would clear his head.

Her voicemail picked up. He didn't bother leaving a message.

Dusk had dropped an orange-purple curtain by the time he pulled back into Raynham's parking lot. His legs were weak from the workout and he struggled up the steps. Even his gym bag hung heavy on his shoulder and it couldn't have weighed more than a few pounds.

He glanced at a LOST DOG flyer on a light post. Was that Lucy? That's a shame.

He hoped Eileen would see he'd called and call him back soon. He was so lost in thought that he almost didn't see the man walking down the sidewalk. The floodlights had yet to register nightfall and the courtyard was painted with deep swathes of darkness. Only the man's movement gave him away. He was otherwise a shadow gliding amongst shadows. Dennis wasn't sure who it was, but hoped they weren't in a mood for conversation.

He nodded a greeting and stepped aside to make room for the man.

No one passed.

He stared up the sidewalk toward the front of the building. There was only cold brick and a few tiny leaves dancing in a breeze on the gray steps. He glanced behind him. The only movement was a mottle-coated tabby darting under one of the cars.

It was just him and the statues. He looked up at one, a nymph playfully hiding her breasts beneath her hands. She smiled, her stone eyes narrow with ecstatic mischief. He usually avoided giving attention to the statues. They bothered him on a deep level. Intellectually, he always brushed the feeling aside. But his instincts were disturbed by the still figures, especially at night. During the day they were tacky, almost comical, but in the dark they were alluring and unsettling.

Thick fingers of shadow caressed the contours of the nymph's form and he had to shake off the feeling that her smile grew wider.

He stepped past her and looked around. Where had the man gone?

His nerves ignited when he realized the man could have only gone one place: he was hiding behind the statues.

Dennis fumbled in the pocket of his jeans for his knife. There was only one reason that someone would hide from him. He had never been mugged, but he had heard enough horror stories from friends on campus to never go out without a pocketknife on his hip.

He took a step forward and tried to focus his eyes on the deep black pooling between the statues and the wall. He stilled his breath and tried to listen for footsteps or clothes rustling.

There was nothing. It was dark and silent.

God, I hope it's not someone being a prankster. He could imagine Mike jumping out and yelling *Boo*—and plunging his knife into the poor bastard's stomach.

He heard a low moan. Froze. Listened. No, it wasn't a moan. It was humming. But whoever it was didn't hum a tune. It was one, low monotone, building slowly in volume.

The lights flickered to life. He almost laughed. It had been an electrical hum as the timer kicked on.

He ducked behind a statue on his left, but no one lurked in the narrow path between the wall and the sculptures. The right side was equally empty.

What the hell?

He stepped back onto the sidewalk, looked behind him, looked to the building. Nothing.

He slid his knife back into his pocket. Had he imagined it?

No. He had seen someone walking down the sidewalk.

They must have gone back into the building. That's the only explanation. They went back inside and he was so lost in his own head that he never heard the door open and close.

He'd been explaining a lot of strange things away lately. His mind refused to grasp that fact. Instead it swam by and traveled far downstream into his subconscious, where it went to work with every odd sight and sound he had experienced recently, eroding the dam of his confidence even as his rational mind moved on to other topics. Deep inside he knew fear—fear of the building, fear of the land it rested on, fear of the very night itself—but his mind clutched to logic like a heroin addict whose stash was threatened. Reason was incredibly addictive and he wasn't prepared to give it up.

He marched through the courtyard and to the front door. He paused as he pulled it open. He had a powerful feeling that someone stood behind him. Watching him. Waiting.

He looked back. There were only the statues, now bathed in dull yellow light, standing in their usual places. The floodlights had packed the shadows away into different crevices, giving the impression that the statues had changed positions. Their heads had turned ever so slightly toward the front door. Their mouths were smiling as always, but their lips were slightly parted. Fingers had shifted in his direction as though they pointed at him, laughed at him. He could almost hear their giggles.

He took a deep breath and shook his head. He was being paranoid. He was all worked up and now his imagination ran away with him. He laughed in an attempt to break his own tension and stepped inside.

Halfway to the elevator he heard a low, faint chuckle. It chilled his blood, and again he tried to shake it off. Rationalize it. How many apartments were on the hall? Someone laughed at the newspaper or a television was turned up too loud. That made sense. He could hear Mike's chortle all the way from the elevator half of the time.

He stepped into the elevator and pressed the button for

his floor. Nothing strange was going on. He just needed a hot bath with some Epsom salts and an hour or so of quiet to clear his head. That's all.

He told himself he was fine and didn't even bother questioning why he pressed the DOOR CLOSE button over and over until he was safely guarded by the elevator's sliding barricade.

★ ★ ★

Eileen's phone rang and she dove across the room for it. Her evening had been spent half-watching television as she pored over the previous week, searching in vain for some clue as to what was going on. She and Dennis hadn't spent any quality time together. They had shared lunch one day when she had ambushed him at work, but there had been no intimacy shared with one another. She had promised herself it wasn't a problem and so felt ridiculous for flying across the room for the phone.

"Hello?"

"Eileen." She was expecting Dennis and the feminine lilt threw her off guard.

"Kirstin?"

"What's up?"

If Eileen had ever been forced to rank her friends, Kirstin would have been given that coveted title of Best Friend. The two had known each other since eighth grade and had gone through all the major ups and downs of being a teenage girl together. Since then they had been inseparable— when they weren't dating someone. In fact, since both of them had started their recent relationships they hadn't spoken much. Eileen put the last phone conversation at three weeks earlier.

"What are you doing tonight?" Kirstin asked.

She thought for a moment about Dennis. "I've got no plans."

"Great! Rick's brother is in a band—"

"Rick?"

Kristin laughed. "Yeah. Rick. *Rick*. The guy I've been seeing for half a year now?"

"That long already?"

"Yeah. Strange, huh?"

Eileen wasn't an overly sentimental woman and definitely not one to keep track of trivial things like the anniversary of her and Dennis' first kiss. She tried to count off how long they had been seeing each other, but the time frame of their first date eluded her. So she counted from the time they first slept together, which was roughly the time he first moved into that awful building.

She was surprised that it had only been three months. Three months and it was already becoming strange. Had he truly been avoiding her? She chastised herself for the paranoia, but the feeling clung to her like the summer humidity. He's just had a rough week, she told herself. Nothing to get upset about. It doesn't reflect on us at all.

She wasn't entirely convinced.

But she had made the decision to let him have a couple of days without her nagging him to see her. She had too much pride to follow him around like a lap dog, after all.

"So," Kirstin went on, "anyway, Rick's brother is in a band and a bunch of us are heading down to the Strip to watch them play. Wanna come?"

"Why not?"

When Eileen finally hung up the phone, she stared at the screen and wondered if she should call Dennis. She decided against it and rushed out to meet her friends.

The bar was heavy with smoke and Eileen, Kirstin, and her friends spent most of the evening dodging the frat-boys that frequented the place. Rick had showed long enough to say hi before announcing he had a six-thirty class the next morning and leaving. The group of girls had laughed and joked and caught up with one another by the time the band filed on stage. Rick's stocky brother waved at their table and picked up his guitar.

The rest of the band took their positions and Eileen's eyes were drawn to the tall, thin drummer. He wore a black T-shirt and blue jeans. A pair of black-rimmed glasses sat on the bridge of his nose and his hair was meticulously sculpted into an early morning mess. She knew him, but couldn't quite place how. Wasn't his name Jason?

Of course. He lived in Dennis' building. He had helped her carry groceries up one night.

The thought of Raynham made her nervous. Despite Dennis' protests, her nightmares had conspired with the television documentary they fought over to push her into the campus library one afternoon. She had looked up Camp Opey and, though an exact geographical location had eluded her, she had pinpointed it to the area of Emory Highway and was positive that the photographs she had seen were taken on Raynham's hill.

She had always been interested in the paranormal, but had never taken it seriously. It was fun to exchange ghost stories with friends, but she hadn't ever considered the implications. Logically, she knew that she was being silly. It embarrassed her and she hadn't told anyone about her research. But what she had read was so awful that she couldn't help but connect the dots in a purely illogical fashion.

An old schoolhouse had sat on the property and, sometime during the Civil War, had become a base of operations for a small Union detachment to interrogate important prisoners. The base quickly expanded into a small fort and a series of rough tents as more and more Confederate prisoners were shipped in.

As the war had dragged on, official oversight of the prison ceased to exist. Disgruntled Union soldiers took out their frustrations on their Confederate prisoners by starving them, beating them, and forcing them into hours and hours of relentless labor without sleep. As the months dragged on, the abuse became outright torture. Prisoners were armed with dull, rusty knives and forced to fight to the death. Legs and arms were amputated for no reason other than amusement. Men were forced to dig ditches, knowing full well that they would be shot in the gut for target practice when they were done and thrown in.

The prisoners slept out in the open, shackled to one another. When one died or was killed, the corpse was left chained to the living. Toward the end of Camp Opey's time as an active prison, the prison guards would starve the Confederates for over a week and then feed them their own dead.

The prison was dissolved shortly before Lee's surrender and the atrocities buried with the tortured Southerners until after the end of World War Two, when historians discovered diaries and letters from Union soldiers who had been stationed there.

If souls did linger after death, if pain could have long lasting effects on the environment, how could such a place not leave an imprint behind? Her mind flirted with a connection between the camp, the thousands of deaths during its days as a tuberculosis hospital, the mysterious doctor and his octoroon mistress, and her nightmare. She couldn't quite connect these things. Each seemed like a separate story, a different explanation offered for different haunted houses in different horror films.

She sat it all aside for the moment and took a drink from the fruity concoction that Kirstin had ordered. The band, while far from amazing, was much better than most of the ones that played around campus. When they finished, the quartet made their way around the bar, sipping from beers and chatting with the small crowd. One by one they made their way by the girls' table, thanked them for coming, and flirted.

When Jason walked over with a beer in his hand, he made a show of doing a double take. "Eileen?"

She laughed. "You remembered."

"How could I forget?" He pulled up a chair. "How have you been?"

"Good."

Kirstin chewed on a straw. "You guys know each other?"

"Jason lives in the same building that Dennis lives in."

Jason took a swig of his beer and glanced around the room. He smiled and waved at someone. "You still seeing that guy?"

As far as I know. "Yep. Still together."

"I sensed some hesitation there."

Kirstin shook her head. "Not Eileen. She's loyal as—"

"A dog?" Eileen smiled.

Kirstin kicked her foot under the table. "I was going to say 'an angel' but, now that you mention it..."

Jason bought the table another round. The conversation continued, the girls exchanging themselves for the band's members periodically as everyone made their rounds-all except for Eileen and Jason. Her because she wasn't so much into the bar scene anymore and him because she stayed seated. It was obvious to Kirstin, who shot Eileen looks all night, but Eileen never thought much of it.

Rick's brother had suggested that everyone trade numbers at the end of the evening and she didn't think twice about exchanging with Jason. On the car ride back to Kirstin's, however, the girls were relentless. Eileen shrugged it off, but she couldn't help wondering what might happen should things with Dennis get worse. She felt guilty, both toward Dennis for thinking that whatever was going on was anything more than a temporary rough patch, as well as toward Jason for instantly relegating him to the bench, ready to spring into action should Dennis sprain an ankle.

When she walked through the door of her apartment, she saw that the voicemail light on her phone was blinking. She played the message, anxious to hear Dennis' deep, radio announcer voice. Instead it was Jason, telling her how much fun he had had talking and wishing her a good night.

She slumped into her couch and deleted it. She tried to put it out of her mind and watched TV, waiting for Dennis to call. Sometime after three she put her phone on the charger and went to bed.

★ ★ ★

Mike lay on his side and watched Margot's breasts rise and fall with every breath. He was filled with nervous energy. He wanted to run up and down the halls, to laugh and yell, to wake her and do it all over again.

The light from the bathroom dripped onto her cream-colored flesh. He marveled at how it pooled onto the slight paunch where her abdomen met her pelvis, how it trickled down into the scruff of recently shaved hair and up into the shadow of her breasts. Her face and thighs were firmly drowned in shadow and so his eyes lingered on her torso. The sight of it thrilled him more than he ever could have imagined. Had he just experienced that hot flesh pressing against him? The sweat that glistened over both of them was evidence enough.

Still, the idea was so strange to him. He had just slept with this woman. He had ran his hands and his mouth all over that smooth skin, her hands and voice guiding him to where he needed to go, until they had collapsed into each other, retreated, and collapsed again. Watching her eyes close and her teeth press against her lower lip, hearing her gasp and sigh, feeling the muscles of her body clench— these things had seemed like a dream.

He wanted to rub his hands over her again, but wasn't sure if he should. Would it be rude to wake her, or would she be flattered? Had she even liked it? She seemed to, but he wasn't sure. It could have easily been an act on her part, a miming of the actions and sounds that he would have expected in order to placate his ego. Could she do such a thing?

Of course she could.

He climbed from bed and started toward her bathroom. He stopped, suddenly aware of how naked and exposed he was. He grabbed his jeans from the floor and slid them on. The feeling was ridiculous. They had just seen and felt each other nude for the past hour. But his insecurities were comforting in an odd way and he embraced them.

He shut the bathroom door behind him and stared at himself in the mirror. His face was painted with vivid color. His chest sparkled with sweat. He giggled at the sight of a spike of hair standing on end. It reminded him of Alfalfa from *The Little Rascals* shorts.

The bathroom was as indicative of Margot's taste as the rest of the apartment. She had a fondness for candles, much like his sister had. There were hundreds of them scattered around the apartment, different heights and colors, and all of them half burned. The walls of every room were brightly colored, the bathroom's deep red providing an interesting contrast to the blue of the bedroom and the green of the living room. Two Mark Ryden prints hung on the bathroom wall, small poster-sized oddities encased in black frames. One showed Jesus pulling himself from a red T-Bone steak while a wide-eyed Christina Ricci looked on.

The other bothered Mike. It was a butcher shop where a grotesquely tall rabbit wearing a Hawaiian shirt and a butcher's apron sliced meat with a giant wood saw. Cuts of meat littered the counters and strings of blood-red sausage hung from the ceiling. A pig lay on its side in the background, its cold glassy eyes staring at the wall as blood leaked from a wound in its neck. A little girl in a Sunday dress stood by the meat counter. She held the hand of a squat and miniature Abraham Lincoln. The odd jumble of otherwise innocent (though bizarre) imagery in such a bloody setting, with the expected heights of the rabbit and the former President switched, unnerved him.

He turned away and studied the shower curtain instead. It was a furry pink thing, reminding him of his grandmother's shag carpeting. He brushed his hand through it and marveled at how soft it was.

He lifted the toilet lid, did his business, and flushed. He returned to the sink and scrubbed his hands clean. Catching sight of his hair again he decided it could use similar treatment. He rinsed it with cold water and rubbed his head furiously with a towel. It felt surprisingly good and so he grabbed some scented face wash from the shelf, clenched his eyes shut, and lathered his face.

A splash echoed through the bathroom.

He paused. Had he done that? Maybe he just imagined it. He scrubbed the lather around his face, but stopped when he heard it again.

It had come from the tub.

"Margot?" As soon as he said it he knew it hadn't been her. He had locked the door behind him and she would have had to come through him to get to the tub even if it wasn't.

He shrugged it off and rinsed his face with cold water. Through the running suds, he glimpsed movement in the mirror.

Someone was behind him.

He froze, breathless. The soap burned his eyes and blurred his vision, but he was positive he had seen someone. He turned, squinting, and scanned the room. The bathroom was a fog of shapes fading in and out of focus.

"Margot?" Again, he felt foolish.

He turned back to the sink and rinsed the remainder of the soap from his face. He dried quickly and examined the room in the mirror.

He was alone.

He shrugged it off, grabbed one of Margot's brushes, and went to work shaping his hair into some semblance of order.

Another splash.

He stared at the shower curtain, unsure of what he expected. The sound came again. It was like the tub was full and someone moved around inside of it. But that couldn't be possible. They were the only ones here.

Weren't they?

The thought that someone had been hiding in the tub all night was absurd, but that didn't keep his pores from leaking a nervous sweat.

He took a step toward the curtain.

Splash.

Water scrambled down the side of the tub and darkened the yellow bathmat.

"Hey..." It was all he could manage to say.

Again, there was no answer.

The light flickered above him.

He gasped. Retreated a step. Fumbled for the doorknob.

The light flickered again.

Splash.

Water flooded down this time, rushing over the mat and across the floor, attacking the soles of his feet with its warmth.

His body reacted irrationally, throwing the brush into the shower curtain. The curtain folded into the tub and the brush fell under it with a loud clink.

But no splash.

Mike shook his head. Inhaled. Marched to the tub. Grabbed the curtain. Yanked it open.

The brush lay on dry porcelain.

Had he imagined all of that?

He stepped closer to retrieve the brush and his foot came down onto the wet bathmat. Warm water pressed out from the sides and ran across the floor.

He couldn't wrap his mind around it. There was no one in the tub, no water filling it and splashing over the sides. But he had seen something, heard something. And the damp bathmat? He was tempted to say it had been wet since Margot last showered, but it was still warm, too warm to have sat there for hours.

He grabbed the brush and returned it to the wire basket he had pulled it from. He sat on the toilet and tried to wrap his mind around what had just happened. None of it made any sense. Had he spilled the warm water somehow and didn't realize it? No—he had been using cold water to wash his face. But he had washed his hands with hot water...

He was going around in circles. There was no explanation. It must be stress, he thought. Between poor Lucy and losing his virginity (what did they call that? Performance anxiety?), he must be experiencing some type of altered state. That was the only thing that made sense.

To prove to himself that he was right, he closed the shower curtain before leaving the bathroom.

He followed the bathroom's trail of light back to the bed like a path cut through the carpet. Knowing he wouldn't be able to sleep now, and curious how Margot had judged him, he sat beside her and ran his hand up her stomach and over the mound of her breasts. He stopped at her nipple, gently circling it until he heard her sigh. He leaned over, his mouth meeting hers, and was soon lost in the excitement of her.

Later, when she had gone back to sleep cuddled up next to him, he thought he heard the splashing again. He refused to acknowledge it and forced himself into a fitful sleep.

That night he dreamed of his sister knocking at his door, crying, begging him to talk to her. He ignored her like he did the splashing and pretended to sleep.

★ ★ ★

The room had grown cold. Dennis shivered and clutched the blanket around him, tucking it under his sides like a cocoon. He hovered on the edge of waking, parts of his mind still anchored deep in his dreams, the rest wondering why the temperature had dropped so much.

Creak.

The chair...

Was he having this dream again?

He refused to fall victim to his imagination. That had been happening far too much lately. He rolled onto his side, the blanket twisting tighter around his body.

Creak.

He was fully awake now. His heart beat against his ribcage. Freezing beads of sweat formed all over his body. *This is absurd. Go back to sleep.*

But he couldn't. Just as before, he had the sense that someone watched him. Just as before, he untwisted himself and sat up to look.

Faint trails of moonlight trickled through the window, barely enough to illuminate the rocking chair.

It was empty.

He scanned the room, saw nothing out of place, and grunted. His head pressed back into his pillow.

The room smelled off. The usual scent of dust and dirty laundry hung around him, but there was another scent there. It was sweet and smelled faintly of flowers. There were other fragrances as well: dirt, strawberries, and something exotic. It smelled like—

"Karen?"

He whispered it to himself as a way to make the thought concrete, but now felt awkward having the syllables hang in the air. It felt like a betrayal somehow. He shook it off. He had to be dreaming. His mind was shifting its stored information from frightening to erotic, creating Karen's perfume from nothing.

But why the smell of dirt?

He didn't feel like puzzling it out. He was too tired for that. Maybe tomorrow.

There was another creak, this one more metallic than wooden, and he thought he felt pressure on the end of his mattress. He looked up again, wondering if Mike had come into the room with some ridiculous problem at three in the morning that only Dennis could solve. But aside from the faint light on the rocking chair, the room was black.

The pressure grew heavier and his foot slid down into a

newly formed valley on the bed.

"Mike, what do you want?"

There was no answer. The smell of flowers, fruit, and dirt grew stronger.

His arms fought their way free of the cocoon and he rolled over toward the weight. A deeper patch of black was almost visible against the dark of the room. It was small. No, *petite*. It was turned toward him and, though he couldn't see anything, he had the impression that whoever sat there was smiling.

Fingers lightly brushed his arm, gently they made their way to his hand and gripped it tenderly. It was a soft touch, a feminine touch, and the smell seemed to intensify around him.

He suddenly realized why Karen's scent was so intoxicating to him. It wasn't only an inherent sensuality, it was also a familiarity, something experienced years before, a scent that had imprinted itself deep inside his brain and was connected to all things romantic and erotic. How could he have forgotten?

His eyes filled with tears and he couldn't see. He blinked twice and they were sent running down his cheeks, hot and thick, some pooling on his lips. He could taste the salt. His breathing quickened again, and the pressure building inside of his chest threatened to break his ribs.

He had to be dreaming. There was no other explanation.

"...Allison?"

The fingers squeezed tighter.

He sat up and pulled her into his arms. Her scent overtook him completely, not just the perfume but also the smell of her hair, that unique scent of a shampoo he had never known anyone else to use. The scent of her skin, even; a soft, feminine musk accented with perfumed soap, lotion, gymnastic chalk, and a hundred other tiny fragrances.

Her arms enveloped him, blanketed him in warmth. He had never forgotten the feel of her against him, of her softness, of how she pressed her head against his chest and how her small frame seemed to vanish inside of his arms. She shook against him and his heart broke all over again.

"I'm so sorry," he muttered between sobs.

—Me too—

Her voice lit up the memory centers of his brain and, if he had any doubts that he held her, they vanished instantly.

He reached down and grabbed her face, held it in his hands, tried to study her, but there was only black. He leaned in anyway, his nerves guided him to the exact spot where he knew he would find her lips. They were like warm velvet and tasted of raspberry lip-gloss and tears. He kept his hands on her face as he kissed her over and over again, desperate with his intensity, as though she could fade away at any moment. The palsied trembling of his hands wouldn't stop and it made him miss her lips several times. He could feel her mouth smile at that.

"I'm sorry," he said. "Oh, God, I'm so sorry."

She placed her own hands on his face and held him back, studying him.

—I'm sorry for everything
you've gone through since then.

I didn't know.
If I had known, I never would have done it—

She kissed him again, this time slow and gentle. "Am I dreaming?"

—I don't know.
If you are then I must be, too—

She giggled. God, how he had missed that sound. "But how—"

—Shhh.
That's not important, is it?
What's important is that I'm here—

He nodded and kissed her again. "I killed you," he said, and fresh sobbing shook him all over again.
This time she cradled his head to her chest.

—Oh God, darling.
No. No. No, you didn't.
You were just young and confused.
I'm the one who slit my wrists—

"But you needed me. You needed help. And I wasn't there."

—Don't blame yourself anymore.
Please.
I hate that you've blamed yourself all these years.

If anyone's to blame it's me.
Maybe my father.
But not you—

He sniffed and pressed closer against her. Her fingers ran through his hair and he burrowed as deep as he could into her small breasts. "I should have been a man. I could have gone with you to the clinic, or married you and—"

—Please, Dennis. Please.
Don't do this to yourself any more.
I'm here, baby.
I'm here and I love you
and that's all that matters—

They kissed again and fell back onto the bed. She wedged herself into the contours of his body like she always had. It was as though the two of them had been made for one another, carved from the same piece of stone to fit so perfectly together that there was barely a seam. She rested her head on his chest and their arms found the old places on each other's bodies where they were meant to lay.

—I'll have to leave in the morning—

"...no..."

—But I'll be back tomorrow night.
And the night after that,
and the night after that.
Now that I know the way

nothing can keep me from coming back to you—

He pulled her fingers to his lips and kissed each of them, one by one. "How did you...?"

He could feel the smile stretch across his face.

—Your mother showed me—

"My mother?"

—Mmm-hmm.
She came to take a look at you all grown up,
and then showed me the way—

He started crying again, thinking of his mother and the dream he had had about the rocking chair. Had it really not been a dream?

Allison pulled herself tighter to him.

—She loves you and she's very proud of you—

"Yeah?"

—Of course—

This time the emotions were too much for him and he couldn't stop crying. They were strange tears, tears of joy at Allison's presence, but also tears pulled from a well carved inside of him by the deepest of grief, tears that he had trapped away for so long that it seemed there was no stopping them now that they had found a way out. He cried himself to sleep in her arms.

In the morning he rolled over expecting to find her there, but she was gone. It had only been a dream, he told himself. His pillows were damp from crying, and he thought he could still smell her, but he shook his head. Just a dream.

The hole inside of him grew deeper. Why was his mind so cruel to him? Hadn't he suffered enough?

He fought hard to get out of bed but couldn't. His limbs were so heavy, and his mind so cloudy. But mostly what kept him in bed was the deep desire to just fade away. He couldn't face anything today. He felt like something had been carved out from deep inside of him, some vital thing stolen away leaving the same cold hollow that he had worked so hard to fill after Allison had died.

He grabbed his cell and called in sick to work. He saw that he had a MISSED CALL alert and a voicemail, but couldn't bear to check it. It was likely Eileen and she was the last person he could face right now. What would he tell her? And, worse yet, there was the feeling that he had been betraying Allison's memory by being with her.

Those old feelings were what had kept him from dating for so long and he hated that they had returned. Was he losing his mind? Is that what all of the hallucinations and paranoia had been lately? It made sense. Between work, preparing for school, and early wrestling practice he had been burning the candle at both ends. It was just a matter of time before the wax melted away and the wick turned to ash.

He should just go back to sleep, he reasoned. Hamlet's line drifted through his head: *To sleep, perchance to dream.* Allison might still be in his dreams, waiting for him.

As he sunk back down into oblivion, that preceding line of Hamlet's came to him: *To die, to sleep no more.*

★ ★ ★

"This way." The man climbed into the elevator and pressed a button. Carletta followed him.

She had never been much for small talk. She appreciated men who just wanted to get off. What the hell did she have to talk about, anyway? She was forty-three years old, at least thirty pounds overweight, and her liver was already failing from how much she drank. She had one child in the grave and two more sitting alone in front of her TV right now. The boys' father was supposedly on his way over to feed them but was more than likely passed out at his cousin's again, a pipe in one hand and his child support money slipping from the other. She had lived on the same block of government housing in Lawnsdale her entire life, shuffling from her mother to her mother's pimp to a never-ending series of abusive men. Lately she had been horribly tired, and her dark skin had grown pale and bruised, leaving her worried that she'd caught something. Did anyone want to hear about all of this shit? No, they didn't. So she just did her thing, usually in the back seat of a car, took her money, and left.

As the elevator shook its way upward, she waited for him to start talking. The talkers usually only wanted to talk about themselves, thank-God-almighty, but still asked questions, mostly to be polite. A few were lonely, paying more for the company and the sense of being with someone than for anything sexual. She wondered which one he was. She settled on the lonely type. Why else pay her five times her going rate to bring her way out here into the boondocks?

She almost didn't take it, but a girl in her position could not afford to turn down that kind of money. She had stayed off the hard stuff, thank-God-almighty, but whiskey and weed still cost her as much as her rent. That was also assuming that she and her kids were fed. She marveled sometimes at how little the three of them ate, and yet how fat they all were. Little Clarence hadn't been, but he had spent most of his time outside playing ball. That was exactly what he had been doing when his heart stopped on him. One in a million chance, the doctors said. You'd have a better chance of winning the lottery, they said.

She had never won the lottery, that was for damn sure.

The elevator slowed to a stop without him saying a word and she was thankful. When the doors opened, she stepped out into a windowless room. A cold breeze hacked the warmth from her. She wished she had worn long sleeves, but it had been so hot out when she left. Why was it so cold here?

A single light, the yellow caged type she had seen her father use in the garage when he worked on his truck, hang in a corner. The man pulled it down and began doing something to the wall. When her eyes adjusted to the room she could see it wasn't a wall at all, just a sheet of dirty white canvas. He pulled it down to reveal a series of boards placed up to prevent trespassing. He rolled the canvas up and tucked it under one arm. A tug here and there removed loose boards and he crouched low through the newly created hole.

She watched his light travel on the other side of the boards. He coughed once and said, "You coming?"

She ducked under the boards.

He sat on an old, beat-up couch in front of an open window. He unrolled the canvas onto the floor in front of him. He patted the cushion next to him and clouds of dust flew into the air. It scratched her eyes and smelled ancient.

She sat next to him and stared out the window. At this time of night it looked like a sea of black swam out there. A single lamp cut through the dark like a lighthouse, guiding her eyes like a lost ship to an abandoned supermarket.

The light behind her shifted and she heard a zipper working. She swished her tongue around her mouth, trying to work up enough saliva to do what he paid her for. She turned to him, but he was leaning over the arm of the couch. The light had been placed on the floor, cutting harsh shadows all around. She could see that his pants were still zipped and wondered what she had heard.

He spun around and something flew at her forehead.

Flash of white. Sharp pain. Fingers in her hair. Around her belt. She was hefted from the couch, slammed onto the floor. Pain traveled from her skull down her spine and into her limbs.

Her mouth flooded and she spat blood onto the ground. What was happening? Her mind refused to sort it out. She moaned, tried to work up a scream, but couldn't. She heard the tearing sound of duct tape and then felt its stickiness shoved against her mouth and around her hair. She coughed blood against it, choked a little, swallowed it.

The tape went around her wrists. Her ankles were left

free.

Was this some kind of rape fantasy? No wonder he paid so much.

He rolled her over onto her back.

Any hope that this was simply a pervert's idea of a good time fled when she saw the knife. The dull light from the garage lamp hit the blade and stabbed into her eyes, telling her in one shining moment how this was going to end.

Adrenaline fired through her and she tried again to scream, but the tape did too good of a job at muffling her. She bucked. Tried to kick to her feet.

His boot came down on her knee with a sickening crunch. Sharp explosion of agony. Tears. Whimpers. Blood fell in her eyes, burning, mixing with the snot and tears to form a red slime across the tape.

He mounted her, pressed her weight into the rough canvas. His free hand found her throat, gripped it like a vice, held her head firm against the ground.

He looked out the window. Nodded as if answering someone. Turned back to her.

The knife crawled into her abdomen. The pressure gave way to searing pain as the skin parted. She screamed underneath the tape again. The knife twisted. Warm blood escaped down her side, soaked the canvas under her.

He pulled the knife out and placed it beside her. His fingers found the hole, wormed their way inside at an excruciating pace. He sat back. His hand retreated from her throat. She gasped for air.

He punched her hard, breaking her nose. Her entire body pulsed with hurt.

He grabbed a tire iron, slid it into an open black bag.

Was that the zipper she'd heard?

She closed her eyes and tried to think, but something else thrust into her wound.

The pain was too much and she blacked out.

When she came to everything was black. She was horrendously cold and the rough texture of the canvas pressed tight all around her. The world moved up and down as the life leaked from her side and it took her a moment to realize she was being carried.

Terror flooded through her and she began to squirm. She shifted one way, then another, before coming down hard onto the ground. She blacked out again.

The final time she came to, the canvas was being unwrapped from around her. She stared up at the broken fluorescent tubes that ran like stripes across the ceiling. The ceiling ended in an awning and the stars twinkled in the sky past it.

The mechanical whisper of opening doors was followed by a low *whoosh* like a sharp breath inhaled in excitement. She realized the tape had been removed from her mouth and wrists. Before she could act, hands gripped her like snakes.

"Darling," the man said and rolled her over twice onto cold tile.

The doors slammed shut behind her.

She was finally able to scream.

PART THREE
OCTOBER

"When I speak
My lips feel cold—
The autumn wind."

—Basho

"I prefer winter and fall, when you feel the
bone structure of the landscape—the loneliness of it, the dead feeling... Something
waits beneath it, the whole story doesn't
show."

—Andrew Wyeth

The evening was cold. The air had chilled and a blistering wind brought small drops of icy rain with it. Raynham Place weathered all of this from atop the hill like a giant tombstone—unyielding, immovable, implacable. Dim lights shone from its windows, and the inhabitants fought against the hum of fear that coursed through the backs of their minds. Fear and something else, something they couldn't identify. Part of it was a strong curiosity to wander into the basement, into the woods, into the abandoned supermarket that rested behind it. The rest of it was darker and ran deeper. It was blind rage and cold, unreasoning anger. It was dangerous, compulsive lust. It was jealousy, and loathing, and despair. Above all it was madness, and it thrummed through the building like the subtle movement of electricity behind the walls, bleeding out here and there through outlets and light fixtures and pores in the plaster, filling the individual apartments like a noxious gas that starts at the floor and builds upward on itself until the entire room is poison.

In Apartment 112, Cody Tate sat in front of his television. Some reality show was on, another of the myriad

American Idol clones, but he wasn't paying it any attention. He was dialing his girlfriend's cell phone over and over again, his nerves feeling rawer and rawer with every call. She wasn't answering. Why wasn't she answering? Was that fucking whore out with another guy? Again? They were supposed to have gotten past all that. He stood and paced back and forth, the thumb of his left hand hovering over the redial button. The thumb of his right hand thumbed the top of the small knife hanging on his pocket, expressing an unconscious desire that vibrated from the very walls.

In 315, Sharon Newman sat on the edge of her toilet, the porcelain cold against her naked skin. She leaned forward, her forearms resting against her thighs, as she rocked back and forth. The tears came heavier than they had in a year, heavier than they had come even the day of Daniel's funeral. She thought she was getting used to being alone, getting used to living her life as a widow, getting used to shoving the memory of her husband deep down inside her mind, but she was wrong. She didn't know where the memories came from tonight, or why they were so vivid. She didn't know why she could suddenly smell his musk and taste his lips and feel the scruff on his chin. She bawled like she hadn't bawled since she was a small child and the emptiness inside of her was heavy. It grew and grew, filling her in a cold way that only emptiness can, building pressure inside of her that was so horrible, so unbearable, that she had no choice but to let it out. The large steak knife sat on the sink next to her for just that reason, to let the pressure out. When it was out everything would be better again.

Colleen Peters and her little brother Barry were playing Monopoly in 226, waiting for their parents to come home.

Neither of them knew that their father had dropped their mother's body, bloody from a hundred tiny wounds, into a pond and was on his way to Chicago. He had an old girlfriend there. She filled his every thought and his twelve-year-old daughter and nine-year-old son couldn't be further from his mind.

Matthew Reynolds' evening swim was coming to a close. Though the pool was heated, the air was growing far too cold. He felt a sinking feeling deep in his stomach and heaviness in his limbs. He swam to the side of the pool and rested his arms against it. A painful cramp stabbed his right leg. He ground his teeth together and tried to get it out. He splashed water up over the sides of the pool and, between the noise and the intense pain, didn't notice the tiny, cold fingers that had slipped around his ankle until it was too late.

Reynaldo Lopez shoveled a flavorless microwave dinner down his throat while his children played with tiny cars around his chair. All he wanted to do was go into the basement, sit in the dark, and wait for his darling to come. But his wife was taking her sweet time at the grocery store and he was stuck with his children. Manny snatched a tiny red Corvette from Benito and the younger boy screamed. Reynaldo stood and ordered him to shut his mouth, but his tiny son just kept screaming. He slapped him across the jaw, hard enough to split the boy's lip. It felt good, too good, and Reynaldo slapped him again. It felt almost as good as what waited for him in the basement and he kept slapping.

Above him a different kind of abuse occurred. Morgan Torrance beat her husband about the face and neck with a rolled up newspaper, like someone disciplining a dog that had messed on the floor. She screamed about the dishes, spittle flying from her mouth, as she swung over and over. Josh stumbled backwards, tripping over his feet and falling. She felt strong and powerful, the way she always felt, *needed* to feel, when she took out her day's frustration on him. She had always been the alpha in their relationship and it surprised her when Josh clutched the poker from the fireplace and swung it into her knee. The knee made a sound like falling timber as it caved in. She fell, the magazine flying across the floor and unrolling. Pain radiated from the useless joint in waves. Josh pulled himself to his feet and stumbled over. He looked down on her, his face fixed into a snarl like a rabid wolf. She had the thought, *So this is how five years of marriage ends,* and then the poker came down on her skull again and again and she thought nothing else.

Little Jake Erik sat in his bed, his "Transformers" sheets pulled up to his chest, and begged his mother to leave the lights on. She scolded him, telling him that he was too old for such fears. He would start school this year, she said, and nightlights and bedwetting were things that babies did. "I love you honey," and "Get some sleep," then the light clicked off and the door pulled shut. Darkness crowded in on Jake, smothering him. He slid down into his bed, his tiny hands clutching the top of the sheet so hard that his knuckles were white. He couldn't take his eyes from the closet door, no matter how much he wanted to pretend that his mother was right. When the door cracked open and the long, white fingers crawled out over the frame like the legs of a massive spider, he finally managed to close his eyes. He squeezed them so tightly that sparks went off behind his lids and his cheeks ached. He yanked the sheet over his head and cowered under it, wanting more than anything to avoid looking at the stark white face that he knew was peeking out at him from between his clothes and toys, a hairless face with bloodshot eyes that always salivated as it glared at him. He screamed when he felt its hot breath on the outside of the sheet and when it whispered *Come into the closet, Jake. There are wonders here, dark and bloody, that will stay with you for years.* He kept screaming long after his mother came and clutched him against her breast.

Jack Stark lay sprawled out on the floor of his workroom. His body was covered with sweat from the lights above him, from the bottles of vodka he had indulged in, and from the dreams he was having. He rolled back and forth in his sleep, moaning, wishing that he'd never heard the chewing and tearing sounds as they ate. Wishing he had never heard their voices. Wishing he had never agreed to be their caretaker, or to watch over this building. There was a reason Rudy didn't live here, the same reason his father had paid Jack a ridiculous amount of money to look after things. That madman's will and trust was what stuck him here and now that those things spoke, he questioned his own sanity.

In 116, Tony Parker watched his daughter read on the couch. His time with her always felt so short and she would be back with her mother tomorrow night. He was surprised how much she looked like his ex-wife. Her hair was the same golden color, her eyes and smile had the same mischievousness, her legs were just as long and tan, and her breasts were far too developed for a fifteen-year-old. He slid onto the couch beside her and smiled. She smiled back. He slid a hand along her calf and she froze. She dropped her magazine as he bent to kiss her. She tried to squirm away, to push him off, but it was no use. He twisted one of her arms behind her and maneuvered his knees onto the couch, positioning them between her legs as he undid his belt.

And in a hospital room near the university, Lloyd Trent could still hear the whispering of his darling, still feel the pull of that building and still feel her bugs crawling over him. He had stolen a pencil from an orderly earlier and painted its many names on the wall, smearing his blood over as much of the surface as he could manage. "Eosphoros," "Lightbringer," "Morningstar," and countless other names in other tongues. The pencil lost its point quickly as the lead disappeared inside his flesh and he was forced to resort to the use of his teeth for more paint. He had to get all of the names out, everything that the roaches were whispering to him. "For you, my darling," he chanted over and over again as he coated the wall with himself.

The lives of neighbors are filled with a hundred secrets and it's impossible to know what happens on the other side of a wall. The residents of Raynham Place huddled inside their own walls, ignorant of the things occurring on the other side, as the autumn storms crept in over the hill.

The wind blew hard against these walls and the windows rattled.

Chapter Thirteen

Dennis stood in front of the supermarket's open doors. Inside was darkness, pure and unsullied. It could not be defined by its lack of light. It was elemental, an idea of darkness brought into the world without filter.

Something nudged him, wanted him to enter, begged him to set foot inside. He couldn't. How could a being born into the world of light exist in there? Even to dream about going inside would be death, he knew. It took will, but he looked away.

Allison stood behind him wearing the same red dress she had worn to her winter formal, exposed shoulders and neck wet with the light of the full moon. Her hands swished through dying brown grass around her. It looked so tall reaching up around her, clinging to her waist and caressing her breasts.

Behind her, Raynham expanded and contracted, brick and mortar groaning and creaking with every breath. Its exhales sent a cool breeze rushing towards him, blowing the grass and billowing her dress like a bright, red flame that grew hotter until it threatened to burst free and consume the entire field.

She held her hands out. Crystal blue eyes begged for an embrace. The skin was absent from her fingertips and gray bone shined in the moonlight. The flesh of her hands had greened and mottled, rot gradually receding as it made its way up her arms. He gently, tenderly took her hands in his, careful not to break them.

She smiled.

The decay crawled up her neck, over her face.

Her face drawn tight against her skull, the skin taking the slimy texture of rotting chicken, hair dried to dull-colored straw, and he loved her, loved every contour, every cell that hovered between life and death.

This is what she looks like in her tomb, he thought.

Her eyes were bloated blood-sacs wrapped in soiled gray cloth. Her smile was just as kind.

—Make love to me—

He'd longed to since her return, but they had been denied the comfort. She was little more than shadow when she came to him. They could embrace, sometimes share a kiss, but nothing more.

"How…?"

He heard one of the washing machines in the basement roar to life, the wet tumbling of the clothes inside, and the screeching of a chair pulled across concrete.

* * *

The whispering from behind Dennis' door was maddening. Mike was tempted to knock, to ask *Who the hell are you talking to when your cell phone is out here on the coffee table,* but couldn't work up the nerve. Something bothered him about the late night conversations that his roommate had with himself. There was a rhythm, a cadence of whispers and pauses that suggested someone else was there.

He worried about his friend. He hadn't seen Dennis for weeks and at first had chalked it up to the time he had been spending with Margot. But lately he wasn't so sure it was his own doing. The whispering from behind Dennis' door at night, when combined with the other experiences Mike had been having in the building, kept him on edge. But there was also school to consider. He knew what Dennis' schedule was and his roommate was typically in his room at class time.

Then there was Eileen.

He had run into her at the mall last Saturday and they stopped in the food court for lunch. She expressed her concern about Dennis, grilling Mike for why he hadn't returned her calls in the past two weeks. This had been news to Mike.

"I went by the gym looking for him," she had continued, "and they said he'd taken his two weeks of vacation."

"Well, he didn't go anywhere. Far as I know, he's only left his room for food, beer, and the bathroom."

She had placed her fork down and folded her hands neatly on the table. She made him think of nuns praying in mountaintop monasteries. "I think it's...it's your sister."

He had lost all warmth at that. "Allison?"

"He talked about her a bit recently. I don't know why it's hitting him like this now, but I'm sure all this has something to do with her."

Mike couldn't speak. He wouldn't have known what to say even if he could. After an awkward pause, he changed the subject to Dennis missing class and was thrilled that Eileen followed cue. When they finished, he asked if she was going to come by and see Dennis.

"I don't know. I don't want to ambush him. If he doesn't want to talk to me…Maybe we're over. I don't know."

He felt sorry for her, but didn't know what he could do. And now, listening to his friend again talking to himself, he was doubly confused.

He reminded himself that it wasn't his responsibility and grabbed a Coke from the fridge.

He went to his own room and sat down in front of the computer, prepared to finish an English paper he had been working on. He opened the file and read over the work he had done. It was an essay on *Crime and Punishment,* which he hadn't bothered to read. Instead he had read the Cliff's Notes, as well as the Wikipedia article and a few essays he found online. He had tried to read the book, but the language was too dense.

He opened the cold can on his desk with a loud *hiss*. He sipped and scanned the room, hoping for any distraction from his work.

The supermarket outside his window.

He knew the light in the parking lot burned, though it was hard to see during the day. He was both frightened by and drawn to the building. Ever since he

—*made a sacrifice, freely given*—

glanced at the darkness inside, he had a difficult time

taking his mind away from it. His dreams were haunted by it. He found himself doodling it in the margins of his notepad during class and sometimes even walked its boundary at dusk, careful not to get too close, as he attempted to decipher the illegible graffiti that covered its sides.

And then there were the things he had been seeing in Raynham Place since then. He tried to tell himself it was his imagination, that the shadows he saw and the whispers he heard were products of his own mind, that the presence he often felt at his shoulder was his anxiety manifesting. Yet some feeling deep in his gut told him these things were tied to that building and he had set them free into the world.

He shook his head. That was ridiculous.

Wasn't it?

Margot had filled his head with so many stories of this place, folk tales and ghost stories and urban legends, that he couldn't dismiss the idea.

And there had been tragedies lately, deaths and missing persons. That poor little girl died from cancer.

—God is a bloated predator
eating flesh as He pleases—

Margot had been deeply unnerved by Matthew's mysterious seizure in the pool a few nights ago. He was still in critical condition at UT. Not wanting to upset her further, Mike never mentioned how similar it was to the Callahan kid's episode at the supermarket.

The dying grass around the building, the broken almost-strip mall, the graffiti on the walls—they took his eyes, stole them and refused to give them back. The light tickled the doors, reflecting back like a whore seducing him with fingers of multi-colored light.

There was a sharp cry from somewhere in his room.

He blinked.

It was dark. Had a cloud passed over the sun? He glanced at his clock.

7:23! It was barely five o'clock when he came in here. That couldn't be right.

He went to his computer, looked at the clock in the corner of the screen. It *was* 7:23. He looked out the window again. The way the dark-blue night had collapsed over the hill, there was no mistaking it for cloud cover.

The cry came again.

How did he lose over two hours?

You were staring at that door.

His muscles went rigid. Had he been staring at the supermarket for over two hours and didn't even realize it? That was impossible.

The cry rang out again and his mind finally focused on it. It was his cell phone ringing its high electronic whine.

He stumbled over to the dresser, equilibrium gone, his body threatening to crash into the walls as it pitched one way and then the other. He snatched his phone up and answered it without looking at the screen.

"Mike?"

"...Mom?" He fell down onto his bed.

A pause. "How are you?" She sounded tense, rigid. He could imagine her standing by the phone in the kitchen, refusing to walk any farther than a few feet away even though there was no cord, her free hand pulled tight across her stomach as if her other elbow needed the extra support.

"Uh…I…I'm fine. You?"

"We're alright."

"Good."

Silence.

"Look, Mom. I'm sorry I haven't called."

"I know you are. Hold on." He heard the rustle of the phone being taken away from her ear, her hand covering the receiver as muffled voices discussed something. It was his father, probably sitting at the kitchen table drinking coffee and directing her speech like an acting coach.

"Mom?"

"Michael, I was calling to ask if you've made any plans about your cell phone."

"Huh?"

"Your father and I have been paying the bill since you left, and he…*we* wanted to know when you planned on taking over the payments."

This was why she called? "Um…shit. I don't know. I had to cut my hours back a little at the theater because of classes."

"How are classes?"

"They're alright. Harder than I thought, but I'm doing okay."

"Made any new friends?" In other words, do you spend all of your time with Dennis?

"Not really. I mean, there are some guys I talk to in my classes, but we don't really hang out or anything."

"Are you eating well?"

"Mom, what are you—"

"Your father and I just thought we'd see if you would like to come over for dinner Friday night."

"Oh. Yeah. Sure. Yeah, of course. What time?"

"You know dinner's always at seven."

"Cool. Uh…I guess I'll see you then."

More rustling, more muffled speech. "Bring any laundry you need done and I can wash it for you."

"We have a laundry room here in the building. You guys should come by some time."

"My washing machine's fine, dear."

"No, I meant—"

Rustling. "We'll see you Friday, Michael."

"Okay. Yeah. See you then."

A pause and a click. The call disconnected.

He sat there for several minutes staring at the screen of his phone. He didn't know what to think of the invitation. He hadn't spoken to his parents since everything happened.

He should tell Dennis, see what he had to say.

He sat his phone down and stood. His eye caught the supermarket's doors through the window for just the briefest of seconds.

He turned, and the clock read *8:42pm*.

His head swirled again, the room spinning on an unstable axis. What the hell was happening to him? He careened into the living room.

"Dennis?"

He felt drunk, unstable, as though he weren't entirely flesh. His mind a wet sponge, eyes covered in a thin veil of cheesecloth, skin draped with a thousand tiny strands of spider-web, tickling him, sapping his will.

What was he doing out here?

Dennis. He stumbled toward his roommate's door, didn't bother to knock, shoved it open a little too hard. It swung against the wall with a loud thud, ricocheted, and began to close.

The blanket and sheet were twisted together into a tumor on the bed. A cool breeze blew in through the window, the curtains reaching across the room like a lover's arms. The rocking chair creaked back and forth, back and forth.

Where the hell was he? He hadn't left his room in God knew when.

The wind died and the rocking chair stopped moving.

★ ★ ★

The sun fought into the basement through dust-stained windows, streaming small waterfalls down to form haphazard pools of light on filthy gray concrete. Tiny eddies of dust danced inside of them, floating down, up, and out in indiscernible patterns. Karen unknowingly stood inside one of these, the light rinsing the white T-shirt that clung to her shape like it was carved from stone, soaking her hair in brilliant flame, sparkling over the green jewels of her eyes. She wore a very short pair of blue gym shorts, her legs growing like well-fed ivy into a pair of sandals. The light bathed over every inch of her, accenting every color and shape on her like the morning sun through a stain-glassed window, and Dennis couldn't help but stand silent in the shadow of the doorway and watch her pull her soaked clothes from the washer and toss them into the dryer.

When she noticed him she smiled and all of the shadows fled from the room. "Hey. How long have you been there?"

He took a step toward her. "Not long."

Behind her, he thought he saw eyes watching from the dark. When he looked again they were gone.

She closed the dryer door. "Hey, listen. About that night—"

"Shhh." He wrapped his arm around her waist and drew her to him. Their lips met and she melted against him. Her skin was on fire.

There was a click. A metallic thud.

They pulled away from one other and turned.

The locks that had fastened the strange door closed had fallen to the floor.

Dennis kissed her again and walked over. He picked one up. "Huh. It's completely rusted through."

The door creaked open.

He turned back to her. Her face was flushed, her hands nervously worked at straightening the wrinkles from her shirt.

"Wanna explore?" he asked.

She shrugged. "Why not?"

He took her hand and led her inside.

One tiny window, as filthy as any other in the basement, allowed a single shaft of light to fall into the room, landing on the chair like a spotlight. Its metal frame was seemingly covered in dried blood, though Dennis assumed it was rust like the lock. A faded green pad was loosely fastened to the seat, stuffing bulging out from tiny slits. Leather straps dangled from the arms, an identical pair connected to the front feet.

He glanced to Karen as she made her way around the room. Metal shelves lined the walls, each one covered in thick sheets of dust. Rusted tin cans, old water hoses, and stained tools rested all over. In one corner a thirty-year-old *Charlie's Angels* poster was crudely taped to the gray brick.

"This chair..." he said, but couldn't quite finish the thought.

She came over and knelt next to him. Her smell made his head swim. "Jesus. It's like something from Ed Gein's basement. What do you think it was used for?"

"The Crossroads..."

"What?"

"Nothing."

He stood. She rose beside him. They exchanged a smile and then their hands found each other's bodies again, their lips following shortly behind.

"This is crazy..." she whispered.

He didn't say anything, his mouth busy traveling along the muscles of her neck. He was dreaming, he knew it now, his mind acting with the same sluggish impulses that it did when Allison visited him.

His hand slid up her shirt, found her nipple. She moaned and pressed against him, her fingers guiding his mouth back up to hers.

Something moved behind her, a shadow passing through shadows. He could feel eyes on them and didn't care.

He cupped the backs of her thighs and lifted her, spinning, the basement swirling around them like a tempest, pressing her tighter against him as he came to rest in the chair, her legs maneuvering her into a better position, warm thighs squeezing his hips, velvet hair falling around his face, the exotic scent of her crashing over him like a wave, her hands on his chest, his on her thighs, pressing against each other, not able to get close enough, trying to force themselves together until they were one creature.

The pressure in the room shifted and Dennis felt like hundreds of people had come to watch. Let them, he thought. It's just a dream, right? He was certain of it now—it was too similar to Eileen's dream.

Thinking of Eileen sent a pang of guilt through him. Karen's mouth on his neck erased it.

Through half-lidded eyes he saw movement in the basement, shadows stepping forward and back in the darkness, shuffling with nervous excitement.

Karen's nails scratched him as they wrenched his shirt up and off, her lips pressing against his chest and abdomen like a warm sponge. He saw the boy who hid behind washing machines and in the depths of the pool, his hair slicked to his head and his skin bloated, over-filled, whatever was inside ready to split the seams of his blue-tinged flesh and spill out onto the ground like the slimy cold water leaking from his mouth.

She worked at unfastening his pants and he marveled at her appetite. She smiled up and the glazed look in her green-jeweled eyes told him that she was here too, was a part of this wonderful dream where inhibitions had been expelled like runoff floating downriver.

He saw a group of men in filthy gray coats, their faces covered with shadow, huddling close together on the edge of the darkness, shuffling as they whispered to one another. He saw something white and malicious, its skin reeking of rotten fish, as it moved between the cracks in the darkness. He saw eyes that he was certain could not be human, that had to be canine, staring out from the black with a hunger deeper than he would ever know.

Karen took him into her mouth, her lips like pillows. He clutched the arms of the chair with exquisite desperation and gasped.

There was Dr. Whaley and his octoroon mistress in the corner, the shadows draped around them like sheets on a lover's bed, her naked caramel body pressed against the wall, his bearded mouth suckling at her breasts like a starving newborn, both of them watching Dennis and Karen, watching and approving, aroused to frenzy, lustful, hungry.

Dennis' body quaked and shook. Karen removed her mouth and replaced it with her hand. He moaned as his hips bucked and his seed spread onto the floor below him.

—Ye have spilled offering
and shall reap the rewards—

He grabbed Karen, pulled her to his mouth, spun her into the chair. Behind him a thousand feet shuffled in anticipation. He placed a foot on his shoulder, kissed her ankle, lips trailing down her calf and her thigh. He wrapped his fingers in the soft cloth of her shorts and slid them free, kissed his way back down her thigh, her body clenching tight and lungs sucking in a sharp breath as he moved in.

The door creaked shut.

Her fingers wrapped around the arms of the chair, her pelvis grinding against his face as he worked. The smell of her perfume drowned him, her perfume and the smell of dirt, of a freshly turned grave.

Allison stood behind the chair, her fingers running through Karen's hair. She smiled.

The straps came to life, gripping Karen's wrists, pulling them tight against the chair. She didn't notice or didn't care.

Allison's hands rubbed Dennis' back, crawled underneath his shirt, pressed deep into the muscles there. Her fingers parted his skin and slid into him.

—Fuck her, my darling—

Dennis rose from his knees and jerked Karen forward, the chair screeching across the concrete. He placed her calves on his shoulders and slid himself inside of her.

The others in his dream crowded closer, their breath hot on his back as they watched. Their shapes melted into one another until a sea of blackness surrounded them.

He thrust.

Karen bucked her hips hard against him. She closed her eyes, threw her head back, the muscles in her neck bulging, the veins in her arms standing out against her flesh as she gripped the arms of the chair tighter, tighter, until finally Allison pressed closer into him, inside of him, *through* him, and the pressure building in him grew too strong, and he released it, sending hot fire into Karen with an intensity he had never known.

She screamed.

The shadows retreated.

Dennis pulled back, fell to his knees in exhaustion. Their bodies glistened with one another's sweat.

Her head rolled forward, damp hair falling around her shoulders.

The leather straps loosened and fell away.

She smiled at him and opened her eyes, cold blue eyes shining like the sun reflected from a frozen lake.

Her scent was flowers, lilac, strawberries, and something exotic. Underneath that was the faint scent of dirt.

"Darling," she said and kissed him.

Chapter Fourteen

From Margot Deschaine's Journal:

As I write this, I have the strange feeling it will be the last words I ever set to paper. The dreams have bloomed again, terrible blossoms crowding my head at night and pulling me, sweat-drenched and breath-starved, from my sleep.

I pretend they've been absent for some time, but that's one of the bigger lies I have told myself. They've always been there, lurking around in my subconscious, watching, waiting for a time they could force their way up.

What happened here to cause it this time?

I have come to think of myself as a storyteller in that grand Southern tradition, gathering the macabre tales that flow through this place like a fisherman who sits on a riverbank catching every runt that swims by while waiting for the Big One. I always thought someday I would write a novel, or even a book of poems. I fear now that this diary will be the sole artifact of my life.

The bits of the story here are strange and varied, wild snippets of cloth that, when sewn together, create a coat of many colors no child would wish to wear. I spoke to Jack about it once and he swears it began with a group of Natives slaughtering one another here. My guess is that it stretches back further, if only we knew the prehistoric oral legendry of this place.

Yet each of these things was simply a precursor to the next, a signpost along a sad and tragic trail. The slaughter beget Camp Opey, which beget doctors who thought this particular hill of all the hills in Tennessee would be a good place for thousands of tuberculosis patients to die, who beget poor Dr. Whaley and Calliope, who beget that crane's unfortunate mechanical malfunction, who beget the Crossroads Killer, who beget the Blue Boy, who beget whatever horror is waiting in the halls of this place now, ready to make itself known at any moment.

Dear God, these are simply the tragedies that I know of! What has gone unnoticed here in this place? What goes on now behind locked doors when the lights are out? What has happened to all of the poor folk who have disappeared during my years here?

Will I be next? Something lusts for me, the way I lust for Mike.

Mike... Have I damned you? If so I am truly sorry. I had to have you. I dreamed of you every night, your young flesh pressed against me, and I just had to have you. Perhaps I have lived in this building so long that its desires have seeped into my blood. Like most of us here, it becomes difficult to separate my own impulses from this place's horrid nightmares.

Nightmares...there is a clue there, I think. I've tried to plot it out, but it's no use. A wall has slammed down in my thoughts and all I can think of is the dark behind those doors, the dark that calls my name as sweetly as a flock of mockingbirds singing in the sun.

There are things to be known and things unknown. Nature herself has gifted us with certain faculties that both amaze and horrify us but even we, with our highly evolved cerebral cortices, cannot learn what hides behind the veil. We can only go forth, part the curtains, and discover what the greatest mysteries truly are. Then we may have a story to tell.

My grandfather was a storyteller. People would gather around the front porch of the old country store in Oneida where he'd sit, spinning his yarns about pioneers and revenants. One hot summer night springs to mind, my entire family huddled around his feet, sipping from sweating glass bottles of ice cold Coca-Cola, as he told us one of his stories. He used to say that God was the first storyteller and that the angels were His words. They held the vocabulary of all creation, their dreams shaping reality to His whim. That was the truly frightening thing about the fall, he'd said. That these powerful words were banished to dark places.

A roach just scurried across the kitchen tile. I thought they had sprayed recently?

I'm tired. I need rest my eyes but a moment, a single fragile moment. I hope the dreams pass me by. If they come now, I know the song that they will sing, the story they will tell, and it is the most tragic and delicious thing I have yet heard here.

In our dreams, we can be anything we want to be. We can be anything we fear to be. Yet so many dreams spring from the baser parts of us. Why do we dream so much of lust, of rage, of fear?

If our brains were broken, would these dreams leak out onto the pillow, seep out of our skulls and into the world around us?

So tired.

★ ★ ★

Needing desperately to make sense of things, to ground his ever-shifting reality, Mike shuffled across the hall and knocked on Margot's door.

While he waited, he assessed himself. Things had been changing since he had moved here, especially since the accident with Lucy, and the metamorphosis wasn't limited to his maturing lifestyle. There were the emotions that he had been experiencing, not only with Margot, but also the new found confidence he had, the clarity he sometimes experienced. He couldn't articulate how he felt about these things, but they did not feel natural. It was almost like they had been *inserted* into him, fed to him, some strange type of software downloaded and installed into the directory of his brain.

If that weren't enough, there were the voices. Whispers heard late at night, indiscernible bits of conversation outside his window or in the halls. When he would check, there would be no one there. Other times he could feel eyes watching him, *judging* him, urging him toward a purpose he couldn't fathom.

Was his mind broken?

He wondered if Dennis experienced the same things.

His only rock had been Margot. She had cemented him in reality, anchored him to the here and now. It was as though he had grown roots through her into the very soil here, deep down into the dark, under the foundation and

—through the concrete tube where once hundreds of bodies were
spirited away out of sight of
still-dying patients,
the corpses hauled downhill

where trucks secretly gathered,
a tunnel capped at one end by the road that ran by,
on the other by a giant iron grate,
the supermarket atop it,
a conqueror astride his horse,
the hounds devouring anything that came near
as they had done since the last string of bodies,
their caretaker wishing they would die,
hating them but fearing them,
feeding them still as was his charge
when the fat man's father hired him,
a true disciple that one,
tending the madness here like a garden,
feeding the soil with blood and pain
until that fateful day
when the bone flowers would bloom again—

The force of the thoughts drilling into his head drove him to one knee. Blood trickled from his nose, his mouth burned with the taste of battery acid and

—Jack
Jack
Jackie Boy
Jack and Diane
Jack be nimble
they come for you
they wait until you sleep
and then drag you from your workshop
by hook or by crook
and only the shadows will mourn your passing—

His eyes itched, tears pouring like someone had turned a shower on full blast, ears ringing with

> *—the Scarecrow's roaches return,*
> *the whore's legs both welcome and birth them,*
> *and the walls weep torrents*
> *as the earth turns*
> *and the dreams come to an end*
> *my darling*
> *my sweet sweet darling*
> *help me awaken*
> *these nightmares are splitting me in twain DOYOUFUCK-*
> *INGHEARMEMYCHILDIHAVETAKENYOUROF-*
> *FERING ANDWEAREBOUND—*

When he came to, Margot stood over him, her eyes as raw as fresh meat, her face as pale as bone. She wore a green robe and crossed her arms over her breasts.

He struggled to sit. "Margot? What happened?"

She sniffed back a tear.

"What?"

She turned and closed her door. "I suppose it's about time."

He pressed his palms against the wall and fought to stand. "What are you—?"

"Shhh…." She kissed him. "I dreamed all of this. Do you have the dreams? Probably don't remember them— most don't. I think that's why we were drawn to one another. I can remember, but you…You will be my memory." She took his hand and led him down the hall.

"Where are we going?"

"To gaze out over Paris."

"...Eiffel?"

His mind struggled to press the pieces of the puzzle together, but the picture wouldn't form. Something important was missing, some scattered pieces that others in the building held, who he couldn't say, but his failure to collect the pieces would be disastrous.

When they stepped from the elevator on the top floor, he was struck by how cold it was, the icy wind grappling with dust across the floor. The second thing that struck him was that the sheet of white canvas was gone.

Margot led him to the couch and they sat. Her hand found his and gripped it tight. Across the field, storm clouds rolled through the sky but did not break.

"I feel like I was supposed to teach you something."

He squeezed her hand. "About what?"

She shrugged. "If I knew *that*..."

"What are we doing up here?"

"I wanted you to see."

"See what?"

She leaned over and kissed him again.

When her lips retreated and his eyes opened, her tears still fresh from where their cheeks had pressed together, she was gone.

He jumped to his feet and looked around.

She wasn't there.

He glanced out at the field—

—and saw her walking through the tall grass and onto the pavement of what could have one day been a packed and crowded parking lot. She stepped to the doors of the supermarket, looked up at him, and smiled.

The doors parted, and she stepped inside.

"NO!"

He was in the hall again, on the ground. His head rang like when his father had punched him, his face slick with tears.

My tears? Or hers?

Margot's door was cracked open. He struggled to his feet and pressed it open farther.

"Margot?"

He could feel by the stillness in the air that she wasn't here.

He rushed past the elevator and into the stairwell. The echo of his feet pounding down the stairs was like a crowd following him. He sprinted by the pool, through the grass that he had avoided since the accident, stopping short on the pavement.

The doors were wide open.

A cold breeze blew by him.

He lost his breath when a snake slithered past his feet. It leaped through the air, flying several feet before coming to rest on the concrete again. He was wrong, it was no snake, but a long fabric belt, the same color as the robe that Margot had been wearing in his —what? Dream? Vision?

He stared into the black. There was no movement, no shapes. There weren't even the shades of black that shadows and darkness usually held, no gradation as the light faltered. Light simply ceased at the space where the doors parted.

Something whispered, faint, barely like a voice at all, as soft as two pieces of fabric brushing against one another.

The breeze blew stronger, bits of dry leaves swirling over the concrete, dancing some obscene dance to a tune that he thought he could *almost* hear.

The whispering grew, not in volume, but texture. It thickened as layer upon layer of soft, rustling voice was added, a veritable chorus communicating from the black.

He fell to his knees. They collided with the concrete with the sound of a hollow drum, the pain stabbing upwards into his thighs and vibrating down through his shins. He registered this, but did not *feel* it. All he could feel was the cold, the dark, and the gentle tickling of the hushed voices speaking from inside.

He knelt there and listened.

In the distance, a coyote howled a long and mournful dirge.

Chapter Fifteen

"Hi, you've reached Dennis. Leave a message—"

She hung up and threw the phone across the room. It collided with her couch, bounced once, and thumped onto the carpet.

Smart move, Eileen.

She walked over and picked it up. Nothing seemed broken.

She was so angry she could hardly think. She couldn't remember the last time she had spoken to Dennis. All of her calls went to voicemail. He was never at work when she went by. He didn't respond to her e-mails or Facebook posts. As far as she was concerned, they were through.

But she needed to know why.

Her emotions had been like an airplane running out of fuel, traveling up and down between pure rage, excruciating sorrow, and a deep and powerful feeling inside of her that said something was wrong.

She had spent far too long waiting for him. If they were done then so be it, but goddammit he was going to tell her *why*. She had thought they had something special.

The tears came again, threatening to break over her. She

sniffed them back, grabbed her purse, and headed down to her car.

A half an hour later she pulled up the steep hill toward that God-forsaken building, the sky already darkening behind it, the setting sun casting its odd light on the thing in such a way that she felt it sneered at her.

The idea that the building itself tormented her was not a new one, but she had been giving it more and more weight lately.

Her nightmare had only been one of the reasons that sent her out researching this place in her spare time. The other, of course, was Dennis. Past experience told her that he had likely met someone new, but the part of her that worried about him pointed to the building as the cause of whatever psychological rollercoaster he was riding.

After she had found the information on the atrocities at Camp Opey, she had been compelled to keep digging. Every page seemed to reveal some new and horrible story. There was, of course, that awful doctor and his whore of a mistress. Though some of the details varied from Margot's story, all of the high points were there. His suicide note had made quite a splash with the local newspapers.

The next mention of the place was in a series of stories from nineteen fifty-eight. Local farmers had been trying to have Raynham torn down and the land auctioned to one of them for years, but talk of opening a new general care hospital in the ruins had kept the building in legal limbo. Then, that summer, a group of homeless squatters, "hobos" the newspaper had called them, had taken up residence. The community used their presence as a further reason to destroy the old place and, in order to settle things down, the police drove up there one morning to force the squatters out. What they found was as strange as anything else in the history of the place.

The squatters were discovered in the basement, their bodies ripped and torn to shreds, their bones gnawed on, bits of each of them missing. The police said it looked like a pack of wild dogs had gotten into the building. That in and of itself wasn't so odd, but what was "peculiar," as one patrolman called it, was the fact that all thirteen men had been found lying in a circle around a burned out fire. Not a single one of them had tried to run or flee. It was as if each of them had resigned themselves to their fate, gladly allowing whatever had gotten in to devour them.

During the late sixties, there were reports of "devil worshiping" on the grounds, though never any evidence discovered. Eileen was tempted to ignore that—after all, anything strange in the South was usually chalked up to "devil worshiping." But in light of everything else, she had to consider it.

In the late seventies, as the farmers in the area sold their properties off to real estate developers, a local real estate genius named Mark Cusimano (the father of the building's current landlord) bought the land. He apparently had a grand vision of a series of apartment buildings, gas stations, and strip malls running along this stretch of road. His first project was converting Raynham, still a solid structure even after these years of neglect, into the building it is today. His second project was the last of his many strip-malls.

Reading about all of this brought to mind the story that her uncle Gary had told her. Gary had worked for a couple of weeks on the project, but while he was out of town visiting family in Chattanooga, there had been a horrible accident and construction had halted. A crane had been lifting thousands of pounds of material from the back of a truck. Something went wrong—an electrical malfunction, the papers had said—and the material came crashing down, killing fourteen men and injuring another six. One of the injured was Mark Cusimano. The accident had crippled him for life. It seemed he fell into a depression after that and never finished building the strip mall or continued with any of his other projects. In the late nineties he overdosed on prescription painkillers and bourbon.

Eileen also found evidence to back up the stories of the Blue Boy and of the Crossroads Killer. The story of the Crossroads Killer was particularly disturbing and she had had nightmares about the man for days after reading about it. His name was Micah Scott Weaver, a high school dropout and a seafood clerk at a grocery store. He would park on the side of the road at night and feign car trouble. If a pretty young girl came by to help, he would abduct her and, police believe, take her back to Raynham. He raped and tortured these girls in the most brutal ways for days and then hanged them from a tree at a crossroads out in the country.

Before he hanged himself in prison, he had told a reporter: "I had to hang them out there, you see? The dead get confused at crossroads and have a hard time coming back. There are enough of the dead wandering around as it is. I was afraid of these girls, don't you get it?"

All of these stories piled atop one another, and atop Eileen's nightmare, to create a horrific tale. There was something at work here, she knew it no matter how much her rational mind refused to believe, no matter how many years of science and logic had been crammed into her brain, she *knew*. So many tragedies tied to one place were just not natural.

She parked her car, and for the first time since she was a little girl, crossed herself. She went inside, took the elevator to the third floor, sucked in a deep breath, and pounded on Dennis' door.

Mike answered. "Eileen?"

"Is Dennis here?" She pushed by him and into the living room.

"He's in his room. Like always. I haven't talked to him in days."

She stared at the closed door. "What's that whispering?"

"He...uh, he's been talking to himself."

"Talking to himself? For how long?"

Mike scowled. "I don't fucking know. Am I my brother's keeper?"

Eileen was struck dumb by his sudden change in demeanor. Dennis had always told her about his moods, but she had never experienced them before. She didn't know what to say.

He sighed. "Look, I've gotta go meet my parents for dinner."

"Uh...sure. Yeah. Go ahead."

Mike hesitated. She thought he was going to apologize, but he didn't say anything.

"Is Margot going with you?"

He shook his head.

"How are things going with you two?"

He winced. "Fuck you." He turned and walked out the

door.

Eileen was left wondering what had happened. She had just seen Mike a week ago and he had been his normal awkward self. Had she done something? Said something?

It's the building.

"Eileen?"

She turned to see Dennis closing his door. He stood in front of it, rigid, dressed in only his boxers. His hair was messed and greasy and he wore two or three day's growth of beard on his jaw. A beer bottle dangled from his hand.

She took a step closer and could see how red his eyes were. Had he been crying? Was he drunk? She couldn't tell.

"Hi," she said.

He just stared at her.

"Can we talk?"

He looked around the room.

"Mike's gone."

He nodded.

"I just...oh, Jesus, this is hard." She took a deep breath, blinked back the tears that tried to form. "What is going on between us?"

He shrugged.

"Say something, dammit."

"What do you want me to say?"

"What do I...?" Her voice quivered. "Why haven't you returned any of my calls?"

"I...I don't know. I was confused."

"Was?"

"Yeah."

"But now you're not."

He shook his head.

304

"Why?"

The door creaked open behind him. A woman stepped through, placed a hand on his shoulder.

Jaw trembled.

Stomach lurched.

Breath stopped.

Eileen recognized her from one of the pool parties over the summer.

Karen.

Karen rubbed her hand along the back of Dennis' head. She wore only a T-shirt, a long white "Humane Society" shirt that Eileen recognized as her own, one she had left the last time she was here. When was that?

Why would he let her wear my shirt?

The tears broke free then, crashed down her cheeks with the force of a tsunami, her grief exposed for all the world to see, her torment on display for Dennis and his *whore*, his filthy disgusting *whore*.

She imagined gouging the redhead's blue eyes from her skull, imagined how the bitch would scream for her, how those white orbs would feel when they burst open under her nails and streamed their jelly down the whore's face.

Instead, she turned and ran.

When she was at the elevator, she heard the door shut.

He wasn't coming after her.

The tears pounded harder against the floor.

In her car, safe from prying eyes, she screamed and punched her steering wheel.

She wasn't sure how long she sat there and cried, but when she was done, when all of the grief had poured out of her, anger flooded in to take its place.

She wiped her face dry and reapplied her make-up. "That cocksucker," she said to her reflection in the rear-view. "I knew he was like all of the others, I just fucking *knew* it." Now that she was through crying, she was going to march back up there and...and...

And what?

She glanced at the building, trying to collect her thoughts.

The building...

What was it about this place? Not ready to accept what had happened, her emotions bubbling up and clouding her thoughts, she latched on to her theory that the building was responsible for so much.

Something moved under the lights by the front door. She sat still, watching, as a skinny figure came into view. It carried a toolbox and, as her eyes adjusted, she saw that it was the maintenance man. Jack, right?

He would know what was going on with this place.

She followed him inside. He looked tired, his back kyphotic and his eyes sunken deep into his skull.

"Jack, right?"

He turned at the pace of a drunken tortoise. "What?"

"You're Jack, right?"

He nodded. His eyes were wide, confused, as they scanned her.

"Can I ask you some questions about the building?"

"Manager handles vacancies and viewings. He's here Monday through Friday, nine a.m. to—"

"That's not what I meant. I mean...is there...what I'm getting at..."

"Spit it out, darling."

The elevator doors dinged open. He stepped in. She followed.

"Is there anything strange about this building?"

The doors shut behind them.

★ ★ ★

Allison's voice whispered in his ear. "Let her go," it said. He turned and stared into her cold blue eyes shining from Karen's face.

These dreams were so odd, Allison and Karen having become one person somehow, but he didn't care. They were magnificent. They allowed him to explore his lust with Karen's body while falling madly in love with Allison all over again. He hoped he never woke.

Guilt crept around the back of his mind, guilt at the sight of Eileen's tears which, even if it were just a dream, was something he had promised himself he would never cause. The guilt had another cause. He knew in the logic of this dream-world that Karen no longer existed, that her flesh had become a vessel for Allison.

The patter of rain sounded against the windows. Trees blew hard in the wind outside and thunder rumbled. He wondered at the symbolism of it. Everything in a dream had some deeper meaning didn't it? Eileen had taught him that.

Allison took his hand in Karen's, smiled, and led him back to the bed. "Forget her," she said. "You're mine, now." Her lips pressed against his.

She shed the T-shirt, her glorious body still sparkling with sweat. She climbed on all fours onto his bed. He shed his own clothes and climbed up behind her. As he slid himself inside, she handed him the rolled up towel that sat next to her.

He looped it around her throat, gripping an end in each hand, and wrenched her head back. The towel bit into her neck, her lungs fighting for air, the muscles in his forearms cramping from pulling so tight as he pounded into her. She turned her face, already a light shade of purple, toward him and smiled.

He prayed that he could dream this dream forever.

★ ★ ★

Mike sat at his parent's table and sliced his pork chops in silence. The awkwardness in the room was physical. It crowded around them like dense fog, clinging to them and sapping any will to speak of the past.

His mother poured herself a gin and tonic while his father glared at her. The old man had never approved of her drinking, had hated it in fact, but since Allison's death had seen it as a necessary evil. When she wasn't drinking, she cried.

"So, Michael." His father sat his fork down and wiped his mouth with a napkin. "How's school?"

"It's alright. Difficult, but I'm doing okay."

His father nodded. "And your apartment?"

"It's cool. Big. Hardwood floors. A pool. I love it."

His mother sipped her drink. "That's good," she said.

Then they returned to the strained comfort of silence. After several minutes, Mike's father again sat his fork down. "Your mother and I have been talking."

Mike stared at him.

"All of the nasty business surrounding you moving out," he continued. "We think apologies are in order."

Mike waited.

His mother cleared her throat. "We'd really like you to move back in."

He said nothing.

"Well?" His father's eyes bore into his, searching, *judging*.

"Well what?"

"Aren't you going to say something?"

"You said that apologies were in order."

"I did."

"So I'm waiting for them."

His father's face twisted in confusion. They stared at each other from across the table. Mike folded his hands in his lap and refused to look away.

Realization dripped onto his father's face. "We meant that *you* owe *us* an apology. For the things you said, for your abhorrent behavior, and for leaving me and your mother the way you did."

Mike's face was blank, his voice calm. "*You* kicked *me* out."

His mother swirled the gin around her glass. She fixed her gaze on the melting ice inside. "Michael, your father was just angry. You said some awful things to him."

The old man nodded.

Mike almost laughed. "All I said was the truth."

His father's nostrils flared. His eyes filled with fire and narrowed as they bore into Mike. "You will apologize, young man."

He was silent.

"Then," his mother interrupted, still staring into her glass, "we can be a family again."

This time Mike did chuckle. "We haven't been a family for a long time." He met his father's burning gaze and poured every ounce of contempt that he had for the old man into his own. For the first time in his life he had no respect, no fear for this man.

They stared at each other for a long while. Finally, his father looked away. "Maybe this was a mistake."

Mike laughed again.

"What happened to you?"

"You want to know about a mistake, Dad? I'll tell you about a big goddamn mistake—"

"Watch your mouth, young—"

"See, this mistake was probably the worst, the most horribly unforgivable mistake that a man could make."

His father nodded. Mike knew the old man thought he was about to apologize and it pissed him off.

"It's not my mistake, you stubborn ass. It's yours."

His father's jaw clenched. "Maybe you should go."

"Don't you ever regret the way you've treated your children?"

Mike's mother reached over and laid her hand on his. "Michael, don't."

Mike jerked his hand away. "Doesn't it bother you that you kicked your own fucking son out?"

His father stood. Threw his napkin down. "Get out of my house."

Mike stood in turn. "Fuck you. I'm through following your orders." Their eyes met again and his father's fist clenched at his side. Mike smiled. "Doesn't it bother you that you treated your own daughter like a piece of property?"

"Shut up!"

"That you went out of your way to make her feel like a failure?"

"Don't you talk about her!"

"That you might as well have sliced her wrists open yourself?"

His father lunged for him, their last dinner together attempting to replay itself. But this time Mike was ready, and as the old man rushed in to swing, Mike brought his dinner plate crashing up into his father's temple. Food flew everywhere, little chunks of it hovering in the air as time slowed around him.

His mother screamed. The plate shattered. Blood cascaded down the side of his father's face. The old man spun, confused, shocked, falling to one knee. He placed a hand on the table, pushed himself to standing as his fist swung out blindly, gliding past Mike's nose without connecting.

Mike's knuckles crashed into his father's jaw. He fell back to his knee. Mike hit him again, and again, until he fell to the floor. Mike reached down, jerked his collar up, and pounded fists into his face rhythmically, explosively, like pistons firing, blood splattering on his shirt and on the wall, blood leaking onto the floor, his father's hands flailing, his mother screaming for him to stop but not moving from her seat, his father whimpering like a dying dog, his bones cracking underneath Mike's fists, Mike's hand and arm screaming in pain as the bones in his own knuckles shattered, but he could not stop, *would* not stop, as two decades of abuse and resentment traveled down his arm and into his father's face.

Kill him, the voice in the back of his mind whispered. *Beat him to bloody pulp. Shatter every bone in his face. Crush his windpipe. Stomp on his ribs until his lungs collapse. Kill him! Kill him and take his battered corpse into the dark, offer it to your darling, kill him, blood sacrifice, the doors are open even now—*

He stopped, staggered back. His lungs fought hard for breath. His knuckles sent sharp knives of pain stabbing their way up his arms, into his shoulder, into his head.

The voice inside of him screamed for him to continue, but he was frightened more than he had ever been, even more than when he had listened to the mad whispers calling his name from the dark. He had always had that voice inside of him, had learned to live with it, but now it almost brought him to tears to realize that *it was no longer his voice.*

It belonged to the darkness.

And so do you, my darling. Finish him. Bring him to me.

His mother rushed to her husband's side. She wept as she cradled the old man's head in her arms. His face was unrecognizable, a crimson Rorschach blot stretched across a purple-and-green mottled skull. His father wheezed, rolled around in his mother's arms, his hands still flailing.

What had he done?

KILL HIM GODDAMN YOU!

Mike stumbled like a drunk from the house. His mother's crying echoed after him, accusing him.

The voice in his head taunted him.

Icy rain fell all around him, crashing into his hot flesh, freezing him to the bone. Wind buffeted against him, trying to push him back into the house to finish it.

He felt sick, nauseous, like he was trapped in some fever dream that no matter how hard he fought he could not wake from.

He stumbled to his car, his broken hand hanging useless at his side.

Overhead, thunder rumbled.

★ ★ ★

Jack's long legs reminded her of tall, thin trees swaying in the wind as he shuffled through the basement ahead of her.

"What kind of strange things?"

"Um..." She wasn't sure how to answer that. She laughed. "Well, this is going to sound weird."

"Mmm-hmm."

"But I've been having nightmares."

He paused. "Nightmares?"

"Yeah."

"What kind of nightmares?"

"It involves the building. There was this doctor back when it was a hospital—"

"You've been dreaming about Whaley's fountain, haven't ya?"

She froze.

"Yep. Reckoned that's what ya was dancing around."

"Is that..."

"Common?"

She nodded.

"Don't know about common, but it's recurring, that's for sure." He started walking again and she trotted behind him. "This building gets a hold of all of us sooner or later. Some of us it just gets a little hold of. Others…Well, sometimes it takes a big bite out of some folks." He stopped at a door and fumbled in his pocket for his keys. "This dream was pretty bad, huh?" He unlocked the padlocks on the door.

"…horrible…"

"Mmm-hmm."

"But the dreams aren't all."

They stepped into his workroom. Lights hung everywhere, blasting the room like the sun itself burned inside. Sweat broke out on Eileen's neck.

Jack pulled a rag from his pocket and dabbed his forehead. "You don't live here, do ya miss?"

"No."

"But you know someone that does."

She nodded.

"Someone who's acting peculiar lately."

"Yeah."

"Here's my advice." He pulled a notebook from his shelf. The spine was labeled "Anomalies." He opened it to an empty page, took out his pen, and scribbled. "Just stay away from here. This place ain't right. Some of us have deep roots here. Some of us made promises that they have to keep, jobs that they have to do. But you're not sucked into this place yet. So just get as far away as you can and don't come back. Things are getting worse here. You may not get too many more chances."

One of the lights flickered and Jack's face lost all color.

"What do you mean? What's wrong with this place?"

"I've said too much already, I think."

"But I—"

"It's not for us to know. I shouldn't know as much as I do." He slid the "Anomalies" binder back onto his shelf.

"Jack, listen. I've been—"

He grabbed her shoulders and jerked her toward him. She froze, scared, his beer-scented breath blowing into her face. "Get outta here. Never come back. Ya hear me?"

She couldn't say anything, couldn't move. The intensity of his eyes rooted her to the floor.

"Whoever you know here's lost. If they ain't someone different by now, they will be. Happens to everyone here. It's like goddamn Chernobyl. It's in the fucking air."

"You're hurting me."

He let go of her and she stumbled to the door.

"Listen to what I say, miss. It ain't just piss and vinegar, ya hear?"

She stumbled out into the dark of the basement. What *had* he said? Did he confirm her suspicions, or was he crazy? And what was in that "Anomalies" binder? The word itself conjured images of paranormal activity. If she could only get a peek at it...

She came to a dead end of storage cages. She was so flustered when she left his workroom that she must have taken a wrong turn. She turned to head back, her mind swimming through everything Jack had said, and saw him rushing from his workroom. His hands were full. In one he held a grocery bag with what looked like tubes of hamburger meat inside, while the other held a foot long black case. He fumbled with the locks, slid his keys back into his pockets, and darted down the hall. He bounced off of one of the cages as he passed.

An overhead light reflected off of his keys.

Eileen stared at them, bewildered. They were hooked on a stray piece of wire hanging from the storage cage he had bumped into. Did he notice?

She heard the elevator's doors slide shut and the box rumble up the shaft.

She almost laughed at the timing of it all. She rushed over, unhooked the keys, and darted back to the door. She undid the locks and crept inside. She glanced around the room to see if there was anything else that caught her eye, but the room was mostly tools. She took the binder from the shelf, laid his keys on the table, and then froze. She didn't want to steal from the man, but she also didn't want to get caught having broken into his workroom.

She debated for a few moments until finally deciding that she could take it, read it, and then sneak back down here and leave it outside his door. He would likely suspect her, but so what? If he didn't catch her in the act of breaking and entering, there was little he could do.

One of the lights flickered again and went out.

She shivered.

Eileen left, shut the door behind her, and made her way toward the elevator.

She felt eyes on her as she walked.

The shadows of the basement seemed to writhe in excitement as she passed. She listened, tried to hear footsteps or breathing, but the only sounds were water rushing through pipes and her own footsteps coming down onto the concrete.

As she passed the laundry room she almost gasped.

A young boy stood in the corner by one of the machines, shirtless, staring at her. His glassy eyes and pale skin unnerved her. Something about him was unnatural and he stared at her with an almost sexual glare.

She chastised herself for being frightened of a child, but hurried off just the same.

Once outside the building, she felt a little safer. A little more secure. Her depression and anger at Dennis flooded back again and she almost broke down crying before she even made it to her car.

Thunder rumbled above her and she thought she felt the first few drops of icy rain splash against her scalp. Finally she was in her car, the binder safe in her passenger seat, and driving away from this damned place.

★ ★ ★

The cold stabbed him like daggers, hacking bits of warmth from him with every gust. Where had this goddamn wind come from? It was too early for this kind of weather. Jack ran through the forest, his gun case in one hand, the hamburger meat in the other.

He had been their caretaker for far too long. They were tied to this place somehow. Mark had hinted as much during one of his drunken rages. Jack had turned his head for too many years, had fed them in exchange for pay and the hope that they wouldn't go looking elsewhere for food. But there was something else, something that he hadn't admitted to himself until now.

Feeding them kept the pain away.

He had been one of the survivors of that horrible accident decades ago, and the pain that he had lived with had been damn near crippling. There were times when he thought about ending it all. But when he fed these things, when he kept up his end of what had surely become some kind of infernal bargain with this place, the pain went away.

He didn't care about that anymore. Things were getting worse and the thought of that grate opening, of those things *saying his name*, was too much. He had to end them.

He slid down the hill. He sat the bag of hamburger to the side and pulled his flashlight from his belt. He had been so wrapped up in his own thoughts that he hadn't even bothered to use it, hadn't thought of the shadows that sometimes writhed and whispered here. He was surprised he hadn't had an accident rushing through the dark woods, but he had made this trek so many times over the years that his body knew every step.

He shined the light onto the tunnel. With thunder overhead, an icy rain showered the earth.

The grate was open.

He fumbled with his gun case. Pulled the pistol out. Shined the light into the trees around him. Listened.

Rain smacked against fallen leaves.

He aimed the flashlight down into the tunnel. The light died against the deep black inside.

He cleared his throat. "Dinner time, boys!"

Something growled behind him.

He spun.

One of them stood on the hill above him. He shined the light into its eyes, hoping to disorient it, but it didn't so much as blink. He raised his pistol—

—and something hit him from behind.

He fell forward into soggy leaves, the flashlight flying from his hand. He rolled onto his back and tried to scramble away, but sharp knives clamped into his calf. He screamed.

Black shapes swarmed around him. Hot drool dripped onto him. Their breath reeked of decay, their fur of rot. Another one bit down into his other ankle, crushing the bones. He screamed and fired off a shot. He heard a whimper, but it didn't let go. He squeezed the trigger again and again, unloading the clip into the thing until it finally opened its jaws and fell limp to the side.

He aimed at the one on his calf, fear taking hold, not realizing he had fired too many shots.

Click, click, click.

The air was knocked from him as one slammed its front paws onto his chest. It lowered its head toward his face, hot diseased breath crawling over him and making him gag.

"I told you we would taste you." It grinned.

They dragged him screaming into the tunnel and fell on him, their jaws ripping muscles away, crushing bones, dragging his guts from his body and stringing them down the tube.

The last thing he saw was the grinning one, the one that spoke, holding his severed forearm on the ground with its paws, ripping meat away as it laughed.

★ ★ ★

Mike stood outside of his car, the cold rain pelting his face like jagged pebbles. Raynham loomed over him like his father once did, dominating him, demanding *respect*. His hand, already swollen and purple, throbbed. He felt dazed still, didn't even remember driving home.

Thick ribbons of filthy ice water ran through the parking lot, crashing against the curbs like surf. His eyes were drawn to something sparkling, some shiny thing catching the light while being washed away. It bobbed upward, a larger piece breaking the surface. It looked like one of his anime figurines.

It slammed against the curb hard enough to split into two pieces before being dragged under.

Come to me, Michael.

The voice had traveled through so many permutations since he beat his father nearly to death. His own, the voice of the strange whispers he listened to in the dark, Dennis, Eileen, his parents, Margot.

I need you inside of me, Margot's voice echoed in his head.

The drenched branches of the willow hung to the ground like a dying man reaching for the earth. The wind hit them hard, each individual leaf swaying like raised hackles even though the limbs barely moved. Every so often they would part long enough for him to see Karen inside, her hair drenched, a white T-shirt soaked through to transparency, the pink buds of her nipples shining through as she spun around and around, smiling at Mike all the while.

Dance with me, Michael.

His head felt like it was splitting open. He thought of Zeus birthing Athena from his skull. His stomach was a roiling mass of acid. His hand felt like it ripped itself apart.

He needed to lie down. Close his eyes.

Karen laughed.

He ignored her and walked through the courtyard. The nymphs fondled their breasts as he passed, moaning while the satyrs laughed.

Don't you want us anymore, Michael?

He stumbled through the doors and to the elevator. The box was crowded with no one. They whispered and joked and pressed Mike into the corner. A woman who didn't exist brushed her hand against his crotch, her perfume clinging to his face like a shroud. He closed his eyes, head swimming, body rocking back and forth.

The doors opened and he maneuvered out. He crashed into his apartment, the door banging hard against the wall. Dennis stood at an open window, the cold rain invading the room with every gust of wind. A small puddle formed at his roommate's feet, but Dennis didn't seem to notice.

"What..." Mike almost toppled over. He leaned against the arm of the couch with his good hand, closed his eyes, tried to right himself. "What are you doing?"

"Your sister always liked dancing in the rain."

He couldn't make sense of what Dennis said. His sister? He needed to rest. He fell into his room, collapsing onto his bed. The walls undulated around him, the room pitching back and forth like a ship at sea. A cold wave crashed against the hull, spilling ice water in through his window. He shouldn't have been able to see the supermarket from his bed, but his window pitched upward until it was fully in view.

The parking lot was white, vivid, every color and shadow accented with a dozen busted and filthy yellow lights. Every lamp was lit. How?

Margot slid into bed next to him, her cold hands running up and down his body.

"Where have you been?"

She smiled. Her open mouth held an endless void. "Don't be silly, Michael. I never went anywhere." She kissed him and his lips went numb from the cold.

"You're dead." He didn't know why he said it, but he knew it was true.

She laughed. "Of course I am."

He sat up. His room was empty.

He was alone.

His window was closed. The walls were stable and still.

"...what the fuck is happening?"

Covered in sweat, his skin felt like it was on fire. He climbed from his bed and stepped over to the window. He fought it open with his good hand and let the cold wind crash into his face. He looked out on the tall grass dancing in the field, out onto the supermarket.

All of the parking lot lights were still on. How could that be? He thought he had hallucinated it, but there it was. He leaned out, the rain pummeling the back of his head. The doors stood wide open, long shadows dribbling out onto the sidewalk like wretched vines gasping for sunlight.

I need you in me, Michael. Oh, God, I need you so bad.

"Darling," he whispered.

★ ★ ★

Eileen had driven through the sudden rainstorm down Emory Highway. She hated driving in the rain and, when the wind threatened to push her car from the road and into a ditch, she decided to stop at a Subway and wait out the storm.

She sat in a corner booth, the "Anomalies" binder open

in front of her. She nibbled on a sandwich as she flipped through it, her mind losing the battle of deciphering Jack's strange electrical readings. If she were to trust her first instinct, the readings seemed to indicate that the elevator had been functioning without power being driven to it for the past year. But that, as well as the other little oddities she thought she read, was impossible. That was just too bizarre, too much of a leap past the simple idea of ghosts and into the realm of fantasy.

She flipped a few more pages in until she stumbled upon a series of hand-written notes scrawled across the pages in a rainbow of inks. These were almost as difficult to decode as the electrical readings. She flipped to the last page and saw what Jack had scribbled as she stood in his workroom:

Some girl here. Having the nightmare about fountain. Have to mention to Margot whenever she gets back.

The nightmare? Have others had the same dream that she did? She flipped a few pages back.

More whispering from radio. Ones from the roof sound like soldiers issuing marching orders. Ones from the basement sound like children singing a lullaby. Ones from laundry room sound like two people screwing.

She flipped a few more pages in. Newspaper articles were taped to the pages. There were several on the Crossroads Killer. That didn't surprise her. But there were others, scores of articles dating over the past twenty-five years. Put together they were a litany of disappearances, suicides, accidents, and crimes of passion. She had taken a Statistics of Criminology class last semester and knew that so many violent crimes in one place weren't statistically possible. Even in areas of high gang violence, the pattern here wouldn't have made sense.

"Eileen?"

She looked up, half expecting to see Dennis. It was Jason. She quickly closed the binder. "Hey. How's it going?"

"Not bad. Just grabbing a bite to eat. You?"

"Just had to get in from the storm."

"Yeah. It's a little hairy out there. If it weren't for my Jeep, I don't think I would drive in it, but that thing handles like crazy. Mind if I join you?"

She shrugged and moved her things out of the way. He slid in across from her and unwrapped his sandwich.

"What are you working on?" He pointed at the binder.

"Uh...Just some Statistics homework. Nothing exciting."

"Definitely sounds dull."

She shrugged again.

"Excuse me for asking, but are you alright? You seem kinda down."

She didn't like to talk about her personal problems, especially with someone she didn't know very well, but she felt oddly comfortable with Jason. "Dennis and I just broke up."

"Oh. Shit. I'm sorry to hear that. By 'just broke up' you mean...?"

"Like, half an hour ago."

"Damn. I'm sorry. You wanna talk about it?"

"What's to say? I caught him cheating on me."

"Karen, huh?"

Eileen just stared.

"I'm sorry. I...well, I've seen them together a couple of

times and—"

She held her hand up. "I don't want to know."

"Yeah. Of course. Sorry."

"It's okay. Actually, do you mind if we talk about something else?"

"Sure. What would you like to talk about?"

"Ummm...let's see..." She smiled. "I dunno. How about your band?"

"Okay. What do you wanna know?"

She asked perfunctory questions about how the group had met, how long they'd played together, what cities they'd played in, and he answered with long and funny stories. When they were done eating he walked her to her car. She was about to ask him to call her sometime when she saw that her tire was flat. She knelt to get a closer look and almost broke into tears.

"What is it?"

She stood and slammed her fist down onto the wet roof. "Someone slashed my goddamn tire."

He knelt to get a look himself. "Jesus."

"Shit!" She kicked the hubcap.

"Do you have a spare?"

"No. I let Kirstin use it the last time she got a flat."

Jason looked around. "Tell ya what. I've got AAA but, like a dumbass, I don't have the info with me. Why don't we ride up to the apartment, I'll give them a call, you can have a glass of wine and relax a little and then we'll get this whole thing sorted out."

"I couldn't."

"I insist." He smiled.

She smiled back. "Thanks."

★ ★ ★

Dennis stared out the window as the storm grew more and more furious. Was he still dreaming? He had a hard time telling these days.

The weather report, if it was indeed real and not something sprouting from his subconscious, said that the storm looked to be one of the worst in the last ten years. Flash flood warnings were springing up all over the Valley and a tornado watch was in effect. He didn't care. He was too busy watching Allison dance.

She swirled under the tree, her shirt soaked through, Karen's hair hanging wet in her face, dancing in tiny circles, smiling and waving.

Headlights fired up the hill, cutting through the low branches of the willow and setting Allison on fire. She stopped dancing and stared as a Jeep drove past. It pulled into the parking lot and screeched to a halt. Allison raised Karen's hand, index finger extended, pointing at the Jeep, her eyes locked on Dennis.

He followed her finger and watched as one of his neighbors (he couldn't remember his name) climbed from the driver's side, walked around to the passenger's, and opened the door.

Eileen stepped out.

The two of them darted through the rain and toward the building.

—She's going to fuck him.
She's been fucking him,

taking his cock deep inside of her
when you're not around,
laughing with him about you,
thinking of him when she's been with you.

He shook his head. Looked back down to the tree.
No one was there.

He turned and glanced at the television. A weatherman
stood in front of a shopping mall as rainwater flooded the
parking lot. Dennis closed his eyes. His head felt filled with
cotton. He shook it clear, looked down at the Jeep again.

This was no dream. He was awake now and Eileen had
gone into the building with that guy.

Allison slid Karen's cold, wet hand down his cheek.

—He's sliding her pants off as we speak,
lover—

"...no..."

—Oh, yes.
Make them suffer for mocking you—

She turned his face to hers and kissed him with Karen's
lips.

—I would never do that to you, would I—

"No. You wouldn't."

—But she is.

He's sliding his cock inside of her
right this second,
asking her to tell him
how much better a fuck he is than you.
It's shameful.
Disrespectful—

"What should I do?"

—Go, my darling.
Go earn your respect—

Chapter Sixteen

Michael. I need you.

I'm afraid.

I know. Everyone is, at first. But there's no reason to be.

I'm sorry I wasn't there for you.

I forgive you, just like I forgave Dennis. Come join me. Margot's here, too. She wants you with us.

What happened that night? Why did you do it?

You know what happened.

Not everything.

I was pregnant. I had known for about a week. I told Dennis and he said he couldn't handle it. That I should get an abortion.

I didn't know.

It wasn't his fault. He was young. Confused. That's what Dad and I had been fighting about when I came to your door. Dad refused to let me do it. He was going to force me to have the baby, said I could stay until it was born, but then he wanted me to move out.

Oh my God, Allison. If I had known that's what you were fighting about—

Would you have opened your door then?

…

You were young, too. We all were. We were children dealing with too much. I probably needed to be on anti-depressants.

Dad would never have let you.

I know. That's why I never saw a doctor about it. I suppose it was inevitable I'd do what I did. I'm only sorry that you had to be the one to find me.

There was so much blood...

In here, there is no blood. There's no flesh to cut, no tears to shed. There's no pain. Only cold. Only black.

I feel like I've lost my mind.

You have.

I'm still so scared.

It's okay. I'll help you through it, darling.

What should I do?

You know what to do.

Chapter Seventeen

Eileen sat on Jason's couch and sipped from a glass of Merlot. She watched the rain pound against his window as he crashed around in a drawer behind her, the light of his candles fluttering across the walls. She had never seen a man with so many candles. It was a little odd. Surely he wasn't gay? No. It was obvious that he was coming on to her.

"Having a hard time finding it?"

He laughed. "A bit, yeah."

"Can I ask you something?"

"Sure."

"You ever notice anything weird about this place?"

She heard the drawer slam and another open. "What do you mean by weird?"

"Well...um...this is going to sound crazy, but...*supernatural.*"

"You mean like ghosts and stuff?"

She took another sip. "Yeah. I guess."

"I used to find this place strange. Sure. I mean, it's different from anything we've ever been taught, anything that we're used to. Ya know?"

"Yeah."

"But when my darling whispers to me at night, it's so beautiful, so perfect."

"Your darling?" She turned around, but he had gone around a corner. She heard him rummaging inside of another room.

"Yes. She's my muse, really. I give her what she needs and she inspires me. Satisfies me. Provides for me."

Eileen was confused. Who was he talking about?

"Have you heard her yet?"

"...who?"

He walked back into the room, a large combat knife hanging from his hand. "No. I suppose you haven't."

"Um...look, Jason. I don't mean to be rude but you're not making any sense. What's with the knife?"

He glanced down at it and laughed. "Sorry. This is probably a little unexpected, huh?"

She laughed back. "Yeah. I'd say so."

He walked over to her, smiled again, and grabbed a handful of her hair. He wrenched her head back, the glass of Merlot spilling onto the floor. She started to scream but the cold blade at her throat killed all sound. "Now, I hope I'm not going to have to use this. Yet."

Tears leaked down her face. What had happened? What was he doing? This had all seemed so *normal*.

"...please," she whimpered.

He pulled the knife away and reached for a roll of duct tape sitting on the coffee table.

Panic flooded through her. She knew she had one chance.

She bucked her hips, her hand shooting toward his throat. He fell to the side, crashing into the coffee table, strands of her hair still twisted between his knuckles.

Candles fell to the floor, wax splattering over the hardwood.

Eileen was up and at the door. He thundered behind her. She spun, the light catching the knife as it flew toward her face.

She ducked and scrambled to the side. The knife slammed into the door several inches deep. He planted his foot against the door and jerked it free.

"Dammit, Eileen, I—"

As he spun around, a nail file slammed into his collar bone with a crunch.

She backed away, her keys jangling from the embedded file, blood soaking his shirt. He grabbed it and pulled, screaming, but it wouldn't budge.

She dove for her purse. It skidded across the floor, the contents spilling everywhere.

Her keys jangled behind her.

She grabbed for the pepper spray as he gripped her ankle.

★ ★ ★

The hall leaned over Dennis as he crept toward Jason's apartment. Some of the light bulbs must have died. The shadows were deep, almost tangible. They clustered around him as he flexed and unflexed his fingers.

His heart felt like it was going to explode in his chest. It pumped acid through his veins and all he could think of was destroying something.

A grunt drifted down the hall. As apartment 234 came into view, the door cracked open. Candlelight flickered in the doorway.

He peeked through the crack.

Jason, naked, his back to the door, the muscles of his shoulders and buttocks tensed. Head tilted back. Eyes closed.

He turned. Stepped away. Muscles quivered. He could taste blood. He saw fire, great sheets of flame painting the hallway, erupting from the floor, reaching upward, grabbing at the ceiling, pulling it down onto everyone's heads. A pressure built inside of him. If he didn't release it, didn't lash out soon, his muscles would rip themselves from his bones.

He took a deep breath. Closed his eyes.

He heard a whimper. A grunt.

"Shut up, bitch." Very faint.

Eileen would never let someone talk to her like that.

Dennis went back to the apartment. He nudged the door open.

She was on her stomach. Her hands behind her back. Wrists held together with duct tape. Jason twisted atop her, fighting with her belt. She squirmed and bucked, pressed the buckle into the floor. Blood ran down his chest onto her jeans.

The candlelight ricocheted from the tip of a knife hanging loosely from his hand.

The next few seconds were little more than snapshots.

Eileen's eyes wide as she scrambles backward.

Jason looking at her, angry.

Dennis' shoulder colliding with Jason's hip.

The knife hitting the ground, spinning, sliding.

Jason's head bouncing from the hardwood floor.

Dennis snarling, his fists firing like pistons, Jason's face crushed under the blows.

Blood splattering onto the wall, the sofa, the floor.

Jason's fingers scrambling for the knife, breaking as Dennis grabs them and snaps them back.

Jason's scream cut off by an elbow smashing into his windpipe.

The fog cleared. Not completely, but enough for Dennis to realize that the weeping, bleeding lump of flesh underneath him couldn't harm anyone any more.

A quivering ball whimpered in the corner. Shadows covered it. A part of Dennis realized it was Eileen, wanted to go to her, tell her everything was okay. But his instincts still had him.

Blood dripped from his fists. The burning in his knuckles told him that some of it was his own. His nostrils flared wide, taking in the scents of the room: thick burning wax, the coppery smell of blood, the acrid musk in the air.

He grabbed the roll of duct tape from the floor.

Jason tried to say something as Dennis strapped his wrists and ankles together behind his back. Dennis slammed his face into the ground again with a loud crunch.

Crying from the corner. "Ohgodohshitohgod."

He grabbed Jason by the ankles and jerked him toward the bathroom.

"Dennis? What are you doing?"

He hefted the squirming, bloody mess up and into the tub.

—Bleed it for me, my darling.
Bleed it like a pig for me—

He marched back into the living room and grabbed the knife.

"Dennis?"

He stared at the crying thing in the corner. A face slowly came into focus.

Eileen? Why was she crying? Why were her clothes ripped?

—Bleed them all out for me, darling.
The whore should leak out onto the wooden floor,
slowly,
slowly.
Stick her in the gut and leave her.
I want to drink her pain—

Eileen fought her way to her feet, her face bruised and swollen, her shirt ripped open to reveal a scratched, pink breast dotted with blood.

—Yes, blood!
She has so much of it in her.
Spill some of it for me—

"Eileen?"

He shook the fog off and went to her. He sliced the tape from her hands and held her close. She pressed herself against him and cried.

"I didn't—"

"Shhh…" He cradled her head in his arms.

They stood like that for several minutes, rocking back and forth as Eileen cried harder than she ever had before.

When she had finally calmed, he took her up to his apartment. She shuffled slowly, staring at her feet the entire time.

"Do you want me to call the police?"

She nodded, then turned and went into the bathroom and closed the door.

Dennis felt sick to his stomach. He stumbled over to the corner table and grabbed his phone. A part of him wanted to go into the bathroom and hold Eileen as long as she needed him to, but she needed privacy. Another part of him wanted to march back downstairs and take that goddamn knife and—

—YES!

YES, BABY!

OH GOD!

SLIDE IT INSIDE OF HIM!

DO IT!

I WANT YOU TO WASH THE FLOOR IN HIS BLOOD!

I WANT TO SWIM IN HIS INNARDS—

He sunk down into his couch and closed his eyes. Allison's voice sounded like it was in his ear, just the way it sounded in his dreams. Was he losing his mind?

He flipped open his cell phone and dialed. He was greeted with silence. He looked at the display to see a NO SERVICE message flashing at him.

He tried the landline next. All he was greeted with was static. Goddamn storm.

He went to Mike's door and pounded. There was no

answer.

He pushed the door open. Mike's phone sat next to his computer. Dennis picked it up and dialed 911. Again, he was met with silence and NO SERVICE.

"Fuck." He smacked his hand against the wall hard enough to shake some of Mike's actions figures from a shelf. He stormed back out into the living room.

He knocked on the bathroom door. "Eileen?" No answer. "Baby, my phone doesn't get a signal so I'm going to find a phone to call from, okay?"

"...okay..."

He wanted to say more, but had no idea what he could possibly say.

He went across the hall and banged on Margot's door. No one answered.

Frustrated, confused, worried, he did the only thing he could think of. He went back to Jason's apartment. He stepped inside and looked around. No sight or sound of the bastard. Dennis peeked back into the bathroom.

There he was, beaten, bloodied, and broken, lying in the tub, his consciousness elsewhere. Just looking at him disgusted Dennis.

—Finish him for me.
Please...
I'm aching for you to—

Dennis grabbed the phone in the living room, but there was no dial tone. The storm had severed all communication to the building.

He paced to the window and pressed his forehead

against the cold glass. He closed his eyes and listened to the wind howl outside, the rain firing like machine guns against the building.

When he opened his eyes they were drawn to the supermarket's parking lot.

All of the lights were on.

He saw movement on the concrete. Someone walked toward the building. He tried to focus through the rain. Whoever it was carried a large gas can, like the kind of emergency can that Eileen used to keep in her trunk. What were they doing?

The figure paused and glanced back at Raynham.

"Mike?"

His roommate turned back toward the supermarket. What the hell was he doing?

Mike walked up to the supermarket and started pouring gas onto the ground.

"Jesus Christ!" Dennis darted out the door.

★ ★ ★

He had been listening to the siren call of the market since he had taken poor Lucy's body inside. He realized that now. All the dreams, the whispering, even Margot—it all came from that deep black. It called to him, had seeped into his blood, had almost forced him to kill his father. He could resist it no longer. He had to plunge himself inside.

He had taken the heavy gas can, an old aluminum model like his father had always used, from the trunk of the car. Eileen had showed it to him when she sold him the thing, relating a story about how she and her sister were stranded in the mountains as teenagers when her sister's car had ran out of gas. It was heavy. He guessed it held three gallons. His fingers ached around the handle. He wished he could switch arms, but his swollen and shattered hand couldn't even flex its fingers.

As he waded through the field, already muddy from the downpour, he felt strong. Confident. Determined. If he had to step into the darkness, he would make sure that he was the last.

Cold, slimy grass clutched at his skin like fingers from a thousand corpses. His clothing was soaked through, and he shivered from the chill. The whispering from inside the blackness had made so much sense to him. His darling waited for him, needed him, *hungered* for him.

He stepped onto the cracked concrete of the parking lot. It looked so strange illuminated, as though he were getting a glimpse of what it would have looked like had construction not halted, what it would have become if his darling had not been so hungry.

He stopped and glanced back to Raynham. Was Dennis up there somewhere? Did he know what horrible wonders slept beneath the earth here?

The darkness writhed like ebon serpents stretching from between the doors and sniffing the air. A few of them slithered out into the rain, the heavy drops vanishing into their non-flesh.

One of them struggled out to Mike's foot, wrapped itself around his ankle. Its touch was searing cold. He hissed and yanked his foot back.

The serpent slithered away. It seemed offended.

Mike bent over and pulled his pants leg up. His ankle

was white, ringed in a purple-red-black mottling that had gone completely numb.

He unscrewed the cap. The smell of gasoline wafted up and smacked him in the face.

—Come to me, Michael. Come my darling—

He splashed the gasoline onto the boarded up windows of the place, careful not to get too near the tendrils of black that reached for him. He soaked the base of the support columns underneath the awning.

Then, without hesitation, he raised the can high over his head. He had to use his broken hand to steady it, and the pain was excruciating, but he ground his teeth together, clenched his eyes shut, and poured.

The gasoline cascaded over him like baptismal waters, burning fumes filling his lungs with every breath. It rinsed the pain away from him, rinsed away all of his weakness, caught every one of his sins in its flowing grasp and carried them off.

The waterfall dwindled away until the can only dribbled onto his soaked head. He sat it down with a loud *clank* and took a rag from his back pocket. He wiped the gasoline from around his eyes and opened them. The fumes burned his retinas, clouded everything in front of him, and wrenched tears from his sockets. But he had never seen anything so clearly in all of his life.

Faces swam up at him in the black. Each was dark and still, carved from obsidian. Their empty sockets stared at him, unmoving lips allowing whispers to escape. Everyone that he had ever known and loved whispered to him from those still mouths.

He took the rag and wiped it through his hair until it was damp. It went easily into the mouth of the can, almost as though the metal chewed and swallowed it. He thought for a moment that it would fall completely in, but it hovered about the lip just long enough for him to roll the tip up and hang it over the side.

He took Margot's lighter, a Zippo she had loved so much, and lit the rag. The tip smoldered for a moment before igniting.

"Mike!"

He turned to see Dennis rushing toward him. His roommate stopped before coming under the awning, staring wide eyed at the darkness struggling its way out into the night.

"Jesus Christ..."

"You see it now, Dennis?"

"What...what is..."

"It's the darkness inside of us. It feeds on it, bathes in it, pools it all in its heart."

"What?"

"Margot knew. So does probably everyone here. No one knows all of it, but everyone has a piece of the puzzle. Awful pieces."

"You're not going in there, are you?"

Mike nodded. "I have to. It's gotten hold of me. I didn't know that when I brought Lucy up here it would take it as a sacrifice, but it did. I'm bound to the thing."

"Lucy? What are you talking about? What's in there?"

"I think it's a Fallen Angel, but I could be wrong."

"You're not making any sense. Let's get away from this

thing, go inside, talk about—"

"It's too late for that. My darling needs me in her. And I ache for it, Dennis. I have to enter her, just once. Her nightmares are getting worse, making everyone's nightmares in that building worse. It feeds from all of the shit that people do here. Each time it feeds it wakes a little. I can't let it wake up."

"But, Mike, that doesn't—"

"You've always been like a big brother to me. I'm sorry for everything."

"There's nothing to be sorry for."

"She came to me for help, you know."

"Who?"

"Allison."

Dennis couldn't say anything to that.

"The night that her and Dad got into a fight. The night she..." Mike sniffed and a tear rolled down his face. "She came to my door and knocked. She was crying and just needed to talk to someone. But Dad had me so brainwashed at the time. I was afraid to. Isn't that fucked up?"

"It wasn't your fault, Mike. If anyone was to blame it was me. She called me that night and I didn't answer."

"You were scared. But me...? I pretended to be asleep. She beat on my door and cried and begged for someone to talk to and I pretended to be fucking asleep."

Dennis was crying now, too. "Mike, please..." He took a step toward his friend.

"No! Don't! Stay right there!"

Dennis stopped. The ribbons of black writhed around the gas can, curious as to what was inside.

"I pretended to be asleep and she went into the bathroom. I heard the water running and later, when I came out to piss, I found her. There was so much blood. So much..." Mike looked into the dark.

What are you doing, Michael? You know I forgive you, baby. Just come to me.

Mike grabbed the can.

Dennis took a step toward him. "Mike, I—"

"I'm sorry," Mike said and touched the flaming rag to his shirt. The cloth ignited, flame swimming over him, embracing him. Soon his jeans had caught fire, too. His skin bubbled and screamed under his clothes, his blood boiling inside of him. The pain drowned out all sounds, all sights. The only thing that existed was the fire draping over him.

The flame smothered his face as it raced to his hair. The smell of burning cloth filled his nostrils, followed by the smell of bacon left in its own grease too long. He knew he smelled himself.

He screamed, fire leaping down his throat, and stumbled into one of the columns. Flames shot up it, catching the underside of the awning on fire. He clutched the searing can, glowing from the heat inside, to his chest. Margot stood in the darkness with arms outstretched and he rushed toward her, ricocheting from the walls as he did. The pain was excruciating as he plunged into the black.

And then he felt nothing.

And then he was nothing.

And it was glorious.

★ ★ ★

In the dark it screamed.

Chapter Eighteen

The flames hugged him as Mike careened through the open doors. Dennis screamed, darted after him, but the tendrils coiled back upon themselves, blocking the way and following Mike into darkness.

The flames leaped from his body as he plunged his way in, catching every beam and timber on fire.

A giant gust of wind carried the flame in Dennis' path like a wall. The building shouldn't have gone up so quickly. Much of it was stone and glass.

But it did. The awning was completely aflame. Chunks of it fell to the concrete. A sheet of fire draped over the boarded windows, leaping out into the parking lot and racing toward the rest of the half-finished buildings.

It wasn't possible. But there it was, fingers of fire dancing their way from building to building, igniting each in turn, like

*—Chinese paper dolls
burned in sacrifice
for the King of Hell—*

like

*—a wicker man
stuffed with screaming children
ignited for the Gods—*

like

*—candles lit in church
for Christ's glory—*

Dennis stumbled back, his head unsteady. Whispering floated from the burning maw of the supermarket, whispering that he couldn't make out, could only tell was confused and hurt.

The flames raced across the rooftops and through the foundations and he knew where it would head.

He turned and sprinted through the rain toward Raynham.

The field of grass caught fire behind him.

★ ★ ★

Miles below, a brilliant flame that reminded it of the beginning ignited. Memories of light and warmth flooded in and it nurtured them, sending them out along what passed for its body, feeling them in every cell, every atom.

A thousand explosions went off in its cold tomb, each one sending spasms of pain along the thin threads connecting it to all of those tiny minds.

It was too much for them.

They shattered.

It drank it in.

The walls separating its dreams from reality crashed down around it.

★ ★ ★

Eileen sat on the lid of the toilet and cried. Her body shook so hard she worried her bones would break. Nothing in her life would ever be the same. How could it be?

Her nightmare had been brought to life.

A cockroach scrambled across the white tile in front of her.

She heard the front door open. She hoped Dennis had found a working phone.

Feet shuffled across the floor and stopped in front of the bathroom door. There was a soft knock.

She struggled through the sobs to speak. "Did you find a phone?"

A fist pounded on the door.

"Dennis?"

Again.

A roach scurried under the door.

The pounding grew frenzied, shaking the door in its frame.

"DENNIS!"

Roaches flooded into the bathroom, running across the tile and up the door.

Eileen screamed.

Chapter Nineteen

Fire chased him through the field. He glanced back once and the entire sky glowed red. The rain poured harder and lightning arced across the sky.

There were shapes in the flames, native warriors butchering one another, soldiers tossing the bodies of countless prisoners into shallow ditches.

He ran faster.

He sprinted toward the building, cut a corner, and froze. Eileen's nightmare had come to impossible life in the fountain. The stone nymph ground against the satyr, his hands rubbing all over her breasts as he kissed her neck.

—*My woman is for you and yours is mine*—

Dennis turned his eyes away and sprinted by. He was hallucinating. Had to be. Dear God, let him be.

A lifeless body floated in the pool. Something bumped into it from underneath, nudging it toward the wall with a small *splash*. A muffled scream echoed from inside Raynham followed by what sounded like shotguns firing.

He rushed into the first floor hallway.

A pool of blood spread across the floor. A dark trail led away from it and under a closed door. Bloody handprints surrounded the doorknob, dotted the wall around it.

Another scream from somewhere above him.

The elevator *dinged* open.

Dennis gasped.

Marie Callahan hung from the ceiling, a length of water hose wrapped around her neck, her face purple, eyes bulging from their sockets, tongue rolled out over her lips.

He took the stairwell, sprinting up the stairs two at a time. As he approached the second floor landing he heard grunting and slowed. A woman's leg came into view, her skirt hiked up far enough to reveal the swell of her ass.

He rounded the corner and saw her pressed against the wall, clutching a man's head close as he thrust into her, grunting every time.

Her wrists were open and leaked blood down the back of the man's filthy suit.

Dennis slid by and the thick, sour smell of rot hit him. The man turned his head and grunted. His skull was collapsed in on one side, his eyes and mouth sewn shut with black wire.

Dennis scrambled backwards up the stairs, almost falling.

When he reached the third floor the door wouldn't budge. He rammed his shoulder against it over and over until he could squeeze through.

Kurt Hagen and Carl Petrie sat slumped over one another against it, the backs of their heads missing, bits of brain and skull dripping down the door.

He didn't know what had happened to them, but wasn't waiting to find out. He rushed to his apartment and dove in, slamming the door behind him and fastening the locks.

He ran to the window. The fire had made it across the field. It was like an ocean of gasoline sloshed around out there and someone had thrown a match in. They didn't have much time.

"Eileen!"

He went to the bathroom. The door was open, the bathroom empty. Cockroaches ran across the floor and the tub, climbing the walls over the sink.

"Eileen!"

He ran to his bedroom and threw the door open.

Cockroaches swarmed over the walls, the floor, the bed. A few fat, red ones fluttered through the air. They hit the closet hard, thumping against the door like a knocking fist.

Eileen screamed from behind it.

"Eileen!" He ran to it, crunching bugs under his heel. A giant roach sat on the doorknob, flapping its wings in irritation. He swatted it away as another collided with the back of his neck. It scrambled up and into his hair. He rubbed his head frantically until it flew away.

—They're awful excited, aren't they—

He spun around at the sound of Allison's voice. Karen's flesh sat in his mother's rocking chair naked, smiling, her nipples erect. Her legs were spread, one foot propped on the corner of his bed. Tiny roaches covered her inner thighs. A fat one crawled up her abdomen.

His stomach lurched, bile rising in the back of his throat, at the sight of long antennae feeling the air. They twitched this way and that before their owner, a slender brown roach, pulled free from between her legs and dropped to the floor.

Another one soon followed. The horde rushing from the chair and under his bed was too much for him. He put his hands on his knees and vomited.

—Oh, baby. Don't worry.
They weren't in me when you were.
I didn't start birthing them until a few minutes ago.
I don't know why.
Lloyd's nightmares, I think—

He hadn't slowed since attacking Jason but now, facing this thing wearing Karen's meat that said it was Allison, roaches buzzing and chittering around him, gunshots and screams coming from somewhere down the hall, his mind couldn't take it. None of his time with her —with *it* — was a dream. Nothing he had seen here tonight was in his imagination. Mike's death was horribly real.

Dennis fell to one knee, clutching at his hair. He knew he should grab Eileen and run, but all he could do was rock back and forth.

Karen's fingers found his jaw and tilted his face toward her.

—You want this to be over, don't you—

He nodded.

—Oh, darling. It will be.
Very soon.
But the supermarket's gone,
so we'll have to do this

the old fashioned way—

She handed him his pocket knife.

—You should get rid of Eileen first.
Just open a little hole in her abdomen
and my children will take care of the rest.
They're awful hungry.
It won't be quick,
and it will be painful,
but it's the best way.
Then you can open your own veins.
Can you do that—

He stared at the knife in his hands. What was she asking
him to do?

—I'm asking you to do the same thing I did, Dennis. Just open
your veins
and let the floor drink you up.
It only hurts for the first minute or so.
I want you to know what I went through.
You owe me that much—

Roaches scurried over his legs. He stared at Allison's
eyes sparkling from inside of Karen's skull. Was this thing
really her?
She slapped him.

—Of course I am.
I'm the girl that you impregnated and abandoned.

The girl who loved you
and who you forced to kill herself—

Oh God. He had, hadn't he?

—You damned me to this.
Now it's your turn.
Open her gut, baby—

Eileen screamed again.

He glanced to the closet. The roaches sat still on the door, a few of them twitching in excitement.

He turned back to Karen's face, to Allison's eyes. "No."

She shoved him onto his back and mounted his chest. Her thighs squeezed his ribcage.

—Do it, my darling. You owe me—

"No."

She scooted farther up on his chest, grinding her pelvis into his face. Something tickled his lips as it tried to crawl from inside of her and into his mouth.

—Sacrifice is sweeter,
but I suppose I'll have to end you both—

He bucked his hips hard, exploding up into a bridge. She fell from his face and he scrambled over into a sprawl. He wiped the roach, damp with afterbirth, from his mouth.

Karen's body fought to sit and Dennis slammed his fist into her face. He felt her nose give way and hit her again.

This time her jaw shattered and she tumbled over backwards, choking and sputtering. Blood spilled from her nostrils and lips and coated her cheeks.

—*GODDAMN YOU*—

The roaches flapped their wings, agitated. They flew from the closet door, from the walls, from the floor, swarming at Dennis, colliding into him with enough force to crunch their little bodies. They flew at his eyes, his mouth.

He held his hands in front of his face, lowered his head, rushed to the door. "Eileen! Come on!"

She bolted from the closet, frantically wiping roaches from her clothes. He followed her into the living room and slammed the bedroom door shut behind him. They wiped the bugs from each other as several hit the other side of the wood with hard, loud thumps.

A few crawled under the door and Eileen stomped them to bloody pulp. "What do we do?"

Dennis rushed to the window. Flames crawled up the base of the building. "Raynham's on fire. We've got to get out of here."

In the hallway, someone screamed.

"What's out there?"

He opened his pocket knife. "I don't know, but if we stay here..."

She nodded. Took his hand. Squeezed it.

They sprinted to the front door.

He squeezed her hand and threw it open.

They stepped out into Hell.

Chapter Twenty

Eileen had been through so much in the past few hours that her mind was starting to give. This had to be post-traumatic stress, she told herself. This couldn't be happening. The hall was dark. Blue light flickered from an open door with cadence like Morse code, illuminating the dead man propped against a brain-splattered door. She thought she recognized him. Kurt something?

Dennis stopped. "There were two of them," he whispered.

"What?"

"Carl Petrie's missing."

"Was he alright?"

Dennis held the knife in front of him and inched his way down the hall. "Someone had blown his brains out."

Had they stolen his body? She didn't know and didn't want to find out.

The heavy odor of smoke drifted into the hallway. She wiped her eyes with her free hand and glanced behind her, paranoid that Karen and her roaches crept after them. The hall was empty.

As they passed Kurt's body, Dennis nudged it with his

foot. The torso shook and slid down the door, the head making a hollow *thunk* when it hit the floor. Dennis grabbed the handle to the door—

—and was taken off his feet.

Eileen jumped as a dark mass collided into him, lifting him up and slamming him into the wall. The knife skidded across the floor.

The flickering blue light of the television revealed Carl Petrie, half of his face gone, chunks of gore dribbling onto Dennis' face.

One hand tightened around Dennis' throat. With his other, Carl worked a finger into Dennis' mouth.

His left eye no longer had a socket. It turned toward Eileen from inside of a gnarled lump of red flesh.

She screamed.

★ ★ ★

The fat finger tasted like sour milk. Dennis gagged as it forced itself past his lips, over his tongue. It wedged against his cheek and tugged, trying to tear his mouth open like a fish on a hook. The pain was excruciating. Dennis bucked, punched him in what was left of his face, but the thing that used to be Carl didn't budge. He knew he only had once choice.

He bit down hard on the finger. Locked his jaws. Wrenched his head back and forth like a dog.

Cold blood spilled into his mouth. Muscle parted. His teeth met bone. The hand around his neck tightened and stars exploded in his eyes. Carl half grinned at him.

Eileen struck Carl hard in the face. Blood and jelly

plopped onto Dennis' jaw. She hit him again and again, his eye turning to mush, his face disintegrating from the blows. It took Dennis a second to realize she held his knife.

She grunted, cried, hacked at the thing's face until chips of bone flew, until its grip loosened and it slumped over motionless on the floor.

The pressure in his head and neck vanished as he sucked in a breath. It felt like an orgasm. He coughed.

She dropped the knife. "What the hell—"

"I dunno, but we don't have time to figure it out." He scrambled to his feet, grabbed the gory knife, and fought the door open.

★ ★ ★

—*Eileen*—

She looked into an open apartment. The television flashed images of the storm. A woman sat on the couch, a baby in her arms. She rocked it back and forth, her nipple pressed against its mouth. Its head hung limp from its neck, mouth open, eyes wide and cloudy. It was dead.

The woman didn't notice. She continued to cram her nipple into its mouth.

In the darkness at the back of the room, something shifted. Its white form moved between the shadows, between the pages of books on a shelf, between fibers on the carpet.

—*Step inside, Eileen*—

Its voice was high-pitched, yet gravelly.

—The wonders in here will take you away.
The fire is hungrier than I am,
and much slower to work.
You won't like it as much as what I have to offer. Isn't that right,
Sarah?
Didn't I treat Peggy well?
And little Charlie—

The woman on the couch stared at her baby's corpse and nodded.

Something in its voice made a twisted kind of sense. How could they hope to escape? Better to offer herself up than to face what waited for her in the halls.

"Eileen!" Dennis grabbed her by the arm and jerked her into the stairwell. He slammed the door behind her. "Here." He pointed to his face. "Focus on me. Forget everything else, okay?"

"Yeah. Sorry. I—"

Another scream, this time below them.

Dennis inched down the stairs. As they rounded the corner, eyes met hers. They were a woman's. Dead. Glassy. She lay on her back, blood spreading out below sliced wrists, as a wretched corpse plunged in and out of her, grunting through sewn lips.

She held Dennis tighter and turned her head away.

They turned the corner and Dennis stopped. She heard the ripping, tearing sounds, heard the growling, and didn't want to look.

★ ★ ★

A pack of large, black hounds paced around. Their fur was shaggy and splotched with dried blood. Terry Crowley was spread out on the ground between them. They had torn his chest open, his ribs jutting out into the air at odd angles. His intestines were strung around the corridor and the dogs feasted on parts of him. His body twitched, his eyes staring past Dennis, his hand reaching out for help...

One of the dogs made eye contact with Dennis. It stepped forward and emitted a low, deep growl.

The other dogs stopped chewing, dropping bits of Terry onto the floor, and stared.

"Back up." Dennis and Eileen walked backwards up the stairs.

One of the dogs followed.

They darted to the second floor door and dove out into the hallway. Dennis shouldered the door shut, wedging it firmly into its frame. It shook as the dog rammed against it from the other side.

A loud blast. The window behind them shattered.

He glanced up in time to see a large, bald man stomping towards them, his shirtless torso covered in tattoos, pumping a shotgun for a second shot.

Dennis turned to the door across from him and slammed his shoulder against it. Pain shot through his arm. He ground his teeth together and hit it again. It flew open and he fell inside, dragging Eileen behind him, just as another shot fired in the hallway.

He jumped to his feet, slammed the door, grabbed the bookshelf next to it, tipped it over. It crashed onto the ground, spilling books onto the floor, and he shoved it against the door.

The smell of smoke was stronger on this floor, burning his eyes and lungs. His ears rang from the shot.

Eileen rushed into the kitchen and ripped drawers from cabinets, scattering their contents across the tile.

"What are you doing?"

"Looking for something."

"What?"

"I don't fucking know! A gun, a meat cleaver—something to help us get past him!"

The door shook.

Dennis walked toward her, but stopped when he saw the blood. She caught the look in his eyes and looked behind her, where a large red puddle soaked into the carpet. Tiny, bloody hand prints covered the wall.

Whimpering. "...no...please..."

Dennis threw his pocket knife down and grabbed a butcher knife from the floor. "Stay here."

"But I—"

"Shhh!"

He tiptoed through the apartment, following the sounds to a bedroom.

An old man sat in a corner. Three other bodies lay across the room, butchered like pigs. Crimson gashes carved up the man's face, neck, chest and arms.

"No," he pleaded. "Please. It's me. Grandpa."

A group of young children walked toward him. None looked older than eight or nine. They were splashed with red stains. Their hands and jaws dripped blood. Each gripped a knife, except for the little blond girl in the green dress in back. She held a cleaver.

A dark headed boy stepped forward. "Grandpa," he said, and plunged a steak knife into the old man's throat.

The children fell on him like a pack of hyenas. Wild. Frothing at the mouth. Arms a blur. Blades flying. Teeth gnashing.

Dennis rushed back down the hall.

The front door shook again.

Eileen held a Maglite. It was easily three feet long. The fluorescent light of the kitchen sparkled from its blue steel. "Best I could do," she said.

"We gotta go."

The children's laughter echoed down the hall.

The door shook again. This time the bookcase fell over onto its face.

"We gotta act fast. Grab that and pull it away from the door."

"What?"

"Just do it!"

Eileen grabbed the bookcase and dragged it across the carpet.

Dennis stood next to the door and took a deep breath. He knew he'd have to kill the man. He hoped he could.

It's him or us, he reminded himself.

The man hit the door again. With the bookshelf gone it flew open. He stumbled inside, off balance, expecting resistance. Dennis hit him hard from the side, the knife sliding in easily under his ribs. The man fell over, the shotgun firing a wild shot into the ceiling. Plaster rained down over them as Dennis stabbed wildly, piercing the man's side over and over again. The bald man tried to shove his attacker off, but years of wrestling allowed Dennis to stick to him. It didn't take long for his flailing hands to lose their strength.

Dennis shoved the shotgun away and stood. Bloody bubbles popped on the man's lips as he wheezed.

I killed him.

"Dennis!"

The children shuffled out into the living room.

Dennis threw the knife down, snatched up the shotgun, and pumped it once. He had never fired a gun before and prayed he wouldn't have to do so now.

He moved to grab Eileen's hand, but the little girl swung the cleaver at him. He jumped backwards and kicked her in the chest. She fell on her ass and tumbled over.

Eileen came toward him, but the dark headed boy growled and rushed her, a bloody knife held in his outstretched hand. Dennis aimed and fired.

The stock punched hard into his shoulder. A sound like a thunderclap erupted and the boy's head exploded into a fine, red mist. Blood sprayed from his neck stump as the body dropped to its knees, fell on its chest.

Dear God…What had he just done?

The other children turned toward him, smiling.

He grabbed Eileen's hand and jerked her out into the hallway.

"You…you…killed that boy." He could barely hear her through the ringing in his ears.

"I had to. There was no other way." Was there? Was there something else he could have done? "I had to."

In front of them, the hallway filled with people. They fought and wrestled each other to the ground, biting and clawing. Knives flashed, bats swung. People screamed, yelled in rage. Thick fingers of smoke crawled up the walls.

Behind them, the children shuffled through the door, murder in their eyes.

"Back to the stairs!" Eileen tugged his hand toward the door.

"The dogs—"

"Shoot them! C'mon!"

★ ★ ★

Eileen kept her hand on Dennis' shoulder as they crept down the stairs. Smoke choked the stairwell. Muted yelling echoed all around. Dennis placed the butt of the gun on his shoulder as they rounded the corner.

Terry's insides littered the ground like trash. His body was no longer there. Gory paw prints painted the floor, but the dogs were gone, too.

Eileen felt eyes on her. She turned and looked up the stairs. The amorous corpse stood on a landing. It seemed to stare at her, even though its eyes were sewn shut. Its pants were still open and one hand slowly stroked.

"Dennis!"

He spun and raised the gun. She gripped his shoulder tighter.

The corpse tilted its head back, moaned, and stroked faster.

She had to get out of here. She couldn't take this anymore, was close to collapsing into a corner and screaming. "Leave it."

Dennis nodded.

They stepped past the meat scattered around the floor

and opened the door. Gray clouds smothered their faces. She started coughing and couldn't stop.

Noises drifted into the stairwell—screams, yells, thumps, wet slaps. The undulating red-orange light of the fire shone on the door. Dennis glanced back up the stairs.

Eileen grabbed his jaw and turned his face to the door. "We have to go, goddammit! NOW!"

He nodded and they stepped into the hall.

★ ★ ★

Flames licked up the walls of the first floor hallway, grabbing at the ceiling. Chunks of plaster fell crackling into the fire. Smoke strangled the corridor. Dennis crouched, pulled Eileen down. He coughed hard. "Stay low, below the smoke." She nodded through red, watery eyes. "We gotta move fast."

They duckwalked down the hall, the gun aiming at shapes in the smoke. A high-pitched scream hit them. Grunting. Wet slapping sounds.

A mass of flailing limbs slowly came into view. A snarling, soot-covered face cut through the smoke. Dennis had met him and his girlfriend a few weeks earlier. "Cody?"

Cody Tate ignored him. They crawled closer and he could see Melissa on her back, her face purple and swollen, Cody between her legs. Other men crawled toward her. She screamed.

"Shut up, whore," Cody grunted. He coughed hard. "This is what you want, isn't it?"

One of the other men fought with his zipper as he inched toward her. She shook her head and he punched her.

Eileen screamed and swung the Maglite into the man's face. There was a loud crunch and he fell into a black pool of shadow on the wall. Dark arms erupted from the plaster and jerked him into the black like there was a hole in the wall. He was gone.

Dennis hit another man in the face with the butt of the shotgun. The man stumbled, lunged back for him, but Dennis swung the gun around and broke his jaw. He fell through an open door and black shapes swarmed over him.

A thick, dark ribbon peeled away from the ceiling and wrapped around Cody's neck. It yanked him away and he vanished into the smoke.

Shadows danced around in the hall, bulging from the walls.

Even with the fire raging around Dennis, his skin had gone cold. He met Eileen's eyes. They were wide, her face as pallid as bone.

She grabbed Melissa and pulled her into a sitting position. "Honey, I know this is hard but we have to get out of here. Okay?"

Melissa nodded, her sobbing, beaten face shaking. The three of them rushed toward the door.

The groundskeeper stood in the doorway. He raised an axe and brought it down on a small, crying shape in front of him. Dennis thought it was one of Reynaldo's sons. The axe stuck in the child's chest with a wet *thump*. Reynaldo fought to pull it back out, blood arcing through the air and splattering across his face. He brought it down again.

Dennis aimed and fired. The shot punched a giant hole in Reynaldo's chest and took him off his feet.

The three of them darted out the door.

Freezing rain pelted them like a hail of bullets. They stood in shock.

The statues in the courtyard had come to life.

They twisted and rolled over one another, moaning, grunting, an orgy of stone covering the path.

Melissa screamed again and pulled her hand free of Eileen's. She backed toward the door, shaking her head.

"No! Don't!" Eileen took a step toward her.

A black dog slammed into Melissa's back. She hit the stone stairs face first, one of her teeth chipping away, as the dog tore into her back. Its brethren scrambled out over her, ripping into her flesh.

One of the dogs came toward Eileen.

Dennis fired.

Its hindquarters exploded. It yelped, howled, but didn't stop, crawled toward her on its front paws, guts trailing behind it.

They turned, ran through the courtyard, dodging the nightmarish obscenities around them.

A nymph was on all fours, one satyr in her mouth and another behind her. One satyr took another while reaching around and stroking him. They maneuvered through the horrid maze, slipping in the soggy ground.

Patty Malone lay in the mud, her eyes peeled from her skull. Vibrant flowers grew around her, red roses and blue orchids, piercing her flesh and sprouting from a hundred wounds. Weeds slithered from her empty sockets. As they watched, a white bud sprouted from her mouth and bloomed.

A nymph rose into their path, smiling, its arms open for

a lover's embrace.

Dennis fired off another shot. Chunks of stone showered the air, its arm puffing into dust. He had aimed for its head, but considered himself lucky for every shot up to and including this one. It watched them, still smiling, as they darted by.

There was a crash behind them and he turned to see someone fly through a broken window on the third floor. Their body hit the ground with a loud *crunch*. It reminded him of crushing the roaches.

Outside the safety of the courtyard, the wind crashed against them so hard that they struggled to stay on their feet. The freezing rain soaked through their clothes in seconds. They slipped on the steps twice while running down the hill, but managed to stay on their feet until they reached the parking lot.

Dark clouds surrounded the hill. Rain pounded into their eyes. It was impossible to see. They splashed through the parking lot, careening between cars, trying to find one of theirs.

Dennis rushed to her Prius. "Keys!"

"Dammit. They're in Jason's apartment." They might even still be in Jason's collarbone. She wasn't sure.

One of the dogs slammed down hard on the roof of the car. Hot breath hit Dennis in the face and stank with death.

"Where do you think you're going?" It seemed to grin.

"Here!" Eileen tugged on the handle of his convertible. He stepped back from the dog slowly and fumbled his keys from his pocket.

It jumped down from the car and kept pace with him, sidestepping as it followed, attempting to circle him.

He fought his keys out and tossed them to Eileen.

"You smell tasty," the dog said, bloody drool dribbling from its mouth.

He heard the engine start and the tires squeal behind him.

Was she leaving him?

The dog laughed.

He raised the shotgun.

His foot caught a puddle and he slipped.

The dog rushed him.

His convertible plowed into the thing with bone-crushing force. It flew into the side of a minivan and his car slammed in after it. Metal crunched and bent.

He rushed over to the car. "Eileen!"

"I'm okay," she said, blood trickling from her forehead. She backed the car up. The front end was mangled and the glass over the headlights was broken, but she clicked them on and the bulbs still worked.

Dennis ran around to the passenger side and climbed in. She locked the doors. Rain smacked like pebbles against the car. They were quiet, their lungs fighting for breath the only sound.

The flames crawled up the side of Raynham, lighting the stormy skies over it like a fiery sunset.

They held each other and cried.

★ ★ ★

He smelled smoke. The dark around him receded, pain flooding in to replace it. His body was bathed in agony. He tasted blood.

Cold porcelain pressed against him.

His vision slowly came into focus.

A roach sat on the edge of the tub and stared down at him.

—I'm not done with you yet—

★ ★ ★

The convertible sloshed through the parking lot. Eileen twisted the wheel and floored it, skidding onto the driveway. The back end of the car slid back and forth and she fought hard to straighten it. The wipers and headlights were both on high, but she still couldn't see farther than a few feet in front of the hood. She worried that the rain would short the exposed headlights out before long.

A gunshot fired from behind them. The back passenger side window sprayed broken glass across the seat. Eileen screamed. The bullet punched hard into the console, sending plastic shards flying. She ducked and pressed the pedal harder.

The bottom of the hill was a sea of black.

Her chest tightened. "What is that?"

Dennis was silent.

"WHAT IS IT?"

"I don't know."

"Is it those shadows? Is it?"

A woman darted in front of her. She slammed on the brakes. Tires squealed. The car slid down the wet hill.

The woman kept running. She waved a golf club over her head. A fat man limped over the curb. She swung the club into his back. They vanished into the rain.

The car continued its slide down, weaving back and forth. She pumped the brake, the gas, cut the wheel one way then the other.

The black came rushing toward them.

She tensed. "Jesus Christ, please protect us from—"

They hit hard. Her head bounced from the steering wheel. Dennis hit the window. A tide of dark water crashed against the windshield. She shook her head, wiped the white sparks from her eyes. They were still moving. She pumped the brakes. Nothing happened.

A tree limb floated by her window.

"It's flooded," she said. Water came up to the door handle. It leaked into the floorboards from somewhere.

Dennis rubbed his head. "The engine?"

"The valley. Look."

He stared out the window. "Shit. Are we floating?"

"I think so."

He grinned.

She started to laugh and then he did too. Once they started they couldn't stop, cackling until they were out of breath.

★ ★ ★

The water level reached the windows within a few minutes. It sloshed in through the broken rear window, splashing into the seat.

Dennis looked around. "We've gotta get out."

"I'm not getting in that water. I can't."

Behind them, the hill was a furious bonfire. The red

0

and orange glow had sunken into the very earth. Dennis thought of documentaries he had seen about volcanic activity. The hill was awash in what could have been a lava flow. It was as though he watched the early days of the planet as it fought to form itself, to create something from

—from the void He said "Let there be light"—

the chaos.

The shadow of Raynham Place rose from the flames.

"We need to climb onto the roof. The car's sinking."

She looked around and nodded.

"I'll go first. Hand me the shotgun and the flashlight and then I'll pull you up from the window. You won't have to get into the water. I promise. Okay?"

"Okay."

He rolled his window down and cold rain invaded the car. He gripped the slick fabric roof and shimmied out, splashing into the freezing flood. A current gently tugged at him, urging him to float away, but he kept his grip on the car. He pulled himself around to the hood and crawled up the windshield.

He knocked on Eileen's window and she rolled it down. She handed him the shotgun and the flashlight and he set both to the side. "Now give me your hands."

She reached up and he gripped her wrists.

"Pull yourself up onto the door."

She shimmied until she sat in the open window. Dennis tugged her up onto the roof.

His foot slipped and he fell on his chest.

Eileen's legs crashed down into the water.

"Dennis!"

"I'm sorry. Just pull yourself up."

"DENNIS!"

"It's okay—" The words caught in his throat when he saw why she screamed.

★ ★ ★

Tiny hands gripped her calves under the water. Their little fingers dug deep into the muscles. An unnatural cold seeped through her flesh and into her very bones.

She glanced down and saw a pale blue shape under her.

Dennis tugged on her arms. "Pull!"

She tried to pull herself up, but its grip was too strong. "DENNIS!"

The water splashed up onto her chest as the thing's head crested the surface. It was a boy, his face bloated and blue.

"Mommy?" the Blue Boy asked. Filthy gray water spilled from his mouth.

Dennis' hands grabbed her under the armpits. She dug her fingers into his back. She heard the fabric under him rip. He pitched to one side, jerked her upwards, and she pulled hard. Her foot came down on the open window and she pushed off. The tiny fingers loosened and she slipped from their grip and flopped onto the roof of the car.

Dennis held her and they watched over the side as the pale blue shape swam away.

The fabric top tore at one end from their weight. They scooted toward the windshield, their weight evenly spaced across the glass and the spine of the convertible's top.

"Look." He pointed toward the trees.

She squinted through the rain and saw twin balls of light rising through the branches. They rose higher and the faint noise of whirring engines could be heard.

"Helicopters?"

"Yeah. Police or rescue I guess. Hell, I don't care if they're news choppers. Grab the flashlight and shine it up so they can see us."

She clicked the Maglite on. She was afraid it wouldn't work, but the bulb came to life. She shined the bright beam straight into the air. "Thank God."

Another splash and something scurried up the hood.

★ ★ ★

He turned to see Jason, his naked body a tangle of fresh wounds, scrambling on all fours up the hood.

Dennis grabbed the shotgun. Aimed. Fired.

Click.

He pumped it and squeezed the trigger again.

Click.

A blade flashed. His thigh screamed as a butcher knife pounded into his leg. Dennis roared from the pain, tried to kick Jason in the face with his good leg, but Jason pulled the knife out quickly and slashed at Dennis' throat.

Dennis fell backwards out of the way of the blade. Before he knew it Jason was on him, grabbing his wet shirt and pulling himself up over the windshield, his broken face slick with blood and black water, his busted mouth a snarl. The blade shot up over Dennis and fell toward his chest.

Eileen swung the Maglite into Jason's face. There was a sickening crunch and he tumbled over backwards onto the hood. He fought himself up. Dennis struggled to one knee. Eileen flashed by him.

She brought the heavy flashlight down into Jason's skull again. He dropped the knife. She slipped, falling on her ass. He struggled to his knees and she swung wildly, hitting him under the jaw. He flew onto his back. She dove onto him, bringing the Maglite down over and over into his face. She growled and cried.

The beam of light arced up and down from the tree line to the water as she bashed him in the skull.

Blood and bone erupted into the air. His hands reached for her neck. She crashed the light into his elbow, shattered it. He moaned. She cracked him in the face. His hands fell to his sides. Arms twitched. Body went limp.

She didn't stop, screaming through her tears, her arm a blur, the blue steel dripping gore, the light filtered through a red sheen of blood. His skull disintegrated.

By the time Dennis pulled her off of him it was impossible to tell that the lump of red mush that connected to his neck had ever been a face.

Her tears stopped. Dennis hugged her tight from behind, but she just stared at the dead body in front of her. Her breath was hard and loud.

She kicked its foot and it slid off of the hood and into the water. The current dragged it under.

She leaned back and Dennis winced. She pulled his shirt off of him and wrapped it around his leg, pulled it so tight that he ground his teeth together, and then tied it off. "I don't know what I'm doing."

"Looks fine to me."

"I'm just doing what I see on TV."

He laughed. "That was me with the shotgun. I doubt I could win any marksman awards with that thing, but luckily it was a shotgun and we were close range and…" He thought of the child's head turning into mist and went silent.

The fire blazed behind them, its light reflecting from the clouds and causing the night sky to glow. Dennis thought about Mike burning and Allison bleeding out in a tub of steaming water.

Eileen scooted close to him and raised the light back into the sky. Its beam shot high into the dark clouds. The helicopters were loud overhead. A large white searchlight draped over them.

They held each other and shivered.

EPILOGUE

The flooding had kept emergency services away from the hill for almost forty-eight hours. By the time Lieutenant Graham and his men were able to make it to the site, the apartment complex and all of the abandoned buildings around it were nothing but soggy debris.

Muddy ash covered the hill. The fire had blazed out of control and consumed everything. He found it odd that a fire could grow so fast during such a rainstorm. It wasn't unheard of, but still rare. Luckily it had limited itself to the area around Raynham.

He removed his helmet and scanned the area. Police and medical personnel joined his men in searching through the rubble for survivors. He didn't hold out much hope. When the rescue helicopters flew through during the fire, all they had found were a young couple stranded on the roof of their car at the bottom of the driveway. They had been in shock and didn't give much information on what caused the fire or how many people had made it out of the building. He couldn't blame them. He could tell by the destruction that it must have been like Hell getting out of here.

The helicopters circled the building for nearly an hour after that, trying to help more survivors to safety. But no one else left the building before the flames finally dragged the roof in and it collapsed. He was surprised that it had crumbled. Again, such a thing wasn't unknown—at high temperatures stone cracks and breaks—but he himself had never had to deal with such a mess. This was easily the worst fire he had ever seen in his years with the department, maybe even the worst fire in Knox County's history.

The bodies they had recovered so far were burnt beyond all recognition. They would have to be identified with dental records before their families could be notified. He hated that part and could sympathize with every person who had a loved one living here. He and some of his men had gone to New York after the Towers came down to help with the rescue efforts. Not knowing if their spouses and children were alive affected some of the families much worse than when they were definitively told that the person hadn't made it.

Some of the charred bodies here showed strange wounds—missing limbs, gaping holes in their torsos, throats parted open—that suggested a riot. He refused to speculate about it until the investigation was finished and autopsies had been performed, but wondered if something had barred the doors. He knew that had happened during Katrina. When a mob of people panicked during an emergency, violent rioting was inevitable.

Sergeant Best ran up to him, his yellow jacket was covered with mud and soot. He fought to catch his breath. "Lieutenant. I think we've got one."

"Show me."

The Sergeant led him to several firefighters and police officers clearing away a small pile of rubble. His heart pounded in his chest. He had prayed all morning that they would find even one person alive. If they could find one, then maybe there were others. They could be trapped in the rubble, or have made it into the woods (where search teams scoured with packs of hound dogs even now), but just one person lifted morale and redoubled search efforts.

He scrambled onto the pile, where an ash-covered hand dangled over bricks. He dove in with the men, pulling debris away until he saw her. She was naked, her shapely body covered in filth. Chunks of plaster clutched at her red hair. She sucked in a breath and crystal blue eyes met his.

A roach rested on her sternum and Lieutenant Graham smacked it away.

She reached up to him, tears filling her eyes. "Don't move," he said. "You may have internal injuries."

She wrapped her arms around his neck and pulled herself up. She was inches from his mouth and he fought the urge to kiss her. God, she was beautiful.

She leaned close to his ear.

"Darling," she whispered.

About the Author

Originally from Knoxville, TN, award-winning author BRAD C. HODSON currently resides in Los Angeles. His short fiction can be seen in a number of anthologies and his film, the zombie comedy *George: A Zombie Intervention* is available nationwide. When not reading or writing, he likes to lift heavy things made of iron and drag chains attached to other heavy things across fields. He also likes cooking, international travel, and writing about himself in third person.

Darling is his first novel.

For more information, including a bibliography of where you can find his work, please visit:

www.brad-hodson.com